HER HIDDEN LIES

Ivy Bishop Mystery Thriller
Book 4

ALEX SIGMORE

Dark Woods Press

Oakhurst is a town that knows how to keep its secrets, but some shadows are impossible to ignore.

After the devastating fallout from her last case, Detective Ivy Bishop is thrust into another chilling investigation. A family in the quiet town of Oakhurst is being terrorized by an unseen stalker—someone who watches their every move, knows their every secret, and seems to be impossible to catch.

With her boss, Nat, still missing, Ivy is left to navigate the growing darkness alone. The case begins to unravel in unexpected ways, and Ivy can't shake the feeling that this stalker is more than just a threat to the family—it's a harbinger of something far more sinister.

As she continues to dig, each new clue draws her closer to a truth that has eluded her for years. The stalker seems to know more about Ivy's past than she does herself, and the lines between the hunter and the hunted begin to blur.

As the danger escalates, Ivy senses that the answers she's been searching for her entire life are within reach—but will come at a cost. The deeper she goes, the closer she gets to unraveling the mystery that has haunted her since that night fifteen years ago, but she must be prepared for a revelation darker than any she's faced before.

Chapter One

Ivy didn't even remember driving. It was as if her body had moved on its own, getting in the car without any input from her brain. And yet she found herself on the road, the darkness stretching before her, blurred by the constant torrent of rain.

Her muscles acted independently, turning the wheel, applying the accelerator and following the road as her headlights cut through the black of night. Beside her in the passenger seat was her service weapon, the rain from the gun soaking into her upholstery.

It was like her mind was lost in a chasm with no way out. Even though she tried to pay attention to the road ahead of her, it all kept coming back to what had happened at the cabin. She recalled walking up to the front door with Alice, the cabin looming large in front of them. The hope had been to find some evidence that could shed light on what had happened to Ivy when she was young. The house had been some part of a scheme Nat had been running fifteen years ago, though with little to no information about it, they were going in blind. She hadn't known what to expect when they arrived.

Ivy's stomach turned at the exact same time she turned the

wheel onto a familiar street. The pain in her gut was intense, almost like a foreign object had lodged itself down there. She even ran a free hand over her midsection to make sure she wasn't bleeding out. But there was nothing but soaked fabric beneath her skin.

She pulled the car up to the familiar house and killed the engine before looking over at the warm lights inside. The house always seemed so inviting; it was no wonder her autopilot brought her here instead of her own place. Not that she'd had the wherewithal to change course even if she'd wanted to. It was like her mind was stuck and she couldn't figure out how to jar it loose again.

Ivy's body stepped out of the car of its own accord, soaking up the pouring rain as the deluge continued. She'd neglected to turn on the heater in the car and found herself shivering from the cold. Making her way up the sidewalk, she lost sight of it for a moment as images from the cabin took over her mind's eye. All she could see was the inside of the home. The smell of cedar and pine filled her nostrils and the feel of the rough-hewn logs cascaded under her fingers, stacked one on top of the other to form the walls. She and Alice had approached the building slowly, looking for any threats. The cabin had been dark, no lights on outside or in. And no vehicles anywhere on the property. It had the look of a place long deserted, but you could never be too sure.

As Ivy reached for the door, she could practically see Alice's determined gaze. Ivy had given her a weapon which she wielded like someone who'd never picked up a gun before. Ivy showed Alice how to cover her— as she'd be the first to go in this time. They tried the handle; Ivy jiggled it just to be sure, but it was locked. She'd have to kick the door in.

But before she could, it opened in front of her and the scene in her mind melted away.

"Ivy? Honey, what are you doing?"

Aunt Carol stood before Ivy, her face etched in concern and worry.

"I... I didn't know where else to go," Ivy found herself saying without meaning to.

"Here, come in, girl. You're gonna get sick," Carol said, grabbing on to Ivy's arm and pulling her into the house. Ivy looked at the woman's grip around her bicep, something that should have sent a jolt of electricity surging through her—and yet there was nothing.

Aunt Carol closed the door behind her and led her into the living room, the sound of Ivy's soaked boots squishing with each step. The house was so warm that it hit Ivy like a blast furnace and she began shivering even harder. Carol pulled a blanket off the back of the couch and wrapped it around Ivy's shoulders.

"We need to get you out of those wet clothes," she said. "What happened? Weren't you and Alice supposed to be headed to that cabin of yours?"

"We did," Ivy said. "We were there." She didn't even recognize her own voice. It was like the voice of a small child, one who didn't comprehend the dark realities of life. "I... I don't even know what I'm doing here."

"What happened?" Aunt Carol said, coming back in front of Ivy. "Is Alice okay?"

"I... don't know," Ivy said honestly. When she'd left, Alice was still there, yelling after Ivy. Screaming at her, in fact.

Something greater than concern crossed Aunt Carol's face, but it was gone in an instant. "Here, let's get you into the bathroom. I want you out of those clothes immediately. You still have some of your stuff here." She practically pushed Ivy down the hall towards the bathroom, a move that on any other day would have been nearly unbearable for Ivy. But for some reason now, it no longer mattered.

She helped Ivy into the bathroom, sitting her down on the small toilet and undoing her boots before moving on to her socks. At the same time she reached over and began running water into the tub.

It was as if Ivy was aware of what was happening, but she couldn't do anything about it. Her body wouldn't respond to the inputs from her brain; they just kept going back to what had happened at the cabin, over and over again. Before she realized it, she was being helped into the warm bath water, lowered down by Aunt Carol until she was completely submerged. All at once her fingers and toes began to tingle as the nerve endings all warmed at the same time.

"I want you to stay in there until you've completely warmed up," Aunt Carol said, her arms full of Ivy's wet clothes. "And in the meantime I'll get all of this cleaned up. And I'll be back to check on you in a few minutes."

She left the door slightly cracked on her way out. Aunt Carol. *She had come to Aunt Carol's for a reason.* Somewhere, her brain must have gone into some kind of protection mode and sought out the safest place it could imagine. It wasn't a surprise it had been here.

Without warning, Ivy plunged her head into the water, completely submerging herself. Immediately she came back into herself, feeling like she'd just come out of some bad dream or nightmare. The hot water was the rudest wakeup call she could have received. She shot out of the water, taking a deep breath that must have sounded something like a scream because Aunt Carol came rushing back in.

"Ivy? Are you okay?"

Ivy stared back up at her, breathing heavily but blinking over and over again as if doing it for the first time in three hours. "I don't know," she finally said.

"So nothing happened at all?" Carol asked, taking a

seat across the small kitchen table from Ivy as she placed two cups of steaming decaf in front of them.

"Not really," Ivy said, running her hand through her mostly dry hair. The bath had done wonders to warm her up and she was beginning to feel more like herself, but some part of her remained foreign. She didn't like it— nor could she explain it. "We went in, it was empty and that was it. I left."

"But Alice stayed behind," Carol replied.

Ivy's heart was thudding in her chest. But she'd positioned herself in a way that made it look like she was sitting casually at the table, doing nothing more than sipping a cup of coffee. "She wanted to keep looking."

"And you left her there alone?"

If she was honest with herself, Ivy didn't know *where* Alice was. She had considered texting her to at least make sure she was okay, but at the same time, she wasn't sure she could face the woman again.

"Alice is more than capable of handling herself," Ivy said after taking a sip of coffee. It took everything she had to keep her hand from shaking. "I'm sure she's fine."

The lines on Carol's forehead deepened, the same way they used to do when Ivy would tell her she got a D on a test at school. She'd never come right out and scold Ivy, but it was the silent judgment that really got under her skin. "And you didn't find anything?" Carol asked. "You were so sure there would be something there."

"Nope," Ivy replied. "Just an empty house. Pretty standard." She could feel Aunt Carol's eyes on her— observing, scrutinizing. She probably wasn't buying it, but she was confident Aunt Carol knew when to leave well enough alone. Dealing with Ivy through her teenage years had taught her that if Ivy wasn't ready to talk about something, no amount of prodding was going to get her to open up.

The older woman sighed. "Well, I'm sorry it was a bust. I know how much you were hoping to find some answers."

Before she could say anything else, Ivy's phone buzzed. The only time Ivy ever turned on the ringtone was when she was expecting an important call and couldn't miss it. And because most of her calls were at the same level of urgency— working for the police department— it meant her phone was perpetually on vibrate. And yet, she could almost feel like this call was more urgent, just by how the phone was rumbling on the table. Like someone had turned up the voltage. Ivy snatched up the phone to see a familiar name on the screen. Inwardly she cursed. She'd known this call had been coming and yet some part of her hoped it never would.

"Bishop," she said, doing her best to remain stoic and professional, even though he probably didn't deserve that right now. But it was taking everything Ivy had not to fall to pieces and she couldn't worry about anyone else at the moment.

"Ivy, what's going on?" her partner asked on the other end, his voice frantic. "I just got a call from Alice. She said you just ran out on her."

"I didn't run out on her, *Jonathan*," Ivy said, keeping her voice measured. "We looked over the place and there was nothing there. There wasn't a reason to stay." Her partner, Jonathan White, while more experienced as a detective, also had the reputation of a rule-follower and someone who didn't like to deviate from the "book." And while they'd become closer over the past few months after Ivy's promotion, she still wasn't a hundred percent ready to trust him. She wasn't a hundred percent ready to trust anyone, though if she could tell anyone about what happened in that house, it would probably be Jonathan. And yet, she knew she couldn't tell him the truth. Not the *real* truth, anyway.

"That's not how she made it sound," he replied.

"Because she's a reporter and she blows everything out of proportion," Ivy shot back. "I assume she left?"

"She said she was calling from home. Ivy, what happened?"

"*Nothing*," Ivy reiterated, throwing a glance at Carol. "How many times do I have to say it? We investigated the house. There was nothing inside. That was it." The very fact he was questioning her meant that Alice hadn't revealed what had *really* happened. Which was odd, considering how angry she'd been when Ivy left. She thought for sure Alice would spill her guts either to Jonathan, her boss, or all over the news the following day.

She could practically feel his exasperation on the other end. "Fine. If you say so. And you're okay?"

"I'm fine," she said, perhaps a little too harshly. "Thank you," she added, trying to recover.

"And you're back home?"

"I'm over at Carol's," Ivy said. "I'll… probably stay the night here."

"Alright," he replied. "See you in the morning."

She hung up and placed the phone face down on the table again. It was impossible to miss the scrutiny on Carol's face. But the woman never said a word, just sipped her coffee and waited for Ivy, like she usually did.

"I'll… get your handgun back from Alice later," Ivy finally said, running her finger around the edge of her cup. Her heart rate was finally starting to come down. "I forgot to grab it before I left."

"That's okay," Carol finally said. "I've got plenty more."

This elicited an eyebrow raise and a smile from Ivy, despite herself. She took a deep breath and let her shoulders drop for the first time since she'd approached that cabin. All she wanted was a good night's sleep.

But given what had happened, she wasn't sure she'd ever be able to sleep through the night again.

Chapter Two

THE FOLLOWING morning Ivy was up early, her sleep having been predictably broken and downright frustrating. Gathering her now-dry clothes from the laundry room, she grabbed a cold breakfast burrito from the fridge as she headed back out before Carol was up. She left a note on the fridge thanking her for everything last night but wanted to avoid another round of the same this morning. The last thing she wanted to do was dwell on this any longer. She just wanted a shower in her own place, clean clothes and to get back to work.

An hour later she was fresh and feeling more like her normal self. And as she drove over to the office she found it almost easy to forget all about the cabin. All she had to do was ignore the five missed calls from Alice and the still-wet spot on her passenger seat where her sidearm had laid the night before. And as she entered the precinct, she'd found she'd done just that.

"Bishop," Officer Ann Touley nodded as she passed.

"Touley," Ivy replied. She'd been on the beat patrol with Touley a few times back before her promotion, though she hadn't seen much of her since other than the occasional passing in the corridor.

"Ayford wants to see you," she said, causing Ivy to pause. She checked the time; it wasn't even eight yet and Ayford was already here? It seemed her new "temporary" boss wasn't wasting any time. But given the conditions with which they'd come to work together, Ivy couldn't fault the man for wanting to get a head start. With her previous boss and *backstabber* Natasha "Nat" Buckley gone, no doubt he had been playing catch-up all weekend.

"Thanks," Ivy said and headed straight for the man's office, bypassing her desk. Jonathan's monitor was still dark, meaning she'd beat him in as well. She wasn't looking forward to another barrage of questions, but if Alice had decided not to tell him about last night, then maybe she could get away with the bare minimum and get him to drop it before it became a whole *thing*. And honestly, what business was it of anyone else's anyway? The cabin was supposed to be a clue to *her* past. As long as Ivy was satisfied with what had happened, then that should be the end of it.

Ivy knocked on her new boss's door that had been left open by a sliver.

"Come in," the man said, his voice sounding more like a growl than words.

"Morning," Ivy said, entering into the small office. "I'm not sure we've ever formally met but I'm—"

"I know who you are, Bishop," Lieutenant Michael Ayford said. "Take a seat." The office was the complete opposite of Nat's overcrowded and frankly, filthy office. Ivy wasn't sure if Ayford had done it himself, or the room had come that way, but the walls were painted in a rich forest green, giving the room a cozy feel, despite being in the middle of a police department. The wall to the left featured awards of all kinds, mostly wooden frames with gold plaques, all polished to a shine. And behind the man, up against the window, were a series of plants, each completely different from the other.

Nearby sat a small spray bottle, presumably to keep them healthy.

Ayford himself was dressed in a no-nonsense suit, his jacket hanging on a nearby rack and colorful suspenders carefully wrapping over his shoulders. The nameplate on the front of his desk was so polished Ivy could see herself in its reflection. She had to admit she didn't look as rested as she thought she had when leaving her apartment this morning.

"Before anything else, we need to address the elephant in the room," Ayford said, folding his hands in front of him and pinning her with his gaze. "Buckley."

"What about her?" Ivy asked.

"I'd appreciate a little more formality, Bishop," he said. "You'll address me as *sir* in this office, understand?"

Ivy winced. She'd gotten so used to a casual approach to the relationship with her boss with Nat that she'd become a little too comfortable in how she addressed her superiors. It happened all the time with Captain Armstrong, though he was usually so upset with Ivy that something as small as addressing him formally never seemed to matter.

"Sorry, sir," she said. "What about Lieutenant Buckley, specifically?"

"I'd like you to explain the situation to me," he said. "Beginning to end."

Ivy's forehead creased. "Beginning to end, sir?"

He nodded, apparently serious.

Inwardly, she threw her hands up. Her relationship with Nat was long and complex. But if he wanted the whole thing, she had no problem telling him all about how Nat betrayed her.

"I first met Nat— Lieutenant Buckley when I was twelve," Ivy said. "She found me wandering the streets of Oakhurst, apparently in a daze. She got me to the hospital, tried to find my family only to discover they had… disappeared."

"Disappeared," he repeated.

"Yes, sir," Ivy said, swallowing hard. So maybe this wasn't as easy as she'd thought. She continued, telling him about how Nat had been almost like a surrogate sister to her for many years, helping her get in with Mrs. Baker at the orphanage and even after she was formally adopted by Aunt Carol. She had been the one to recommend Ivy to the department and eventually promote her to Detective. However, during all that time she had been lying to Ivy about what had really happened after she was found. Ivy had only recently discovered that Nat had worked with another unknown man to cover up the details of her family's disappearance, all of which had something to do with the cabin, though she still didn't know what. However, she didn't reveal the part about the cabin to Ayford. She'd already had one too many people inquiring about it and, frankly, didn't need any more.

Ayford drummed his fingers on the desk for a few minutes after she finished. "Lieutenant Buckley recommended putting you on suspension," he said. Ivy nodded. "I've spoken with Armstrong about it. We both agree her judgment may have been impaired when making that recommendation. And considering the work you did on the Rouge murder case, we're willing to put that to the side for now." He pinned her with his gaze. "But let me be clear. You put one foot out of line, or if I even get a whiff of something smelling off, you're going to be on desk duty for the foreseeable future. Got it?"

"Yes, sir," Ivy said. She couldn't blame the man. All she could do was focus on her job and on delivering solid results. She hadn't had the chance to work without Nat looking over her shoulder and was anxious to get back to her caseload as soon as possible.

"Okay, that's it," he said. "Get back out there."

"Thank you, sir. I look forward to working with you," Ivy stood, ready to head out.

"Bishop, one more thing," Ayford said as she reached the

door. "This… *issue* of yours, the physical contact. That's not going to be a problem, is it?"

Ivy stopped cold. No one but her partner and Nat were supposed to know about that. Had Nat written that down somewhere and Ayford had found it? Or had he brought Jonathan in over the weekend and he'd had a loose tongue?

"No, sir," she said, thinking back to when Carol had guided her the night before. Normally that should have set Ivy off, but it was like she hadn't even felt it. "Not at all."

"Good," he replied. "Make sure it stays that way."

As Ivy made her way back over to her desk, she found Jonathan already there, working away. Checking the time again, she realized she'd been in Ayford's office for nearly half an hour.

"Morning," Jonathan said, looking up quickly before returning his attention to his computer. The word was cold and indifferent. She'd pissed him off by being so dismissive last night and now he was returning the favor.

"Good morning," she said, taking a seat across from him, her voice softer. "About last night—"

"We don't need to talk about it," he said.

"Jonathan, look, I'm sorry, okay? I wasn't in the best headspace."

He stopped typing and looked around his monitor. "Are you okay now?"

She nodded. "Yeah. I just… needed a good night's sleep." He was about to ask another question but she stopped him. "I still don't want to talk about it, though. Okay?"

He took a deep breath, but then seemed to stop himself. "Were you in with Ayford?"

"Yeah, he just gave me the third degree about Nat. Made me explain our entire relationship."

"Can you blame him?" her partner asked.

"I guess not. Do you know if anyone has heard from her?" As far as Ivy knew, Nat was still somewhere in the vicinity of

San Francisco, if the tracker her friend Oliver had placed on her phone was to be trusted. And as far as Ivy was concerned, she could stay there. Oliver told her he'd let her know if it looked like she was on the move again.

"Not that I'm aware of," Jonathan replied. "But they're not going to wait around forever. Eventually they'll determine she abandoned her post and she'll be let go from the force."

Good. Ivy couldn't help the bevy of harsh thoughts directed at Nat. The woman had covered up what had really happened to Ivy's family and now had run away. Even if Ivy tracked her down in San Francisco, she'd never talk. And it wasn't like Ivy had hard evidence. All she had were a few strange instances that didn't line up. That and Nat's duplicitous behavior. If only she could find the man Nat met with the other night again. The two of them had worked on it together, and when Ivy confronted him on the side of the road he'd definitely known something. But he'd disappeared off the face of the earth.

"Hey, you didn't say anything to Ayford about…" Ivy indicated her hands.

Jonathan furrowed his brow. "What?"

"My… *thing.*"

"No," he replied. "Why would I? I've barely even talked to Ayford."

"Somehow he knows," Ivy said, sighing. It must have been in Nat's files somewhere. Despite her telling Ivy she never made a record of it. Just another lie.

"Is he benching you?" Jonathan asked.

"Not unless it becomes a problem," she replied.

"Then we just need to make sure it doesn't," he said, giving her a quick smile. Some of that warmth she was used to had returned. Good. Hopefully he'd just drop any more questions about the cabin.

Just as Ivy was about to get started with her day, her phone vibrated in her pocket. When she saw it was Alice calling yet again, she silenced the call and let it go to voicemail for a sixth time. She would have to deal with that sooner rather than later, but right now she had work to do.

"What's on the docket this morning?" she asked, shoving the phone back into her pocket.

"Stalker case. Just came across the feed," Jonathan said, reading off his screen. "Been fielding calls from a woman complaining of someone watching her house. Apparently, she's insistent enough that Ayford wants someone out there to see if it has any merit. Want to check it out?"

"Sure," Ivy said, standing back up. "I'll take all the fresh air I can get."

Chapter Three

Even though the weather usually wasn't what most people would think of as "pleasant" in western Oregon, Ivy still considered it superior to anywhere hot. Most of the days were temperate and usually involved some kind of precipitation. Today was no exception. The rare storm from last night had left a low-hanging fog around town, drenching it in a cool mist that gave Ivy goosebumps when they got out of the car in front of the modest, two-story home in the upscale Blakehurst neighborhood.

The houses out here were all on the larger side, probably three-thousand square feet or better, and their plots were large, yet still all lined up in rows on either side of the road. Behind the house stood a dense forest of pine and deciduous trees, forming a natural barrier to the property lines. Today, because of the mist, the tops of the trees faded into the sky like someone had blurred them away with a paintbrush.

"Nice house," Ivy said, staring up at the stonework on the front of the building.

Before they could even make their way up the walkway, which was bordered on both sides by local plants embedded into a rock garden, the door to the home opened and a woman emerged, dressed in yoga pants and an oversized sweater. She wore a scowl like it was her job and marched toward them unrelentingly.

"Are you with the police?"

Jonathan nodded. "I'm Detective White. This is Detective Bishop. You're Mrs. Quinn?"

"That's right," the woman said, her words sharp. "About time someone got here. I've made no less than nine calls to your department. What took you so long? I reported this five days ago."

Jonathan put on his best public-facing persona, which was good because Ivy didn't respond well to abrasive people. Especially *entitled* abrasive people. "May we go inside?" he asked. "You can tell us what's going on."

"No, you don't need to go *inside*," she said, her gaze glancing at their shoes for a brief moment. "You need to go in the backyard where I saw that man."

"Man?" Jonathan asked, pulling out his notebook. "The information from the call said you couldn't identify if it was a man or a woman."

"Look, what does it matter?" Mrs. Quinn huffed. "Some stranger is traipsing around my backyard where my children play and no one is doing anything about it."

"Don't worry, our specialty is traipsing trespassers," Ivy said. Mrs. Quinn came off to her as someone who was used to getting her own way through force or abuse and Ivy wasn't going to be the woman's punching bag.

Jonathan glared at her while Mrs. Quinn flared her nostrils. Ivy gave him an *I couldn't help it* face as he turned back to the homeowner. "Which way to the backyard?"

The woman was shooting daggers at Ivy. Finally she pointed around to the right of the house. "Over there, use the gate. I'll meet you out back." She turned and headed back into the house while Jonathan and Ivy made their way over to the gate.

"That doesn't help, you know," he said.

"Sorry," she replied. "It just slipped out."

"Try to keep anything else from slipping out, huh?"

"Sure." It wasn't like Ivy to be snarky on the job, but there was just something about Mrs. Quinn that rubbed her the wrong way. She struck Ivy as the kind of woman who expected the world to revolve around her and her children, and who might not be above inventing scenarios out of boredom. Then again, there might actually be something here. She needed to take her partner's advice and wait until they'd had a proper look.

"Lock on the gate is busted," Ivy said as they pushed through. It wasn't a particularly high gate, just forty-eight inches, and it was the type made of black metal bars. The "lock" itself was plastic, but had long since deteriorated so it didn't latch properly anymore.

"According to the report she didn't see him by the gate. She saw him in the back," Jonathan said.

"Still, someone wouldn't have any trouble getting in this way." She searched the ground for any footprints, but there was nothing but grass and stones that transitioned the small walkway through to the back. Though once they were off the stones, the soft ground gave slightly under their weight.

"He was over there," Mrs. Quinn said as they rejoined her around the back of the home. Right off the back was an expansive patio with deck furniture that had been covered for the winter. A couple of those large heaters that resembled streetlights were scattered around the deck, though they were all off as well. Children's toys littered the deck and the backyard, though there was no sign of anyone else.

The woman pointed hurriedly in the direction of the pines along the back of the property. Ivy followed Jonathan across the yard, looking for anything that might be out of the ordinary. In some areas the grass was depressed, probably from the children playing. As they reached the edge of the property, the ground dropped off about four or five feet before being overrun with trees.

"No fence back here?" Ivy called out as they began searching the area for anything that might be significant.

"Never needed one," Mrs. Quinn called back. She was still standing at the edge of her deck, her arms wrapped around herself due to the chill. "The children know not to go into the woods."

Ivy turned to look at the home again. The back of the home was practically all glass, floor to ceiling windows on both floors. If it had been a sunny day, she probably wouldn't have been able to see in the home, but she could easily make out the kitchen and living rooms from here. No doubt Mrs. Quinn kept a sharp eye on her kids. Still, the lack of a fence along the property line was just asking for trouble.

She took a few tentative steps into the shade created by the pines and noted it was significantly darker here. A child could roll down the small hill easily, though it wasn't steep enough for them to get hurt. The woods itself extended out as far as Ivy could see, until the underbrush became so thick the details of individual trees were lost.

"Quiet back here," Jonathan said. "You almost wouldn't know you were right up against a neighborhood."

"What kind of parent doesn't fence their yard?" Ivy asked, looking back through the trees to Mrs. Quinn, arms still wrapped around herself.

"The kind that probably never takes her eyes off her kids," Jonathan said. He paced through the woods, parallel to the property line, pulling out a small flashlight and shining it along the ground.

Something caught Ivy's eye and she bent down to examine what turned out to be a discarded candy wrapper. And beside the wrapper was the outline of a boot print. "Jonathan." He made his way over, shining his light on the area which illuminated the boot print even further.

He bent down beside her. "Not enough of an impression to get a shoe type. But looks like maybe a size ten or eleven."

"Think the candy wrapper belonged to the same person?" Ivy asked.

"It's worth bagging," he suggested.

Ivy fished an evidence bag from her inside jacket pocket, flaring it out and using a nearby stick to pick up the wrapper and slip it into the bag before sealing it.

"Here," Jonathan said, running his light further into the woods. More prints every few feet led back into the brush. Not every footfall had created a print, but the ground had been soft enough to leave a trail. "Guess she wasn't lying after all." He shot Ivy a smarmy smirk.

"Could have been a hiker that got lost," Ivy suggested. But even she had to admit it was strange. Why would a hiker walk all the way up to the property line, stay long enough to eat a candy bar, then leave?

"Follow the trail?" Jonathan suggested. She shrugged. Why not? Might as well figure out where it led. Jonathan went back to the property line and called out to Mrs. Quinn that they'd be back in a few minutes. She began peppering him with questions from there but he didn't stay long enough to answer. Instead, he rejoined Ivy as she began following the footsteps.

"Where *does* this back up to?" Jonathan asked as they made their way through the woods. The footprints disappeared every now and again before reappearing in a muddier part of the woods. Finally, they came upon one that had pressed so far into the mud they could clearly see it was a combat boot of some kind.

"I'm not sure," Ivy said. She wasn't familiar enough with the geography around this part of town to know what was behind here. There was a good chance it was nothing but woods for miles. "That's military-grade, isn't it?"

Jonathan bent down to take a closer look. "Maybe." He pulled out his phone and snapped a few pictures. As he did, Ivy thought she spotted something through the brush. She pushed forward, leaving Jonathan behind until sticks and branches were pulling at her sleeves and legs. Finally, she broke through the brush to find she stood on the edge of a hiking trail.

"Shit."

"What?" Jonathan called out from behind her.

"It's a trail," she called back. "In each direction." There were still prints in the soft mud, but the ones they'd been following were lost among the dozens of others. She grimaced before turning back and rejoining her partner. "That's it. That's where he came from. Peeled off from the hiking trail and made his way through until he reached the house. Then, presumably went back the same way."

"Well, that's that," Jonathan said, standing back up. With the potential for hundreds of footprints there was no way they'd be able to track these prints further. But it didn't necessarily constitute wrongdoing either. "Want to go deliver the news?"

"Not really," Ivy replied.

"Too bad, that's the job."

Ivy sighed and hung her head as they made their way back to the home where Mrs. Quinn had taken up residence in one of the covered deck chairs, staring daggers at the woods. She promptly stood up as Ivy and Jonathan emerged.

"Well?" she asked as they made their way across the lawn towards her.

"We found evidence *someone* was back there," Jonathan said. "Do you know the hiking trail that runs back behind your house?"

"Of course," she replied. "That's the low ridge trail. But it's hundreds of yards back."

"It looks like someone might have peeled off the trail," Ivy said. "Before reaching your property. Maybe nothing more than a lost hiker."

"If it's a lost hiker, why have I seen him more than once?" Quinn asked. "At least three different times he's been out there, always dressed in black. One time my *kids* were in the yard, playing. And he was just there in the woods, barely visible… watching them. Do you understand?"

"Yes, ma'am," Jonathan replied. "Is there anyone you know of who might want to threaten or intimidate your family? Anyone who might engage in this kind of behavior?"

She shook her head. "My husband is well-liked at his job and I'm head of the neighborhood HOA. I've never had a problem with *anyone*."

"No one who might be jealous, or have a reason to harm your family?"

The woman huffed. "If I knew who was doing this, I wouldn't need you people out here to find out."

"Yes, ma'am," Jonathan replied. "But unfortunately, without a suspect, there isn't much we can do at this point."

"Nothing you can do? Someone is *terrorizing* my family," she spat.

"You may want to invest in a fence for your backyard," Ivy said. "Preferably a high one that you can't see over. It would not only provide security but keep your children from going where they shouldn't."

"That's your solution?" she huffed, crossing her arms. "A fence? Half the reason Jerry and I bought this property was because of the view from the back. And now you just want me to cover it up?"

"I'm sorry, Mrs. Quinn, but there's really very little else we can do. Just keep a sharp eye and if you see the man again, call us immediately," Jonathan said.

"God, you people are worthless," the woman said, turning and heading back inside. "Show yourselves out, you know the way."

"Well, that went about as I expected," Ivy said as they returned to the car. "What now?"

"Hold the evidence until something else develops," Jonathan replied.

Chapter Four

T HE REST of the day remained relatively uneventful, as she
and Jonathan returned to the station to file their report on the
Quinn situation before moving on to the other stack of cases
that populated their desks. It turned out Ayford was a lot more
structured than Nat, and required updates on all their open
cases, as well as step-by-step progress reports. It had taken Ivy
the better part of the day to pull that information together
before she'd had yet another meeting with Ayford, this time
also with Jonathan. They'd both gone over not only their open
cases, but the case they'd just finished up regarding Father
Rouge. Ayford wasn't convinced there wasn't something else
that couldn't be done about the resolution of the case— that
was— until he read Ivy's report.

Ivy couldn't exactly blame the man— he was coming into
a new situation, covering a much larger team than he'd originally signed up for. It made sense he wanted to get a handle
on every case that had been dumped on his lap. At times
during the meeting, Ivy could practically *feel* the anger at Nat
radiating off the man, though he never broke his composure.

Finally, quitting time came around and Ivy had never been
happier to get out of the office. While Jonathan hadn't asked

her any further questions about the cabin, she could sense the inquiries were right on the tip of his tongue. It was a relief to be out from under his gaze all day. He meant well, but sometimes even the words that remained unsaid were the loudest.

And while she wished she could go straight home and take a long bath— it felt like the end of a forty-eight-hour day— she had an errand she needed to run first.

As she pulled up to the now-familiar house, she was surprised to find the entire yard had been trimmed. The grass that had been knee-high only two days ago was now as short as an army recruit's haircut. In fact, it was almost too short— it looked like whoever had trimmed it cut it so close she could easily make out brown patches. However, the lawn looked tidy and someone had taken care to clean up the edges as well. Just as Ivy got out of the car a small little dog came bounding around the house, yipping as he reached the chain-link fence, trying to scramble over it.

"Hero!" Ivy said. "Where did you come from?"

"Hey, Vee."

Ivy looked to the porch of the house where Oliver stood, his weight supported by a single crutch. His blonde hair was wet against his head, combed back so it didn't fall in messy strands around his face. He was dressed in sweats, but it wasn't hard to see from the grimace on his face it was causing him pain.

"What are you doing out of bed?" Ivy demanded, coming through the gate and giving Hero a couple of rubs on his head.

"What?" Oliver asked innocently. "I had to take a shower."

"You're not supposed to be doing anything other than the absolute essentials," Ivy replied.

"Showers are essential," he replied. "I only got one sponge bath the whole time they had me in the hospital. I smelled like a men's locker room."

She couldn't argue the point. When she'd helped get him back home yesterday, he'd sported a very particular odor.

"You cut your grass too?" she asked sarcastically as she made her way up the walk with Hero right on her heels.

"I had someone come over this morning," he replied. "I figured Hero needed more space to run around. And… maybe you were right. Maybe it was a security risk. If it looks like no one is home, no one else is going to be watching out for us."

On her first visit here a couple of months ago, Ivy had joked Oliver had been hiding booby traps in the wilderness that had been his front yard. But now that all the grass was gone, there was nothing but a normal lawn underneath. Hero, for his part, seemed to love it, dashing back and forth as Ivy headed to the porch, doing his best to outrun himself every time. Ivy still hadn't received a full explanation as to what had caused someone to come into Oliver's home and beat him half to death, but considering he had just been discharged from the hospital yesterday, she wasn't about to pressure him until he felt better.

"Jeez, what happened to you?" Oliver asked. "You look like you've been awake all night. How did it go at the cabin?"

"I don't want to talk about it," she replied. "I just came by to make sure you didn't need anything."

"A phone call would have sufficed," he replied.

She shrugged. "I guess I'm just making sure you're not getting into any more trouble."

He held up a trio of fingers. "Scout's honor. Not like I can do much anyway until I replace my equipment. You wanna come in for a drink?"

When she'd made her way over, Ivy had expected to find Oliver on the couch halfway to Toontown on painkillers. Seeing him up already was a good sign that he was serious about his recovery. "Sure."

He turned and headed into the house with Hero close behind him. "C'mon in."

"Can I—" Ivy said, stepping forward.

Oliver smiled. "That's okay. I know the physical contact thing is still tough. I can make it on my own." He hobbled down the hallway, leaning heavily on his crutch as she closed the door behind them. Considering how Ivy had found him a few days ago, it was a miracle he was walking at all. The little dog jumped excitedly at Ivy before running into the kitchen ahead of Oliver. It took him a long time to make it back to the kitchen as well, before he slowly lowered himself down into one of the chairs, wincing as he did.

"Would you mind getting me something?" he asked.

"Sure."

"I left my meds in the living room."

Ivy headed back down the hallway to the makeshift bed that she and Aunt Carol had made up for Oliver the night before. It was messy, indicating he hadn't gotten much sleep. She grabbed the bottle, giving it a shake. It still felt full from yesterday.

"Have you been taking any of these?" she asked as she returned to the kitchen.

"Been trying not to," he replied. "But the shower was tough. I thought maybe the pain would subside but it's only getting worse."

She set the bottle down before him. "That's what they're for."

"I know," he said, grimacing as he opened the first bottle. "But you know how addictive these things can be. I don't want to get hooked on them."

"Yeah." She hadn't thought of that. "Maybe just half a pill then?"

"Good idea." Ivy got up and retrieved a knife from the kitchen drawer as a rumble of thunder rolled in the distance. She handed it to him before sitting back down.

"Do you have something for dinner?"

"I was just going to order takeout," he replied.

Ivy huffed and got up again, going to the fridge.

"Vee, really, it's not a big deal."

"We got you groceries for a reason," she replied. "And you're going to use them."

He chuckled. "Yes, ma'am." Ivy got to work pulling out the basic ingredients for a chicken broth, realizing just how much she was being like Aunt Carol in the moment. But it also helped to have something to do.

"Sure you don't want to talk about last night?" Oliver asked, gulping down one of the pills.

"Sure you don't want to talk about who broke in here and attacked you?" she shot back.

"*Touche*," he replied. The thunder rumbled again. "How's ole' pencil neck doing?"

Ivy shot him a glare, a frown across her lips.

Oliver grinned, then winced again at the pain of the movement. His face was still swollen from the beating and would be sore for weeks. "Sorry, couldn't help myself."

"Jonathan is fine," she replied. "I'll be sure to tell him you asked."

She poured a box of chicken stock into a large pot before putting it on one of the electric burners, then got started chopping the vegetables. Hero looked up at the noise and came over to sit at her feet, wiggling his tail.

"What's, uh… what's happening at work? You know, with… everything."

Ivy slid the vegetables into the broth, setting the cutting board down for more. "Organized chaos. We've got a new boss, who is now overseeing *two* departments until Nat either comes back or is formally let go."

"How is that?"

"Tense," she replied. "But okay. For now." She paused

cutting for a moment. "I don't suppose you've seen anything else?"

He shook his head. "Tracker still shows San Francisco. Maybe that's her final destination."

Ivy sighed. "I just wish I knew what the hell was going on. I wish she hadn't been so cowardly. She knew I'd figured it out. Why couldn't she just face me?"

"People are selfish by nature," Oliver replied. "You caught her in a lie. She probably decided running was the best way to get ahead of the situation so she wouldn't have to deal with it. Think about it. If she's been holding on to this secret for fifteen years, you think she's just going to come out and admit it?"

"I hoped so," Ivy replied. "I thought she had enough respect for me to at least give me that much. But apparently, I was wrong." She slid the carrots and onions into the soup just as it was beginning to bubble. She turned down the heat to a low simmer, opening the cabinets and looking for some spices.

"I'm not going to give up looking for that other guy," Oliver said. "As soon as I get my equipment back up and running, I'll start working on it for you."

"Good luck," she replied, plucking some basil flakes and oregano out of the cabinet before sprinkling them in. "I have a feeling if that man doesn't want to be found, he won't be."

"You said he was older, right? In his sixties?"

She nodded. "And very straightforward. Could have even been an ex-cop. At least, that's how he came across."

"Did you consider talking to the sketch artist down at your station?"

"And give my new boss more ammunition against me? No thank you," she replied. "I think it's best to keep all of this off the books. Especially now that Nat's gone. Before, when she was still around and could take the fall for some of this, it was different. But there's no one left to blame. And if something goes wrong, guess who they'll be looking at?"

"That's a good point." He shifted in his chair which got Hero's attention. The little dog came trotting over, then put his front two paws on the chair, looking to be picked up. "Sorry, bud, can't right now. Maybe in a few days," Oliver added.

Ivy watched them for a few moments. The dog so wanted to hop onto Oliver's lap. "Do you want Carol to take him back?" Ivy said, having finished adding all the ingredients. "She wouldn't mind. I don't want you to have to run around after him while you're trying to get better."

"We'll be okay," he said. "He makes me get my fat ass off the couch. In fact, I'd probably still be there if he hadn't had to go out this morning."

Ivy eyed the small dog. "And you're sure there's no chance of those people coming back? You were damn lucky they didn't hurt him last time. Next time might not—"

"There won't be a next time," Oliver said. "I'm going to make sure of that."

Ivy frowned. She didn't like his tone of voice. It was as if he was looking for revenge. And he was in no condition to take retribution out on anyone. It bothered her that he might even be considering it. One thing was for sure: she needed to get to the bottom of what had happened *before* he went off and did something else stupid that might get him killed this time.

She wanted nothing more than to tell him all of this— to figure out just what had happened to him. But she was in no position to ask. Not unless she wanted to delve into the specifics of her own experiences last night, which were off the table completely.

"Here you go, better than anything you'd get from a fast-food joint." She filled a bowl and set it in front of him, the steam rising up from the soup.

"Never thought I'd see the day when Ivy Bishop actually cooked something," he replied with a grin.

"Desperate times and all that," Ivy said before filling a

bowl for herself and taking her seat. As they began to eat, drops of rain splattered against the windows and the makeshift covering over Oliver's broken window.

"Guess I should get that fixed next," he said, pointing to the broken window with his spoon. "Especially if this rain doesn't plan on letting up anytime soon."

But Ivy barely heard him. She was lost in her thoughts of the night before; the rain having brought it all back again. As Oliver continued to talk, Ivy found herself falling deeper and deeper into the hole once again.

A hole with no bottom.

Chapter Five

"Bishop!"

Ivy hurried down the hallway of the precinct, a coffee in one hand and a file folder in the other as she rushed to meet with Jonathan. She'd gotten in early, in hopes of getting a jump on some of the cases they had parsed through yesterday after their outing. But apparently Lieutenant Ayford was an early bird as well, seeing as he was there no more than fifteen minutes after Ivy. He hadn't greeted her with much more than a gruff nod when he came in and Ivy had hoped that would be the end of their interaction for the day. But from the sound of him bellowing her name she guessed that had been too much to hope for.

"Yes, sir?" she asked, poking her head into his office.

"Did you and White investigate this Quinn case yesterday?"

She nodded. "We did. Our report should be in the file. There wasn't much we could do, though we did find some preliminary evidence. It's already been processed."

"Well, you're going back out there," he said, his gaze stern.

"Why?" she asked.

"Because one of her kids is missing."

~

"Did we miss something?" Ivy asked as Jonathan drove back out to the Quinn home. The call had come in first thing this morning, after the mother had discovered her son missing when he didn't come down for breakfast. An APB had been put out to all units to be on the lookout for the boy along with his description. Since they didn't know who could have taken him, they had little else to go on.

"There wasn't anything to miss," Jonathan replied, his face stern as he drove. His words were clipped, which meant he was as aggravated with himself as Ivy was. As soon as Ayford had given them the news they'd jumped into action, calling in tech services to meet them there. For once, Ivy had allowed Jonathan to take the wheel. His face had been a mixture of frustration and distress, and she thought maybe he needed to take charge. Not that she was happy about the situation either. She was forced to admit she'd been distracted yesterday, and her head hadn't been in the game. Coming off Sunday night, she hadn't been in the right headspace to investigate the case; she just hadn't been willing to admit it to herself.

It was like fumbling an easy catch. There had been a clear, credible threat to the Quinn family and she'd just brushed it off as an errant hiker. Of course, there was still the possibility this was all some kind of misunderstanding and the boy had just run away during the night, but Ivy didn't think that was the case.

Despite Jonathan's reassurance, they should have taken a closer look, maybe gone inside the house. As investigations go, they'd been sloppy. She should have been more focused— more intent.

As they pulled up to the home there was already a white county van on site, along with two black and whites, their lights flashing as neighbors across the street stood out on their porches and watched the commotion.

"This is going to be a train wreck," Jonathan muttered.

"Hey," Ivy said, putting her hand on his arm briefly before removing it again. Despite the pain, she was finding it easier and easier to do lately. And for him, she was willing to endure it. "We work with what we have. And this time, we won't miss anything. You still have the photo of that boot print from yesterday and the candy wrapper is in evidence. It might not have been a total waste."

He sighed, turning the engine off before nodding. "We need to fix this."

"Agreed," she replied.

They stepped out of the vehicle as Officer Toombs approached. "How does it look in there?" Jonathan asked.

"Wife's pretty shaken up," Toombs replied. "Husband is on a rampage. Girl is up in her room. Burns is here, but she didn't want to get started until you two gave her the go-ahead."

Jonathan nodded. "Appreciate that. Keep an eye on any onlookers. Our kidnapper might have stuck around to watch the aftermath of his handiwork."

"Yes, sir," Toombs said and headed over to one of the other officers who was keeping an eye on the perimeter.

"I hate the idea he could be right here," Ivy said. "Relishing the scene."

"Sometimes they can't help it," Jonathan replied. "Especially the narcissistic ones. They love seeing the chaos they cause. And occasionally they're so confident they won't be caught they like to stay close."

Ivy looked at the nearby neighbors, some of whom were walking down their driveways towards the house. "You think one of the neighbors might be responsible?"

"They know the home and neighborhood better than anyone," he replied as they made their way past the gate to the backyard and up the steps to the porch. "We'll need to speak with all of them anyway, see if anyone saw or heard anything last night."

The front door was already cracked open when they reached it and Ivy could hear raised voices from inside.

"—don't care what you do as long as you do *something*," a man— presumably Mr. Quinn— was yelling.

Jonathan took the lead as they entered the house to find a tall man in a white button-down shirt and black slacks pointing his finger at Officer Kilgore. "And another thing," he added before catching sight of Jonathan and Ivy out of the corner of his eye. His finger immediately dropped as he addressed them. "*Finally*. Took you people long enough."

"Mr. Quinn, I am Detective White. This is my partner, Detective Bishop." Upon hearing their names, Mrs. Quinn stuck her head around the doorway.

"*You*," she practically growled before pushing past her husband. She was still in her robe and her hair was up, her makeup looking like it was about halfway done. Dried tear marks had cut lines through her makeup and her eyes were red-rimmed. "No, you, get out. I want someone else."

Ivy and Jonathan stopped in the middle of the hallway as Mrs. Quinn barreled towards them. "I tried to tell you yesterday, but you wouldn't listen. And now my son is missing. He's *gone*, do you understand that? He's *GONE*." She grabbed Jonathan's lapels as she nearly collapsed into him. He had to hold her up as she began a fresh round of sobs.

"Brooke," her husband said, coming up behind her and taking her by the arms. But still she held tight to Jonathan's coat. "*Brooke!*"

Finally, the woman let go, her cries of anguish only increasing as she turned and cried into her husband's shoulder.

"Give me a moment," he said, keeping his voice even as he led his wife back to the room she'd come from.

Jonathan motioned for Officer Kilgore to follow them, which he did.

"I'm glad that was you and not me," Ivy said, once they'd disappeared around the corner.

"It's understandable," Jonathan replied. "She did the right thing. She called us out here to try and prevent something like this from happening."

"Take a look around," Ivy said. "This can't be random. It has to be someone who knows them."

Her partner nodded. "More than likely." To the right of them was a home office which housed a desk and a small library, as well as a bevy of photos and awards that had been hung on the walls. The room itself looked out onto the street through a bay-style window with floor to ceiling panels, though Ivy recalled not being able to see inside from the street. And because it was overcast this morning, she was beginning to think the windows weren't regular windows but instead double-paned, in order to keep intruders from looking into the home. A lack of any curtains or window dressings meant they never closed this window, despite it having an expansive view.

While Ivy searched the office, Jonathan stood in the hall-way, poking his head into the dining room which was on the other side of the doorway. It was as large as the office, but had a lower ceiling and a table that could seat at least eight.

On the office desk was a small laptop, and a few other photographs, mostly of the Quinn family. One was of Mr. Quinn shaking hands with someone who looked important, though Ivy didn't recognize his face.

"Sorry about that," Quinn said, returning to them and causing Ivy to look back up after inspecting the desk. "Albie is her world, especially now that our daughter is older. Now, tell me how you're going to find my son."

Mr. Quinn wasn't the kind of man who minced words. Nor was he the kind who seemed to take *no* for an answer. He seemed to Ivy to be the kind of man who would command a room. And given his height— probably six-two or six-three, and his impressive stature, he was more than likely used to doing so.

"Mr. Quinn—" Jonathan began.

"Call me Jerry," he interrupted.

Jonathan shot Ivy a quick look. "Let's start from the beginning. Can you tell us what you know?"

"Someone broke into my house and kidnapped my son, that's what happened," he replied.

"How did they break in?" Ivy asked.

The man paused. "I'm sorry?"

"You said they broke in. Was it through a window? Or did they use one of the doors?"

"I... don't know."

"Were all your doors and windows locked last night, Mr. Quinn?" Ivy asked.

"No," he replied. "My wife likes to keep some of the upstairs windows open, especially when it rains. She says it helps her sleep. It's a habit my daughter has picked up."

"May we take a look at the rest of your home?" Jonathan asked.

The man furrowed his brow for a moment, then held out his hand, indicating they should go ahead.

Ivy took a quick look at the wooden staircase before beginning to climb. It had been outfitted with an expensive-looking runner, though there were bits of dirt and debris on the carpeting.

She glanced at Mr. Quinn who wasn't wearing any shoes. "Do you normally wear shoes in the house?"

"My wife doesn't like when we do," he replied. "Sometimes the kids forget."

"Has anyone from our office been upstairs?"

"No. Just my daughter."

Ivy motioned to Jonathan. "We should get Burns to examine this."

"Dirt?" Quinn asked.

"If it was tracked in by the person who took your son, yes," Ivy said. "Do you believe they may have come in through the upstairs windows?"

"The only windows we keep open were the ones in our bedroom," he replied. "And I'm a *very* light sleeper. I didn't hear a thing all night."

"Did you wake up at all?" Ivy asked.

He paused a moment. "No, I don't think so."

"I'll be right back," Jonathan said, headed for the backyard to retrieve Burns and her team.

"My wife told me you were both here yesterday," Quinn said. "She said your advice was to *build a fence*."

Ivy inwardly winced. "I apologize," she said. "Yesterday was a tough day for me. I've been dealing with some personal issues and I let them get in the way of work."

Quinn raised his eyebrows, then sighed. "I can't say I don't understand," he replied. "I have those days once a week."

"What do you do, Mr. Quinn?" Ivy asked, thinking about the pictures in the office.

"Once upon a time my family came from coal. But times change. I'm on the executive development board for green energy for Oakhurst and the surrounding counties. We approve or deny any and all new green initiatives for the valley."

"Any contentious approvals or denials lately?"

"Sure," he said. "Happen just about every time. No matter which way you cut it, someone is always unhappy."

"Anyone unhappy enough to follow you home? Target your family?"

Before he could answer, Jonathan appeared back around the corner with Burns in tow, her short, silver hair pinned back out of the way as usual. Burns had been on site during Ivy's first real case and in every instance she'd worked with the woman, Ivy had found her to be competent and more than capable.

"Bishop," Burns said as she approached the stairs.

Ivy nodded. "How have you been?"

"Never better," she replied, looking at the dirt that had been left on the stair runner. "I'll get a sample of this. You two keep going."

"Do you mind showing us your bedroom?" Ivy asked Mr. Quinn.

"I told you, there's no way he could have come in through there. I would have heard him," Quinn replied.

"Even so," Ivy insisted. "Indulge us."

Chapter Six

As THEY HEADED up the stairs of the Quinn home, Ivy noticed more dirt spots on the runner, calling them out to Burns below, who said she'd pull samples of each. Ivy, Jonathan and Mr. Quinn were all careful to avoid stepping on them. She also insisted Mr. Quinn not touch the railing. They'd need to dust for prints everywhere.

The stairs led to a small landing where a couple of chairs sat beside each other, one of which was covered in toys. "This is the kids' play area," Quinn said. "Or… it was when they used to play together."

"Do they not get along?" Jonathan asked.

"My daughter is a teenager," he replied. "Thinks she's too mature for her younger brother." Though as he said it, his gaze trailed off down the hallway, presumably towards his son's door.

"Our bedroom is right here," he said, indicating the first door on the landing near the railing. "We set it up that way so we could hear them if they ever tried to sneak past."

Ivy didn't comment, but Quinn must've really thought he was a light sleeper if he was willing to believe that. In her experience, not as many people slept as lightly as they thought. The door was partially cracked and Ivy decided to pull on a nitrile glove before entering, just in case. The bedroom was typical enough, a bed, a couple of pieces of furniture and a door that led to an en-suite bathroom. Two large windows framed either side of the bed. There were no dirt prints in here like there had been on the stairway, but she could see definite impressions in the carpet. But they weren't clear enough to determine if they'd come from Mr. Quinn or someone else.

Heading over to one of the windows, she noted again the lack of any curtains or drapes. "How dark does it get in here at night?"

"Dark enough," Quinn replied. "We have tinting on all the windows that blocks out UV and lowers how much light comes in. At night it's almost pitch black."

Ivy nodded and unlatched the window, noting it opened sideways rather than up and down like most other similar windows. Below was a straight drop twenty-five feet to the ground and it didn't look like there was anything to climb onto. The backyard stretched out before her out to where the property line touched the woods. "Nice view."

Quinn slumped down on the bed, his hands between his knees. "It's why we bought the house."

If someone had come through these windows they would have needed a ladder to get up here. But because of the way they opened, someone could fit through them easily.

"Mr. Quinn, may we see your son's bedroom?" Jonathan asked.

He seemed to gather himself before standing again. "This way." He led them back down the hallway, passing the door on the left before coming to a door on the right.

"Wait," Ivy said as he reached for the handle. She edged around him, careful not to touch and opened it herself with her gloved hand. "Please stay out here for a moment." Jonathan followed her in as they took in the room.

The bed was a mess of sheets and covers, looking like a tussle had taken place. So why hadn't the boy cried out? Even if the Quinns had slept through the intruder gaining access to the home, surely wouldn't the kid have tried to call for help?

For an eight-year-old, though, the room was tidy. A pile of toys sat in one corner, while sports posters dominated the walls. Ivy noted this room was on the same side of the home as the master bedroom and had a view that looked out on the backyard as well. Maybe this stalker person had been watching the boy— Albie— for a while now, plotting his move.

"What do you think?" Jonathan asked as they made their way around the room.

"It doesn't make sense," she replied. "A struggle indicates the kid was awake when he was taken. Even if the kidnapper used chloroform or something similar, it would have taken a second to take effect. So why didn't he yell for help?"

"Too scared?" Jonathan offered.

"Maybe." She took one more look at the room. "I dunno. I just don't like it."

"Burns is going to need her people to work the room over," Jonathan said, scanning the room. Ivy approached the window, noting it was the same as the ones in the primary bedroom— the kind that opened sideways. It was large enough that a full-grown person could slip in and out of it easily. But unlike the other windows, this one had a latch with a little lock on it that kept it shut and out of the boy's reach, presumably so he wouldn't accidentally open it and fall out.

"Couldn't have come in through here," she said. "Window is locked from this side."

"It's always been that way," Quinn said from the doorway. Ivy turned to face him. "When we moved in here, the windows were old and the house was drafty. Updating them with these new ones saves us a fortune in heating bills. And the tinting keeps anyone from being able to see inside, giving us all the privacy we need."

"Even at night?" Ivy asked.

"Especially at night."

She grimaced. Even if the person Mrs. Quinn had seen was watching the house, he wouldn't have been able to see inside. "Any other windows on this side of the home?"

Quinn nodded and they followed him further down the hall to the last door. It led to another bedroom that was being used as a storage room of sorts. There was only one window in here, but it was partially blocked by totes and boxes. Ivy didn't see an assailant making his way through all of this stuff without making any noise.

"Let's see the rest of it," Jonathan said.

Quinn led them to the other side of the hall, showing them a bathroom with a small window that faced to the front of the house. Kids' toothbrushes sat in a little cup by the sink and there were rubber ducks on the edge of the tub. A small curling iron had been left on the counter, unplugged.

"Ugh," Quinn said, reaching for the iron. "Jasmine has started getting into doing her hair more. I've told her a thousand—"

"Don't touch it," Ivy said. "Don't touch anything else."

"You think the kidnapper came in here and curled his hair?" Quinn asked.

"No, but if he didn't know the layout of the house, he may have checked a few rooms before finding your son. It's possible he errantly touched something. We'll need to check every-thing. Has your daughter left her room?"

"Not to my knowledge."

Ivy nodded to Jonathan, who indicated Quinn take them to the last room upstairs. The door was decorated in stickers and a little nameplate that said *Jasmine* in rainbow letters.

"Jazz, hon?" Quinn asked as he knocked. "The police are here. They need to see your room."

There was some shuffling inside before the door opened a moment later, revealing a miniature Mrs. Quinn, right down to her bright blonde hair. Her eyes were puffy, though Ivy caught a look of defiance in the girl's face.

"This will only take a second," Jonathan said. Jasmine moved to the side and Jonathan went into the room while Ivy stayed at the door.

"Do you mind if I ask you a few questions?"

The girl looked at her dad, who nodded, then she shrugged.

"Did you hear anything last night? Anything strange?"

Jasmine shook her head.

"Did you wake up at all?"

"No," she replied. "I slept really hard. I didn't wake up until Mom started screaming this morning."

Ivy noticed the door to her room had one of those holes in it that could unlock the other side with a small pin or paper-clip. "Do you normally keep your door locked at night?"

Her gaze shifted. "No. I'm not supposed to," she said.

"But you do, don't you?" Ivy asked.

She shot a quick look at her dad again before looking at the floor.

"It's ok, hon. You're not in trouble," Quinn said.

"Yeah… I usually unlock it before my parents wake up."

Quinn turned to Ivy. "My wife doesn't like to have closed doors in this house. I've tried to explain to her that making a teenager keep their door open is like trying to beat up the ocean. It's useless, and you're always going to lose."

"Why do you keep your door locked?" Ivy asked Jasmine.

She shot another quick glance at her dad. "Because of my mom."

"She… isn't the best with boundaries," Quinn added. "And you know how teenagers like their privacy."

Ivy couldn't blame her. "Do you know if your brother locked his door too?"

Jasmine nodded.

"Looks pretty clean," Jonathan said, sweeping the room with his eyes. "No errant footprints as far as I can see. No locks on the windows, though. And it overlooks a roof peak where someone could climb up if they really wanted to."

"What?" Jasmine asked, her eyes wide with terror.

"Oh, I mean, they'd have to be really strong and use a ladder," Jonathan said, going a little red in the face.

"Dad?" Jasmine physically grabbed onto her father.

"No one is coming in your room," he said reassuringly. "But maybe we'll keep the windows closed for a while, huh?"

"Do you normally keep your windows open?" Ivy asked.

Jasmine nodded. "I like the fresh air. It helps me sleep."

"And were your windows open last night?" The girl nodded again.

"Is there anything else?" Quinn asked.

"If you both wouldn't mind waiting downstairs," Ivy said. "We need to have our people take a close look at both your bedroom and your son's room."

"How is any of this helping you find Albie?" Quinn replied.

"If we know the circumstances of *how* he was taken," Jonathan replied, "We'll have a much better chance of finding the person behind it."

Jasmine stayed close to her father. Even though she was young, she looked like she had inherited his height. She'd probably be as tall as he was in another few years.

Quinn huffed. "Fine. Jazz, let's go see if we can't help your mother." He led his daughter back down the stairs, passing Burns as she made her way up.

"Well?" Burns asked, snapping off one glove and itching a spot over her left temple.

"May have come in through the master bedroom," Ivy said. "Or, I suppose this room. I'm not sure how else someone would have gotten in."

"Back door looks like it's probably the egress location," Burns replied. "We found a partial down there while we were waiting. And a few prints in the back yard leading to the woods."

"So they ran off into the woods with the kid?" Jonathan asked.

"It's the smart way to go. Avoid any neighbor's cameras out on the street."

"We need to check the ones on the house, just to be sure," Jonathan replied.

"Toombs already asked when they got here," Burns said. "All they have is one of those doorbell cameras and it didn't catch anything in the front of the house."

"That's it?" Ivy asked. "In a house like this?"

Burns held up her hands in a *What are you gonna do?* gesture.

"Let's check the backyard again," Jonathan said. "Are your people still out there?"

Burns nodded. "Talk to Jason. I've got them combing the backyard."

"Also, I'm sending you the image of a boot print we grabbed yesterday. It's not much, but maybe it will help."

"A boot print?" Burns asked.

"Found it in the middle of the woods," he replied. "No idea if it's related or not."

"And we'll need a full workup up here," Ivy said. "Anything you can get us."

Burns nodded with a solemn look on her face. "We're on it. But don't expect any miracles."

Chapter Seven

As they made their way down the stairs, Jonathan tried not to think about the worst-case scenarios that were currently attempting to play out in his head. They were on a tight clock; every second they didn't find this kid meant he was that much further away. But given their working theory— that the kidnapper had used the woods behind the house to both reach the home and abscond with the child— maybe they weren't as far behind as they thought.

"It's about ten minutes to that trail walking, right?" he asked Ivy as they reached the lower floor.

"More or less," she replied.

"And how long would it take to get off that trail? Say to a car that you'd parked at either one of the entrances?"

Ivy pulled out her phone and tapped away for a few moments. "About thirty minutes in either direction. So running… maybe another ten, fifteen?" She paused. "You're trying to figure out how far ahead of us they are."

He leaned closer to her, noting that she didn't pull away like she had when they'd first begun working together. He wasn't sure if it was something he was doing, or if she was working on her issues on her own time, but Ivy was making remarkable progress on her phobias. Though he wished she would trust him enough to tell him about what had happened at the cabin the night before last. Alice's call had been almost frantic, and she'd been more than pissed off, telling him Ivy had abandoned her there. But that didn't sound like Ivy. Still, he couldn't afford to think about it right now. The seconds were ticking, and he could feel each one deep in his core. "I don't need to tell you," he whispered. "This doesn't look good. Without a suspect... we're shooting in the dark."

She nodded. "It *has* to be someone who knows the family, right? Why else target them?"

He shrugged. "Home doesn't have a lot of security. No alarm system, only one camera and easy access through the back."

"But why take one of the kids? Why not rob them or something? Why would someone want the son?"

"That's what we need to figure out," Jonathan said. He'd been thinking much the same way, that there had to be a personal connection driving this crime. Kidnappers didn't just randomly target victims. At least not in ninety-five percent of the cases.

"Let's try the family one more time," he said. "Then I want another crack at the backyard." Ivy nodded and followed him back to the living room, where Mr. Quinn sat on one of the couches, Mrs. Quinn in his arms, her vision glassy while Jasmine sat on one of the other chairs, her legs pulled up to her chest, lost in her phone. Officer Kilgore stood in the corner while one of Burns's people worked in the open kitchen that connected to the living room. The back door was wide open, its handle covered with fingerprint dust.

"I know it seems like we're treading the same ground, but we need to make sure," Jonathan said. "Are you positive there isn't anyone who wishes your family any ill will?"

Mrs. Quinn just glared at him, though her eyes weren't as

sharp as they had been before. If he had to guess, she'd probably taken something for her nerves.

"No," Mr. Quinn said. "We've received no threats. And no one has so much as looked at our family funny."

"What about Uncle Jack?" Jasmine asked.

"Who's Uncle Jack?" Ivy asked.

"My brother," Quinn said. "Jack has had a… tough time of it lately." He turned to his daughter. "But he'd never break into our home and kidnap you or your brother."

Ivy kept her attention on Jasmine, which was beneficial, because Jonathan didn't think the girl would respond well to him. Especially after his faux pas upstairs.

"Why do you think your uncle might be involved?" she asked.

"Look, Jack is not the problem," Quinn said. "It's someone else."

"I'd prefer her to answer, if you don't mind," Ivy said, pinning Mr. Quinn with her gaze before turning back to Jasmine.

"He asked Daddy for money a while back," she said. "I overheard them. When Daddy refused to give it to him, he said we'd all be sorry before hanging up."

"You heard that?" Quinn asked.

"We all heard it," Mrs. Quinn said groggily, rubbing her head. "You were practically shouting."

"Why didn't you mention this before?" Jonathan asked.

"Listen," Quinn said, standing back up. "My brother is a lot of things, but a kidnapper isn't one of them. Like I said, he's had a tough time and is just going through a rough patch."

"How much money was he asking for?" Ivy asked, watching Quinn carefully.

"Five thousand dollars," he admitted.

"Where does your brother live?" Jonathan asked, pulling out his notepad. Quinn hesitated. "We can either get it from you or we can get it from the DMV. But we're going to find him, Mr. Quinn. Do you want us to find your son or not?"

He sighed. "Fifteen-oh-four Webster Avenue," he said. "Unit eight."

"When's the last time you spoke with your brother?" Ivy asked.

"That day on the phone," he said. "About two weeks ago."

"Does he have a key to this house?" Quinn shook his head no. "But he's been here before? He knows the layout?" The man sighed, before nodding.

Jonathan pointed at Kilgore. "Stay here, update Burns and keep looking for any evidence."

Kilgore nodded. "You want me to call it in?"

Jonathan was already headed for the door. "No, we'll inform Ayford on the way."

Ivy was right behind him. "I assume we're calling in backup."

Jonathan pushed through the door and back outside, trotting for his car. "We need to know if he's home or not. See if there's an available unit that's close. And if he is, tell them not to let him leave."

They hopped in the car and Ivy got on the radio as Jonathan put the car in gear and pulled away from the curb. The crowd was still gathered close to the road and Toombs worked to get them out of the way. But they were nothing more than a blur of faces to Jonathan. He had failed the Quinns yesterday by not doing everything he could have to make them feel secure. He needed to fix this. With any luck, they'd have Albie back home before lunchtime.

"Unit Sixty-Four is on the way," Ivy said after getting off the radio.

"Good," Jonathan said, pressing harder on the accelerator.

"This isn't your fault, you know," his partner said, catching him off guard.

"Who said it was?"

She scoffed. "If there's one thing I know, it's body language. The best way to prevent unwanted physical interactions is to watch people and learn what they'll do. And right now, your lead foot and that steel gaze tell me you're beating yourself up over yesterday."

"Since when did you start going easy on yourself?" He winced even as he said it. She was right, he was on edge and taking it out on her wouldn't do anyone any good. "I'm sorry," he added before she could say anything. "I didn't mean that. You're right, I'm beating myself up because I feel like we could have done something else yesterday. Something to prevent this."

"What?" she asked.

"I don't know."

They were quiet for a moment as he drove. "Sometimes, things just go bad," she finally said. "There's not always someone to blame."

This was new. Coming from the woman who had almost gotten herself killed because she had been trying to find the person who kidnapped her one-time caretaker and the two children under her supervision? Jonathan hadn't even thought about the parallels until now. But in that case they had clear evidence someone had broken in and taken all three of them. The culprit— John Shepard— hadn't been subtle in his work, even though he eventually blamed it on someone else.

But whereas that had been like dealing with a sledgehammer, this was more like a scalpel. Whoever had gotten into the Quinn house— whether it was this *Uncle Jack* or not— had been quiet, stealthy, and left with barely a trace. Two completely different MOs. That, and Shepard was locked up awaiting trial.

Jonathan had to face it; Ivy was right. There wasn't much else they could have done yesterday. Mrs. Quinn hadn't revealed anything about the brothers fighting and without the ID of a specific person, there hadn't been much the police could have done to make the situation any safer. And the Quinns hadn't done themselves any favors. Had it been Jonathan's house, he would have had backyard cameras the day he moved in.

"You know what, don't listen to me," Ivy said. "I don't know what I'm talking about."

"No, I think you do," he replied. "We were working within a lot of constraints, especially since they weren't up front about this fight with the uncle. It's not anyone's fault."

The radio crackled to life.

"Control, Unit Six-Four. We're ten-twenty-seven at the property on Webster Avenue. We have eyes on a vehicle registered to the address. License plate Charlie-Omega-Niner-Lima-Hotel-Four. Presumed suspect is inside the premises."

"Copy Six-Four," dispatch replied. "Stand by for Unit Twelve."

Ivy picked up the radio. "This is Unit Twelve. Copy that Six-Four. Maintain visual and do not engage. We're en route, ETA nine minutes."

"Roger that, Twelve," Unit Six-Four responded. "Holding position."

Ivy replaced the speaker on Jonathan's radio as Dispatch came across again. "All units, be advised. Unit twelve en route to assist Unit Six-Four. Maintain caution and report any changes."

Jonathan shared a glance with Ivy. This could be it. He could only pray that the kid was inside.

Chapter Eight

Ivy couldn't keep her leg from bouncing as they raced to the apartment. She wasn't used to being in the passenger's seat. And sitting here mentally pushing for Jonathan to get them there faster was driving her nuts. If she'd been behind the wheel, she would have cut every corner, rolled every stop sign, even hopped up on the curbs if she'd needed to. Jonathan was rushing, but wasn't moving nearly fast enough. If Jack Quinn had the boy at his apartment, every second that went by was just that much longer they risked something happening to that kid. Or Jack figuring out that they were on his tail. Either way, the boy was in danger.

She also didn't like that they were dealing with yet *another* kidnapping case so close to their case a few weeks back involving Mrs. Baker. Kidnappings were more common than other violent crimes, such as murder, but this many in as few weeks was an anomaly. And it couldn't be the same perp. John Shepard was locked up in County, awaiting trial.

Then again, Shepard had always maintained there had been someone else giving him the orders, someone behind the scenes telling him what to do. And Ivy— with Nat's help—

had discovered what looked like the remains of surveillance cameras at his property.

She shook her head. No, this was more than likely a family dispute, nothing more. She couldn't let herself get bogged down in conspiracies— she'd had enough of that lately. And she didn't want to think about Nat.

"If you don't step on that accelerator, I'm going to reach over and push it down for you," she said as Jonathan slowed for the next corner.

"I'm going as fast as I feel safe to," he replied. "What if someone jumps out in front of the car?"

"What if lightning strikes us dead right now?" she retorted. "C'mon, Jonathan. *Hit it.*"

Her partner grimaced and pushed the accelerator harder, lurching the car forward. "That's more like it."

"You're a bad influence, you know that?"

"That's not news. I've been told that all my life," she replied, grinning in spite of their present situation. She caught him grinning back. She was grateful to be partnered up with Jonathan. Not many other cops would have understood her… peculiarities. And they definitely wouldn't have defended them. But he'd never wavered, for whatever reason.

"There." She looked up to see the patrol car parked along the side of the road near the apartment complex. It was a two-story brick building with a small parking lot, comprising maybe eight or ten units. A metal staircase led to a balcony on the second floor, providing access to the upper units. Ivy grabbed the radio. "Unit Six-Four, proceed to the alley in the back. We'll approach from the front."

"Ten-four," the reply came on the radio. Jonathan pulled past the patrol car and parked in the lot like they were any other tenants as the patrol vehicle turned and circled around the building on the other side.

"How do you want to do this?" he asked.

"Casual, like we're just regular tenants." They didn't need

to spook Jack Quinn, nor did they need him doing anything rash. If they could get him to come out on his own without suspecting anything, that would be the best situation. Not to mention there was a chance he might not even have the child.

"Agreed. Take the lead?"

"Me?" Ivy asked as she was about to get out of the car.

"Sure. More than likely he'll open the door for you before he will for me."

She conceded the point. Especially if she played it up. If Albie was in that apartment, they couldn't ID themselves as cops up front. Which meant she had to create a performance.

Closing the door of the vehicle so it wouldn't slam, Ivy checked her weapon to make sure the safety was off before she began taking the stairs. Jonathan waited a beat, then followed a few steps behind her. They made their way down the metal walkway until she came to apartment eight. She took a deep breath, then knocked once. Jonathan hung back a few doors down, his weapon out and pointed at the ground. Ivy adjusted her coat so her weapon wasn't showing.

"Yeah?" a voice came from the other side.

"Hey, I need some help," Ivy said. "My car won't start and my phone is dead. Can I use yours for a second?"

She saw the peephole darken as face moved in front of it. "Who are you?"

"I'm a friend of Gloria's who lives below you. She already went to work," Ivy said. She had no idea if there was an actual Gloria that lived in this building; she was betting Jack didn't know his neighbors very well.

She practically held her breath waiting for him to respond. Finally, Jack threw the lock and the door opened to reveal a grizzled man with a passing resemblance to his brother. His face was unshaven, his beard grey and messy, and his eyes were sunken in like he'd been up all night. As soon as he got a good look at Ivy a lecherous grin formed across his face.

"Thanks," Ivy said. "It should just take a minute." She

moved to head into the apartment, but found herself blocked by Jack.

"You know," he said. "If I do a favor for you, maybe you can do one for me." He reached out with one hand but before it got halfway to Ivy, she had his arm behind his back and slammed his face to the ground with her knee in his back. It hurt, but she could handle it.

"Go!" she yelled as Jonathan practically jumped over her to enter the apartment.

"What the *fuck!*" Jack yelled; his words muffled due to the fact he was being pressed hard into the metal walkway. A surge of electricity pulsed through Ivy as she held the man down, but she found she was able to handle it so long as she focused on the task at hand. Finding the kid and getting him to safety. A second later the patrol vehicle pulled back around and Deleon and Suarez came running up the staircase to assist.

Ivy stayed on Jack until the other officers had him in cuffs and got him back on his feet, pushing him up against the railing. "Keep him here," she said as she entered the apartment where Jonathan was already going from room to room. "Anything?"

"Not yet," he replied. "As far as I can tell there's no one else here." Ivy made a cursory inspection of the apartment, checking all the crevices and cabinets, or anywhere small enough to hide a kid. Finally, she was forced to admit Jonathan was right. She replaced her weapon back in her holster as she met back up with her partner.

"No sign of him," she said.

Jonathan motioned they should go speak with Jack outside.

"I'm going to wipe the floor with you people," Jack said as Ivy and Jonathan came back outside. "Do you know who my brother is?"

"Where's the boy?" Ivy demanded.

"What boy?" he asked.

"Your nephew, Albie," Jonathan said.

"How the fuck should I know? School?" There was an aroma about the man, a mixture of marijuana and something else Ivy couldn't immediately place. He also reeked of body odor, like he hadn't showered in a few days. Likewise, his apartment was messy. Sink full of dishes, discarded towels on the bathroom floors, bed missing sheets or anything that resembled a cover. Jack Quinn must be going through a *really* rough patch— either that or he was just a slob by nature.

"Where were you last night?" Ivy asked.

The man sucked back a goblet of snot into his throat and looked as though he was ready to spit on Ivy before Jonathan grabbed the man's jaw, forcing it shut. "You don't want to do that. Swallow it."

Jack tried jerking out of Jonathan's grip, but couldn't find a way to do it. Jonathan pinched the man's nose until he was forced to swallow it down. When he let him go, Jack gasped for air. "You son of a bitch," he growled. "I'll pay you back for that one."

"Location. *Now*," Ivy reiterated.

Jack sneered at her. "I was out sellin' Girl Scout Cookies." The look on Jonathan's face made the man grimace. "Delia's. Until eleven. Then here. Happy?"

Delia's was a strip club on the edge of town, notorious for both their clientele and their employees. Ivy was familiar with it as it was a place the Black Pistons loved to frequent. "Did you leave your apartment at all during the night?"

"Yeah, I have a habit of getting up in the middle of the night and taking a walk out to fucking nowhere," he replied. "No, I didn't leave. Where would I go?"

"Your brother's house," Jonathan said.

The man scoffed. "Jerry don't like me coming around unannounced. I don't think that would have gone over very well, do you?"

"Doesn't mean you didn't do it," Jonathan replied.

"Why the *fuck* would I go over there? Just to get my ass chewed out about how much of my life I've wasted again? I've heard that song and dance enough over the past five years and I don't feel like going through it again."

"Can anyone vouch for your whereabouts last night?" Ivy asked.

Jack sneered again. "No. Unless you count the cokeheads that hang out around here. I'm sure they'll tell you all about it, if they could remember."

"The club will have cameras," Jonathan said. "We can check those."

"When's the last time you saw your nephew?" Ivy asked.

Jack shook his head. "I don't know. Christmas two years ago, maybe? I don't even know what he looks like now."

"Why did you call your brother asking for money?" Jonathan added.

Jack turned back to him. "Why do you think? Does it look like I'm rolling in it here?"

"Did you threaten him if he didn't give it to you?"

"I don't even remember, okay?" he replied. "I was drunk off my ass when I called. I barely remember doing it."

"Do you have a criminal record, Mr. Quinn?"

"No," he replied, then winced. "Wait… yes. Petty theft. Eight months ago. Sometimes I forget." He grimaced before whispering to himself. "How did everything get so fucked up?"

"Your nephew, Albie, is missing," Ivy said. "You're telling us you had nothing to do with it?"

A crease formed across his brow. "Missing? He ran away?"

"Kidnapped is more likely," Jonathan replied.

Jack's posture changed immediately, standing up straighter, his eyes sharper. "Last night?" Ivy nodded. "What happened?"

"That's what we're trying to find out."

"How long has he been gone?"

Ivy checked the time. "Approximately eight hours, but we still don't know exactly *when* he was taken."

Jack's eyes shifted from one side to the other, like he was deep in thought. "Did you check the woods behind their house? There's a trail back there—"

"We know," Jonathan said. "We're looking into it. How do you know about the trail?"

"I've lived in Oakhurst all my life," Jack replied. "I used to be an avid hiker, in my younger days. I've been all over every trail his town has to offer ten times or more."

"Then it wouldn't be hard for you to gain access to their property from the trail," Ivy said.

Jack shook his head. "No, I couldn't. At least, not without difficulty. I injured my back about two years ago— it led to me losing my job. I can't walk more than fifty feet before it starts throbbing. If I go more than a mile, I'm laid out for two or three days. As much as I'd like to, my hiking days are over."

"Then you haven't been watching your brother's house from the woods," Ivy said.

"Why the hell would I do that?" Jack asked. "He doesn't want me there so why would I want to be there?"

Ivy exchanged a glance with Jonathan. This was looking less promising by the minute. Still, this man could be lying about his back condition. "We'd like you to come down to the station to answer some questions," she said.

"Fuck you. I'm not going down to any station," he spat back.

"Mr. Quinn, that's not a request. You can either accompany officers Deleon and Suarez or I can arrest you right now."

"For what?"

Ivy huffed. Talking to this man was beyond frustrating. "For the abduction of your nephew."

"Lady, you are off your rocker if you think I could ever do that," he said. "But sure, I'll come down to your station. Why not? I don't have anything better to do today." Ivy motioned for them to lead him down. As soon as they'd gotten him into the vehicle Jonathan turned back to her.

"Do you want to get Burns down here to search the apartment?"

Ivy shook her head. "Did you notice as soon as we told him about Albie his demeanor changed?"

"Yeah, I saw," Jonathan replied.

"It's hard to fake that kind of concern. Unless he'd practiced it."

"Ivy, people can lie."

"Their mouths, yes. But the body is a much harder thing to control. Didn't you see the way his posture changed?"

"You think he didn't do it because he stood up a little straighter?" Jonathan asked.

She turned to him. "I've spent a lifetime reading people. I *had* to. I'm not saying he's innocent, but from what I can see, it's not looking good. Which means we're wasting our time on the wrong person."

"What do you want to do?" Jonathan asked.

"I don't know," she admitted. "But whatever we do, we better do it fast."

Chapter Nine

AFTER DELEON and Suarez left with Jack Quinn, Ivy and
Jonathan did one more quick sweep of the apartment. There
was absolutely zero evidence that a kid had been there
recently, which helped contribute to a growing feeling in Ivy's
gut they were on the wrong path. They ended up heading
back to the Quinn home to speak with the family again and
finish up with Burns.

Except by the time they arrived, Burns was already pack-
ing up.

"Anything?" Ivy asked as they headed for the white van
where she was loading her supplies into the back.

"A couple of errant prints," she said without looking back.
"But they're only partials. I'll have to compare them against
the family." She closed the door to the van and locked it.
"How did it go over at the brother's house?"

"He's headed to the station," Jonathan said. "We'll question him again there."

"No kid, then."

Ivy shook her head. "I'm not sure he's the perp. Did the
family mention anything else?"

Burns took a deep breath. "Mother's out of it pretty bad.

The dad and daughter aren't doing much better. But I'm not sure they know any more about this than you two do."

"Did you find anything in the backyard?" Jonathan asked.

"Just a few soft prints. Nothing deep or defined enough to pull a cast out of. My guys took it all the way back through to the trail behind the home too."

"What about the print we found yesterday?" he asked. "Near the trailhead?"

"Rain must have washed it away," she replied. "But I'll examine the photo."

"Maybe we should just go focus on Jack Quinn, give the family a few hours," Ivy suggested. "We can always come back later."

"Yeah," he finally admitted. "Thanks, Doc."

Burns nodded. "No problem. I'll get all this back to you as soon as I can." She headed to the front of the van and hopped in, pulling away.

Officer Kilgore was leaning up against his patrol car while Officer Toombs was about twenty feet away, smoking a cigarette. The crowds from before had dispersed and they'd taken down the police tape.

Ivy made her way over to Kilgore. "Anything else to report?"

"Ray and I checked the first four houses on each side of the street closest to this one," he said. "No one remembers anything from last night. The Hursts, over on that side of the house, have a motion-activated camera in their backyard which will sometimes go off if it catches an animal in the neighbors' yards, but we checked— there was nothing from last night."

"What the hell are we dealing with here, a ghost?" Ivy asked as she looked down the street. The homes were far enough apart that checking any of them beyond what Kilgore and Toombs had already investigated would be pointless. "Okay, thanks."

"Need anything else?" he asked.

Ivy sighed, continuing to stare down the street. "Yeah. Stay here for a few hours. See if any suspicious characters happen to come along."

"Define *suspicious*."

"Anyone who is more interested in you or that house than they should be," Jonathan said, joining them. "Was there anyone gathered before who didn't live in one of these homes?"

"There was a couple who live on the next street over who were out for a morning walk," the officer replied. "And there was a repairman working on one of the neighbor's houses. That's it."

"Who was the repairman with?" Ivy asked.

Kilgore pulled out a little black notebook. "Uhh, Landon's Plumbing and HVAC. He was checking the heater for the Coves, who live at 4455, three houses that way." He pointed down the street, but Ivy didn't see a repair truck anywhere.

"Did you call Landon's Plumbing to confirm they had a man out here this morning?"

He nodded. "Yep, it had been on the schedule for a week. Routine maintenance."

"Give me that," Ivy said, taking his book and copying down the information. It wasn't much of a lead, but right now she would take whatever she could get. She handed the book back to Kilgore before turning back to her partner. "Should we close up with the family?"

"Better to do it than not," he said. "It's in our best interests to keep things as smooth as possible."

As much as Ivy didn't want to do it, he was right. She wished she could go back in time and persuade herself yesterday not to be so flippant about Mrs. Quinn's concerns. But that was impossible. There was nothing to do about it now but to try and move forward. But she doubted she would ever get the woman to truly trust her.

"Can you take over?" she asked Jonathan as they climbed the stairs to the home again.

"Sure," he said. "You okay?"

"Just… not sure I can face them again. I thought maybe if Quinn was our guy it would be okay. But I don't think he is. Which means we have to tell them we don't know *where* their son is."

Jonathan nodded. "We'll find him. I know we will."

"Yeah, but the question is will we find him in time?"

"You found those two girls in the Baker case," he said. "If I were the Quinns, I wouldn't want anyone else but us working this case."

"That's sweet," Ivy said, "but you know you're full of it, right?'

That produced a laugh between them which was immediately cut off as the front door opened, revealing Mr. Quinn again. His eyes were more bloodshot than they'd been just a few hours ago and Ivy caught the smell of whiskey on his breath. His tie was missing and the top two buttons of his now-wrinkled white shirt were open.

"Well?" he asked.

"No sign of Albie at your brother's house," Ivy said. "But we're not giving up. We have him down at the station for questioning."

"I already told you. My brother wouldn't do something like that," he said. "You need to quit wasting time and do your jobs." He was sounding more like his wife by the second.

"We are, sir," Jonathan said. "Right now. We just wanted to let you know that those two officers will be staying here for a few more hours, just in case you need anything." He indicated the patrol car where Kilgore and Toombs stood nearby.

"We appreciate that; I need to run a few errands," Quinn said. "It helps knowing they'll be here."

"What kind of errands?" Ivy asked, frowning. Why would

he need to leave? Unless he was planning on looking for Albie himself.

"If you must know, to purchase some firearms," Quinn replied. "I'm not staying one more night in this house until I know I can keep my family safe."

"Sir, that may not—" Jonathan's words died in his throat as Quinn glared at him.

"Are you telling me that I can't defend myself?"

"No, sir, just that in situations like this, heightened emotions—"

"Listen here, *Detective*. Someone violated my home. And until I know who it was, I'm not taking any chances. So don't stand there and preach to me about what I should and shouldn't be doing." Jonathan took a step back.

Ivy fished a card out of her pocket and handed it to the man. "Here is my direct number. As soon as we learn something more, we'll be in touch." She hesitated a moment. "How is— your wife doing?"

"How do you think?" he said. "Her only son is missing."

Ivy nodded apologetically. She shouldn't have asked, but she almost couldn't help herself.

"Detective Bishop here just helped solve another case of kidnapping a few weeks back," Jonathan said, trying to recover. "So trust me when I tell you, we are on this. We will find Albie."

Quinn looked between them before his expression softened somewhat. "Just... hurry."

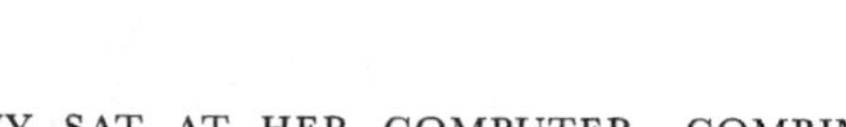

Ivy sat at her computer, combing through everything they had so far. It had been a few hours since leaving the Quinn home and she was beginning to grow anxious. They still had Jack Quinn in custody, though there hadn't been any formal charges or even a full explanation. Jonathan had decided to speak to him alone in hopes he might be able to get something else out of him, but Ivy suspected it was nothing more than a waste of time.

As she was pondering it, her email pinged with a message from Delia's— the club Jack Quinn had attended the night before. Attached was a message from the owner and a link to their camera footage which was on a cloud server. Ivy immediately dove into the cameras, looking for Jack on the monitors. It didn't take her long to find him, leaning over the edge of one of the raised dance platforms, flinging money on the stage before becoming belligerent with one of the security personnel. A few moments later, two bouncers escorted him from the premises and tossed him outside, where he remained motionless for a good twenty minutes before a car finally arrived to pick him up.

Ivy already knew where this was going, but she had to follow it all the way through, no matter what. After observing the name of the cab company on the tape, she picked up the phone and dialed the number.

"Collect-A-Cab," a cheerful woman on the other end said. "Where are you headed?"

"This is Detective Ivy Bishop with Oakhurst Police. I need to speak with your dispatcher, please," Ivy said. "Whoever was on last night around eleven P.M."

"One moment," the woman said as Jonathan passed Ivy on the way to his desk before slumping down.

"Anything?" Ivy asked.

He shook his head, his shoulders bunched up around his ears. "If he's lying, he's the most consistent liar I've ever seen. What about you?"

"Story matches so far— hang on. Hello?"

"This is Forrester. You're with the police?" the man on the other side said.

"Yes," Ivy said, then explained what she was looking for.

"Oh yeah, that call came in around eleven-fifteen, I think.

My driver reported the man was drunk as a skunk. He had to help him in and out of the cab."

"Do you know if he made it back to his apartment after leaving the cab?" Ivy asked, jotting down the notes from the dispatcher.

"Yeah, Omar is a good guy. He said he helped him to his door before leaving him. The guy was so wobbly he wouldn't have been able to stand up under his own power."

"Okay, thank you," Ivy said before hanging up and turning to Jonathan. "Quinn was in no condition to kidnap anyone last night. Video shows him at the club, drunk off his ass and the cabbie confirmed as much."

Jonathan pinched the bridge of his nose. "What do you want to do?"

"We'll have to cut him loose," Ivy said. "We've got nothing to hold him on."

"Great," her partner replied. "Our one lead is a dead end. I'll take care of it," he said.

"Why so generous?" Ivy narrowed her gaze.

"Because you get to inform Ayford," Jonathan replied, patting her on the shoulder as he walked back past.

Ivy's stomach sank at the thought. But she couldn't help place her hand where Jonathan's had just been.

Chapter Ten

Ivy felt like hitting something. Or someone.

The day had been nothing but one disappointment after
another. None of the evidence Burns and her team had
collected ended up producing anything substantial— just a
couple of partial prints that didn't match to anyone in the
family and the dirt on the stairs— which had come from
outside. Their working theory was whoever abducted Albie
had somehow climbed up into one of the open second-story
windows, made their way past the parents or the daughter and
down the hall to the boy's bedroom before taking him and
exiting out the back door, headed back into the woods.

But what didn't make sense was why there was dirt on the
stairs and not beside the windows. It had been raining last
night, so presumably whoever got into the house would have
been wearing muddy shoes. But there was no mud anywhere.
Nothing except that little bit of dirt, which could have been
mud at some point, but Ivy thought it would have been more
plentiful. And why were there no wet spots on the carpets
either? None of this made sense, especially the fact that the
kid hadn't yelled or screamed or *anything*. One of the other

people in that home should have heard something, and yet they'd all been oblivious.

Why would anyone want this kid anyway? There didn't seem to be any financial incentive. Sure, the Quinns were well-off, but not enough to go through the trouble of kidnapping a child and holding him for ransom.

Then again, maybe someone *would* go to that extreme. Tomorrow the plan was to start speaking with Mr. Quinn's co-workers, as well as Mrs. Quinn's friends and acquaintances. The Quinns might not be aware of any outright threats against their family, but that didn't mean they didn't exist.

And yet something about all of this was leaving a very bad taste in Ivy's mouth. Not because it came so soon after the other kidnapping involving Jessa and Taylor, which had ended in the death of Mrs. Baker— but because this seemed eerily familiar in some ways to what had happened to Ivy when she was young.

She hadn't been kidnapped— at least, she didn't think she had— but she'd gone to bed with her parents and her brother only to find herself waking up in the hospital two weeks later with no memory of what had happened to her. Her entire family had gone missing in a single night and she had ended up wandering the streets of Oakhurst, alone, with no explanation. It had been national news at the time, and her story had kept the headlines for months afterward. But as the case had grown cold and no new information came to light, eventually interest had faded, leaving Ivy alone to remember.

Something about this seemed familiar, almost like it was the opposite. Boy goes missing in the middle of the night with no explanation. At least with Mrs. Baker, it was plain to see her home had been trashed and someone had clearly abducted them. But in this case, it was almost *too* clean. And they still had this mysterious man watching from the woods.

The minute Ivy got home, she was going to pour herself something to drink and take a nice, long bath and try to forget about the day. She needed a good night's sleep and a clear mind before going back to work tomorrow. But as she pulled up to her apartment complex, she cursed six ways from Sunday.

Leaning against her car in one of the visitor parking spots, her arms crossed, was Alice Blair. Ivy hadn't seen her since that night at the cabin and judging by the scowl on Alice's face, she was probably still upset at that whole "being left at the cabin alone" thing.

Ivy sighed, pulling into her small garage which sat on the far side of the parking lot. She supposed she should have expected this. Alice wasn't the kind of person who let things go easily. But the fact was, Ivy didn't have time to deal with this, not right now. Going to the cabin had been a waste of time and there was a kid that needed to be found.

"What were you going to do, just leave me hanging forever?" Alice demanded before Ivy could even get out of her car.

"I didn't leave you hanging," Ivy replied, pulling her garage door shut. "I told you there wasn't anything to find in that place and that I was leaving."

Alice's face was practically red with frustration. "Oh, no, that's not how it went at all. And then you just left me there, defenseless."

"You weren't defenseless, you had my aunt's gun," Ivy said, heading for her door. "Which I'll need back, by the way."

"I don't know why I ever thought I could trust you to help me," Alice said. "And here I thought you wanted to get to the truth of what happened to you."

"I do," Ivy said, then stopped with her hand on the door. "Can I… offer you something to drink?"

"Something to drink?" the woman asked incredulously.

"Yeah, you drove all the way over here. Or you can stay out here by yourself," Ivy said, then paused. "Sorry. I'm not the best with people."

Alice crossed her arms. "That's an understatement." The woman huffed. "Fine. But you better have something good in there. And I better get an explanation."

Ivy paused. She'd said something similar to Oliver. Maybe the two of them weren't so different after all. She held the door for Alice, allowing the woman to follow her into the lobby and to the elevator bank.

"You get home this late every day?" she asked.

"New case," Ivy said, pressing the elevator button. "It's… complicated."

Alice softened somewhat. "I'm sure Bianca is already on top of it." She slumped back against the wall as they waited.

"Bianca?"

"You don't watch TV, do you?"

Ivy shrugged. "I'm not much of a TV person, not unless it's for a case."

Alice waved her off. "No one is anymore. Except for people my mother's age and older. Bianca is the newer, better version of me."

The doors opened and Ivy stepped inside, followed by Alice. "Of you?"

"The evening anchor. She took over the desk at KTLV when I took leave to try and get back into field reporting. And to hear my boss talk about it, she's getting the best ratings the station has ever seen."

"Are you having regrets about giving it up?"

Alice pressed her lips into a line. "Not really. But Russ just reassigned my cameraman, which means for the foreseeable future I'll be on my own. And the fact that I barely even covered the Father Rouge story didn't earn me any brownie points."

The doors opened to Ivy's floor and she led the way down the hall. "I can't tell you anything about our current case. You'll have to talk to Lieutenant Ayford."

"I don't really care about your current case. I just want to know why you left me in a creepy fucking cabin in the woods to fend for myself in the middle of the night."

Ivy opened her door and tossed her keys into the small tray on the side table. Alice followed her in but didn't remove her jacket. Just stood in the hallway taking in the apartment, her hands in her pockets.

"Can I get you a beer, or would you prefer wine?" Ivy asked.

"What kind of wine?"

"Umm…" Ivy looked above the refrigerator and realized all she had was a half bottle of Pinot that she'd hadn't finished from the other day. "Pinot Noir?"

The look Alice gave the bottle was all Ivy needed to see. "Beer it is." She pulled two bottles from the fridge and opened them both on the edge of the counter before handing one to her guest.

"Good view," Alice said, stepping up onto the raised platform which took up the far half of the apartment. The giant windows opposite gave a view of the buildings and the town beyond.

"Thanks," Ivy said, pulling off her jacket and tossing it on one of the stools along the countertop.

Alice turned back to face her. Her heels gave her an extra six inches and with her jacket still on, she looked more imposing than Ivy had realized. She was waiting for an explanation, but Ivy wasn't sure she had one. She was right. Ivy *had* technically abandoned her, but it had only been because she literally couldn't stand to be in that place a second longer than she had to.

"Have you ever been somewhere that just… felt bad?" Ivy asked. "Like you can't explain why, you just know you never want to be in that place again?"

"Yeah," Alice replied. "It's called my house."

Ivy furrowed her brow.

"My mother is recuperating in my guest room," Alice said

with a bit of a smile, but upon seeing Ivy's confusion, it disappeared. "Never mind."

"I've been in some bad places before," Ivy said. "Crack houses, abandoned buildings, jails. And sometimes I'll come across a place that just feels… wrong. I don't know why. But all I know is I would never want to stay there for very long. It's like being inside a sickness. You know if you don't leave soon, you'll never be able to."

"And that's what happened to you in the cabin?" Alice asked, looking slightly less skeptical.

"It was like that, times a hundred," Ivy said, staring off into space. She was going back into the memory, trying not to allow herself to fall back into that despair.

"But… we weren't even in there for five minutes," Alice said. "We didn't even get to the basement."

Ivy shook her head. "I couldn't. Besides, the house was empty. There was nothing to find there."

Finally Alice took a seat on one of the barstools, setting her beer on the counter. "But how could you know that? We barely checked."

"The cabin wasn't that big."

"No, but maybe…" Alice huffed. "I don't know. It just seemed premature to me." She eyed Ivy carefully. "And you're telling me that you, a seasoned police officer, didn't want to explore a potential crime scene because it made you feel bad?"

"Not just *bad*," Ivy said. "Sick. To the stomach. Dizzy."

"Dizzy?"

Ivy nodded. The sensations had come fast. She'd felt like she was going to pass out, or throw up. Or both at the same time. It was like when a stranger would touch her, only much more potent. Much more visceral.

"Why didn't you say something?" Alice asked.

Ivy took a long sip of her beer. "Embarrassed," she admitted. "I don't know what's happening. I've already got all these… issues. I couldn't deal with more."

Alice raised her eyebrows and took a swig herself. "I guess that's understandable. Still, you could have let me know. You literally left me standing there."

"I know I did," Ivy said. "I'm sorry. I should have… well, I should have done a lot of things differently. You shouldn't have had to call Jonathan."

Alice waved her away. "Don't worry about it. I like bothering him. He gets so flustered." She paused. "You need to go back."

"Why?"

"Because we didn't finish," the woman replied as if it were obvious.

But Ivy wasn't sure she could go back into that cabin. Whatever had happened there, whatever was causing this visceral reaction deep within her, it was something very, very wrong. And she had a sneaking suspicion it had to do with her family. Despite wanting to know the truth for the past fifteen years, when faced with the opportunity to learn more, she'd been a coward. It was unbecoming. Still… Ivy believed there was some part of her brain that was trying to protect her…the same way it had protected her fifteen years ago by not allowing her to remember. If there was one thing therapy had taught her, it was that the brain had a self-preservation mechanism. And if a person experienced a trauma deeply enough, the brain would effectively "erase" it, in order to shield the person from going insane.

"I mean, don't you want to make sure we didn't miss anything?"

Ivy looked at Alice. The woman was pragmatic, a reporter. She was used to cold, hard facts. How could she understand something like this? How could anyone?

"I don't know," Ivy finally said.

Chapter Eleven

Ivy awoke to her phone vibrating on the side table beside her. She grabbed it quickly. "Bishop," she said groggily.

"It's me," Jonathan said. "We had a hit on that BOLO. Someone thinks they saw the kid with an older man."

Ivy checked the time. It was close to one in the morning. Alice had left after only staying for about half an hour, leaving Ivy with her thoughts. Ivy hadn't tried to get her to stay, either. It wasn't as if they had anything in common and Ivy wasn't out to make a new friend. She had just felt like she'd owed Alice *something* after the other night. And now her conscience was clear… mostly.

Ivy sat up in bed, realizing she'd gone to sleep in her clothes again. "Where?"

"Gas station on the edge of town, headed north."

"How long ago?" Ivy asked.

"About fifteen minutes. Just got the call from the clerk."

She pulled on her boots, grateful for once that she didn't have to get dressed. "And it's a positive ID on the kid?"

"Just a boy about the same age, same hair color. Clerk didn't get a good look at the kid's face. Said the driver kept the kid in the car the entire time. But we have a description of the car and a plate number."

Ivy shoved on her jacket as she grabbed her keys, badge and weapon. "Meet you there?"

"I'm already on my way," Jonathan replied. "I'll send you a pin for the location. We'll be pursuing him north. I've already contacted the staties and had them set up stop points along all the major roads. They should be in place in the next half hour."

"Good," Ivy said, rushing out her door and to the elevator. "I'm headed to you now."

"Ten-four," Jonathan said and hung up. As Ivy waited for the elevator she found her foot tapping more than usual. Finally, the doors opened and she stepped inside, pressing the lobby button. An excruciating minute later the doors opened again and she rushed out.

"Evening, Ms. Bishop," Henry, the doorman, said as she rushed past. "Working late?"

"Crimes never take my sleep schedule into account," she called back as she jogged to her garage, throwing the door open and hopping inside the Datsun. She revved the engine once before backing out in a smooth three-point turn and peeling out of the parking lot at a fast clip.

Five minutes later she was on the highway and headed north in the direction of Jonathan's location. She pushed the vehicle up past eighty, but since it was so late there was very little traffic out and she wasn't worried about causing an accident. She was more focused on nailing this guy and getting Albie back to his parents safely. If she could just do that, maybe everything else would be okay. Maybe it would be okay that she didn't know exactly what was in that cabin, or that she'd let the only lead about what happened to her own family disappear into the night before she could stop him.

Maybe, if she could prevent this tragedy, none of that would matter anymore.

She wasn't even sure why those thoughts were crossing her mind, but somehow it seemed right. Maybe her brain was doing that protecting thing again.

As she drove her phone rang again and she put it on speaker. "Bishop."

"Looks like the staties got him," Jonathan said. "About ten miles north of the pin on one-thirty-eight. Where are you?"

Ivy checked her GPS as she drove. "About twenty minutes out."

"I'm five minutes," Jonathan replied. "Meet you here."

Ivy took a deep breath. The possibility that all this might be over in the next hour was like a weight off her shoulders. Even though she knew it was dangerous to hope, she couldn't help it. She felt partially responsible for what happened to Albie Quinn and needed to right the situation before something terrible happened to the boy. She also needed to get her head straight. The past two days had been a whirlwind, and it had all started with that night at the cabin.

Maybe what she really needed was a vacation— some time away where she didn't need to think about any of this stuff. Now that Nat wasn't looking over her shoulder anymore, she had more leeway for something like that. But then again, was leaving really the right choice?

After what seemed like an eternity, Ivy finally arrived at the location. She saw the flashing lights long before she came upon the scene. Highway one-thirty-eight at this section was a three-lane road, with a passing lane on the ascending side and nothing but wilderness on both sides of the road. The car in question had been stopped on the side, surrounded by two State Police vehicles, the yellow stripes on their vehicles reflecting in the flashes. Jonathan's silver Chrysler was parked behind them.

The suspect's vehicle was a dark minivan, but Ivy couldn't tell exactly what color in the darkness. All she could see were all the lights were on inside and the doors were open. As she approached, one of the troopers flagged her down. She pulled over and grabbed her badge, showing it to the man as she got out of her car.

"Where are they?"

The trooper pointed towards the woods. "I just got here," he said. "Jeffries called in a few minutes ago that the suspect headed into the woods with the abductee."

"Where's my partner?" Ivy asked.

"I assume he's in pursuit."

Ivy pulled out her phone, but out here coverage was spotty and she didn't want a call to Jonathan to accidentally give him away if he was close to apprehending the suspect. She cursed and ran back to her car, pulling out a flashlight from the glovebox.

"If they radio, let them know I'm coming in. Do you have a description on the suspect?"

"White male, dark hair, red ball cap and jeans is all I got," the trooper replied.

Ivy nodded and clicked on the light, dropping down into the ditch on the side of the road before pursuing the others into the forest. She couldn't see any lights or hear anything other than the dripping of water from wet branches, but she continued anyway. She found she could see without the light as the moon was nearly full and it was a clear night, bathing the woods in a bluish hue. Moving quickly and quietly, Ivy kept her weapon drawn but the safety on as she worked her way into the brush, thinking about how the man would be familiar with stomping through the woods if he'd taken Albie from his home and out through the trail in the back.

But as she made her way deeper and deeper, that sickening feeling came back— the very same one she'd felt in the cabin. It started off as nothing more than an errant ache somewhere deep in her gut, but the further she ventured, the worse it grew and she couldn't understand why. She found herself going deeper and deeper into her own head, her movements slowing as the feeling continued to assault her.

Then she remembered. She remembered driving to Aunt Carol's house the night of the cabin. Of feeling like she was almost outside her own body— like she wasn't in control of it anymore. She remembered going to Aunt Carol's house and Carol putting her into the bath, because she was freezing. As she thought of it, a chill ran through Ivy so strong she began shaking like a leaf.

The deafening *crack* of a gunshot somewhere off to her right brought her back immediately and she dropped to her knees, her weapon pointed in the direction of the sound.

"Okay, okay! I surrender!" a man yelled out.

"Show me your hands!" Jonathan yelled as feet rustled through the pine. Lights clicked on about a hundred feet from Ivy.

"Jonathan!" she called out.

"Ivy, over here," he yelled.

That sickening feeling was gone. Whatever had stopped her in her tracks had just… disappeared. To say she was grateful was an understatement and she wasn't about to sit here and analyze it. Ivy rushed in the direction of Jonathan and the other man.

As she ran up on them, Jonathan was on the man's back with cuffs around his wrists while the other trooper— Jeffries — was scanning the woods with his flashlight.

"Bishop," Ivy said, showing Jeffries her badge. "Where's the boy?"

"That's what we want to know," Jonathan said, getting off the man's back and pulling him up to his feet. He was clean-shaven, his hair cut short, though this hat had been knocked off. He wore one of those puffy designer jackets which was now covered in dirt and mud. He glanced at Jonathan, his terrified expression telling Ivy he wasn't going to put up a fight.

"Where?" Jonathan asked again, jerking the man by the shoulder.

"Over there," the man replied, "I left him near those rocks."

Ivy shone her light in that direction, finding a large outcropping of boulders that had erupted from the ground probably a million years ago. She exchanged a quick glance with Jeffries as the two of them made their way over to the rocks.

"You better pray that boy is ok," she heard Jonathan say to the man. "Here, take him."

Jeffries nodded and took custody of the man, pulling the man's shoulders back enough so that he winced in pain.

Ivy shone her light all over the rocks, but didn't see any trace of the kid. She motioned for Jonathan to take the left while she went right, swinging wide around the rocks. As she reached the other side, her light fell on the form of the small child, his knees up against his chest and his arms wrapped around them. His head was down, giving Ivy a perfect view of his brown hair.

"Albie?" she asked.

The kid looked up and her heart dropped. It wasn't him. The face was all wrong. Where Albie had more of a cherub-like face, this kid's face was more in the shape of an upside-down triangle. Still, he was covered in dirt and tears streaked down his cheeks.

"Hey, it's okay," Ivy said, crouching down. Jonathan came around the other side of the rocks, his light falling on both of them but she held out a hand for him to stay where he was. "Can you tell me your name?"

"Michael," the boy replied, though it came out as a whisper.

"Michael, my name is Ivy. I'm a police officer, okay? We're going to get you home."

Something like hope crossed the boy's face and Ivy held

out her hand, as much as she didn't want to. "Here. Let's get out of the woods."

The boy hesitated for a moment before finally nodding. He slowly got to his feet and given the height of him, Ivy could see how he might be mistaken for the Quinn boy. They were about the same height, though from what she'd seen in the pictures provided by the family, they had slightly different builds. Michael took two steps forward before taking Ivy's hand, then grasping on to her, *hard*.

She winced at the sensation, feeling like her entire body was on fire as the kid latched onto her.

"Ivy?" Jonathan asked, holstering his weapon.

"I'm okay, can you just…take him?" she said through clenched teeth.

Jonathan bent down, taking out his badge and showing it to the kid. "Hey," he said. "Wanna hold this for me until we get out of here? It's kind of like a good luck charm."

The kid's eyes went wide and he let go of Ivy, taking the badge from Jonathan. Ivy let out something like a whimper as soon as the kid let go. It was like removing her hand from a live socket, but at least there was relief. Jonathan took the kid's hand, and they led him around the rocks, headed back in the direction of the road.

"You got here in record time," Jonathan said as they made their way back.

"Because I treat the speed limit like a guideline and not a rule," she shot back. The pain had already dissipated. It was getting easier, though it wasn't exactly a linear process. As they passed the point where Ivy had been frozen to the spot, she couldn't help but linger for a moment.

"Hey, you okay?" Jonathan asked, his hand still clenching Michael's.

"Yep," she replied. "Fine."

Chapter Twelve

"CLIVE NAVARRO," Ivy said, opening the folder and setting it down on the table.

The man they'd arrested and brought in sat on the other side of the table, his hands bound with cuffs. Jonathan sat beside her, but his attention wasn't on the file. It was on Navarro, who had sweated all the way through the booking process.

They'd managed to discover he was originally from Sacramento, apparently on his way north to possibly cross the border into Canada. However, he was also an ex-con and hadn't checked in with his parole officer in almost two weeks. They'd discovered he'd abducted young Michael Baird from a grocery store in Medford, not far from the California border.

Even though they hadn't found Albie Quinn, both Ivy and Jonathan agreed it was worth interviewing the man after his arrest. The similarities were too drastic not to. It had been a tense drive back to the station and currently Michael was under supervision, waiting for his mother to arrive from Medford.

"Let's start with an easy one," Ivy said, staring at the man after looking over his rap sheet they'd procured from the California Department of Corrections. "Where were you headed?"

"North," the man said, his voice shaking as he did.

"How far north?" Jonathan asked.

Navarro licked his dry lips. "Pretty far."

"You were looking to cross the border," Ivy said. "Why?"

He shrugged.

"Why abduct the boy?"

Navarro hung his head. "Figured they wouldn't be looking for a father and son. Thought it would be easier."

Ivy exchanged a glance with Jonathan. "Sure it wasn't for another reason, Navarro?" he asked.

The man raised his head. "What?"

"We have your rap sheet," Ivy said. "Two counts of child endangerment, kidnapping, failure to pay alimony, a restraining order. Do I need to go on?"

He shook his head. "That... that's not... it doesn't matter."

"The hell it doesn't," Ivy replied. "According to this, you were terrorizing your ex-wife and son. To the point where you were arrested for attempting to kidnap the child. So we know this isn't your first rodeo." Ivy and Jonathan had discussed their strategy before coming in here. Navarro had an extensive history of kidnapping and could be involved with Albie Quinn's disappearance; they just weren't sure how. But he was the best lead they had, given Jack Quinn had turned out to be a dud.

Navarro didn't reply, just continued to hang his head.

"Why did you really take the Baird child?" Ivy asked.

Navarro took a deep breath. "He looked like Elijah," Navarro said. "I thought maybe... I thought I could start over."

Ivy closed the file, leaning over the table. "Look, Mr. Navarro. I don't really care about you or your twisted sense of family. You're a predator and you deserve to be locked up for the rest of your life. What I *do* care about is another missing boy, about Michael's age and size. His name is Albie Quinn, ever heard of him?"

Navarro shook his head.

"See, I have a hard time believing you," Ivy replied. "Because you just admitted to trying to take another child for your own and get him across the border. Maybe you were passing through town and had some doubts about Michael. Maybe things weren't gelling between the two of you and you decided you needed another kid, someone who might play along a little better."

Navarro looked up, his eyes wavering. "What?"

"How long have you been in Oakhurst, Mr. Navarro?" Jonathan asked.

He shook his head. "Only— only a few hours. We were just passing through."

If that were true, then he couldn't be the man who had been watching the Quinn home. But they still didn't have any solid evidence that the person Mrs. Quinn had seen at the edge of her property was the same person who abducted Albie.

"You sure about that?" Ivy asked. "Are you *really* sure?"

Navarro nodded emphatically. "I've never even heard of this town before," he said. "Honestly, we were just on our way through. If I hadn't had to stop for gas—"

"If you hadn't stopped for gas, you would have made it to the border, is that what you're saying?" Ivy interrupted. Navarro shut his mouth. "What route did you take?"

"We were on I-5 for a while, but I was getting nervous," Navarro said. "I thought it would be better to take the smaller highways for as long as I could."

"Were you on I-5 after you left Medford?" Jonathan asked. He nodded. Jonathan turned to Ivy. "We can pull the camera footage from down there. See if he's telling the truth about his timeline."

But Ivy wasn't so sure. Navarro struck her more as an opportunist, who took Michael Baird because it was convenient. Whoever had taken Albie Quinn had planned it, maybe for weeks. It hadn't been a fly-by-the-seat-of-your-pants operation.

Ivy opened the file folder again. "Let's go back to when you took your son. The *first* time. Did you take him from his house?"

"Hell no," Navarro said, his words gaining strength for the first time. "My ex would have ripped my balls off if she'd caught me in the house. I went to school to pick him up before she could get there."

"And the second time?" Ivy asked.

"Soccer game," Navarro admitted.

"And after that you were arrested and charged. And you were told once you got out, if you ever went within a thousand feet of your ex-wife or son again, your parole would be revoked and you would be in prison until your sixties." Navarro didn't reply. "What I don't understand is if you knew the punishment, why go for some random kid rather than your son if you were going to do it anyway?"

"I wasn't," he protested. "At least, not originally. I tried making it work in Sac City, but my parole officer was a real piece of work. Almost felt like I was back in jail again. I knew there was no way I could get close to Elijah again. I was headed north— a new start and I stopped in Medford. I… I hadn't planned it. I just saw him standing there, looking around. And it was so easy. No adults around, no parents. I thought maybe things could be different."

This was looking less helpful by the second. Navarro was a piece of trash and a coward. And he'd be spending the prime of his life behind bars, that much was for certain. Despite time served, he'd violated parole, attempted to flee the country and kidnapped *another* child. There would be no easy way out of this.

Ivy exchanged a glance with Jonathan, who gave her a subtle shake of his head. As much as she wanted the two cases to be connected, there just wasn't anything here. Navarro hadn't been in town long enough and the MOs didn't match. But she couldn't let this be for nothing.

"I just have one more question for you, Mr. Navarro. How would you abduct a child from their home, hypothetically?"

"What?" he asked, looking up.

"Say you weren't scared of your ex-wife ripping off your balls. How would you go about abducting your son from his home?"

The man's brow formed a deep "V" shape. "I wouldn't."

"Why not?"

"Because... too much can go wrong," he said. "It's too risky. Unless the kid was bedridden or something, I'd just wait until he was out in the open. Less chance of getting caught, easier to get away."

"Humor me," Ivy said. "Let's say you're a glutton for punishment. How would you do it?"

The man shifted in his seat a few times, clearly uncomfortable. "Well, I guess I'd have to get familiar with his schedule. Try to figure out when he was home alone, or at least unsupervised. Then I'd get a nice toy, something really expensive. Something to draw him outside."

Ivy wanted to throw up. There was no part of her that was sorry for Clive Navarro. There were people who sometimes made the wrong decisions, but he was a predator through and through.

"What if it was a kid you didn't know? What if it was Michael? How would you take him from his house?" Ivy pressed.

"Ivy," Jonathan said, placing his hand on her shoulder. She shrugged it off.

"Like I said, I wouldn't," Navarro replied. "There's no reliable way to get the kid that way."

"You wouldn't go into the home?" Ivy asked.

"Hell no, you think I want to get shot?" Navarro replied. "There are easier ways to get kids, trust me."

"I think we're done here," Jonathan said, standing up. "Mr. Navarro, the California State Police will be along in a few hours to collect you and bring you back to Sacramento. We're handing your case back to them."

"Could I… maybe get some water?" he asked.

Ivy closed the file folder and left the room without responding. Navarro could die of thirst for all she cared.

"Hey," Jonathan said, catching up to her as she made her way back to her desk. "What was that back there?"

"Just trying to get into his head," she replied. "I want to know why Albie's kidnapper went to the trouble of breaking into his house and stealing him in the middle of the night when apparently there are *so many* other easier targets out there. What is it about Albie that makes him special?"

"And you think berating a felon is going to give you the answers you need," Jonathan replied.

"I think right now I don't have a lot of options, and we need a lead," she said.

"The only problem is we can't trust someone like that," Jonathan said. "He'll say anything to try and get out of doing more time."

"Seemed pretty reasonable to me," she said. "I happen to think he's right. The kidnapper could have just as easily waited until Albie was at school or another event. But he didn't. He took him from his *bed*. So either he's extremely lucky, or he's extremely skilled and knew he wouldn't get caught. And based on what we have so far, I'm thinking it's the latter." Ivy sat back down at her desk and rubbed her temples.

"Go home," Jonathan said. "I'll take care of the report."

"I can do it."

"Ivy, it's four in the morning," he replied. "One of us should get some sleep."

He was right. She was exhausted. She'd had a hard time falling asleep after Alice's visit. And now she'd been up another three hours. "You willing to fall on your sword?" she joked.

"No, I've just seen how you are in the mornings when you don't sleep well," he replied. For a second she thought he was serious until she caught the hint of a smirk on his lips.

"Ass," she said. "Fine. I'll leave you to it. Thanks."

"No problem," he replied. "I figured since I woke you up, I owe you at least that much."

"How about we reconvene at ten?" Ivy suggested. "Start fresh again."

Jonathan grinned. "It's a date."

Chapter Thirteen

Despite heading back home for a few more hours of shuteye, Ivy found that even when she was in bed with all the lights off, she couldn't stop her brain. She couldn't quit thinking about what had happened in the woods, and how familiar it had felt to what she'd felt at the cabin. To what had put her in that almost trance-like state when she arrived at Aunt Carol's. Had Jonathan not taken a warning shot and stopped Navarro in his tracks, Ivy might still be out there, just staring up at the sky like a turkey in a rainstorm, prepared to drown.

After a solid two hours of tossing and turning she finally got up and took a long shower, hoping it would at least calm her down some. She found standing under the shower head the only place she could truly relax because it shut out the entire world. She could close her eyes and pretend like she was in the middle of nothing, the white noise from the water and the constant pressure reinforcing the feeling of drifting. It was like being in one of those depravation tanks, except the budget version.

She thought back to her conversation with Alice— about leaving the cabin only moments after entering. About the effect it had on her psyche. Something happened to her the moment she stepped in that cabin and she wasn't sure what. Ivy recalled being nervous, and even a little excited about going inside to find whatever could be in there. But the moment she put a foot in that building she knew something was wrong about it.

It was almost as if the cabin held a negative energy. Not that she believed in that sort of thing. But that was the only way she could think to describe it. And then, in the woods only a few hours ago, she'd had the same sensation again. That sense of despair, of pain… or hopelessness.

But that didn't make sense. The cabin and the woods beside Highway 138 were nowhere near each other. They weren't even in the same county. So how could they be connected?

Finally she realized she wasn't going to get the answers she needed standing under the shower. After taking a few minutes to get ready, she fixed herself a frozen waffle and ate it on the way to her car. She thought about stopping for a quick coffee from one of the drive-thrus, but figured she could just get one at work. Ivy wasn't a coffee snob and the brews they had in the office were good enough. All she needed was for it to keep her awake. Even though it was barely eight, she figured she could get a start on the investigation until Jonathan arrived. She appreciated him taking one for the team last night, for what little good it did her. She felt no more rested than she had a few hours ago.

But as she made her way into the office, Lieutenant Ayford was already there, in the kitchen, fetching his own cup of coffee.

"Bishop," he said, giving her a quick nod. "You and White resolve that kidnapping last night?"

"Yes, sir," she replied, grabbing a cup from the cupboard. "Turns out it wasn't related to the Quinn case. But it was good timing. If we hadn't made the announcement on the news, the gas station clerk might have just let them go without another thought."

"And you're sure there's no correlation with your current case?"

Ivy liked this. Being able to talk to her boss without worrying if he was going to stab her in the back or not. Or if he had ulterior motives. This was how it *should* have been from the beginning. "I don't see how. Assuming he was telling the truth, Navarro was only passing through town yesterday. The timeline doesn't match up. And based on his record, he wouldn't have broken into the Quinn home to get the kid."

"Why not?" Ayford asked.

"Because he's a coward," Ivy replied. "I think whoever kidnapped Quinn isn't someone who can be rattled so easily. And given how little was left behind, they're going to be a professional."

"Didn't I see some partial prints gathered?" he asked.

"Yes, sir, but those could be from visitors or friends. We have no way of knowing if they belonged to the kidnapper or not."

Ayford leaned against the counter, taking a sip from his mug as Ivy brewed herself a cup. "So what's your theory?"

"Sir?" she asked.

"Your theory. On what happened?"

"Oh." Ivy hesitated. "I'm not sure I know yet. The evidence seems to show someone *did* get into the house, though I still don't know how. And since the boy has no history of running away or sleepwalking, I have to believe he was taken by force."

"Where? And why?"

"That's what Detective White and I are going to try and find today," she replied. "We plan on interviewing anyone who has crossed paths with the Quinns over the past six months. This was a personal attack; whoever took Albie knows this family… intimately."

"What makes you say that?"

"It's like Navarro told us. Why go to all the trouble when there are so many other easier targets out there?"

Ayford nodded, taking another sip. "Okay. Keep me updated. If you didn't see it come through, we cut Jack Quinn loose. We were coming up against a wall and I didn't see we had enough to charge him."

"No, that's fine," Ivy replied. "He was a long shot anyway."

Ayford pointed a finger at her with the cup still in his hand as he walked back to his office. "Keep on it. The answers are there, Detective."

Ivy turned back to the coffee machine with a miniscule smile on her face. Ayford seemed like a reasonable cop. Things might have started off a little rocky but so far she couldn't complain. He was giving her the leeway she needed without being overbearing, a micromanager or patronizing. Was this what it was like for everyone else in the department all the time?

"Morning… again," Jonathan said an hour later as he rounded their desks and took a seat. Ivy pushed a doughnut his way on a small plate.

"Here. Touley brought them in. I saved you one before they were all gone."

Jonathan gave her a half smile. "Oh. Were there any sugar-free ones?"

"It's pronounced *thank you*," she replied, grinning.

"Right, that was rude. I apologize," he said. "*Thank you*."

"That's more like it." She took a sip from her mug, having warmed her coffee up about ten minutes before Jonathan arrived.

"Did you get any more sleep?" he asked.

"Yep, like a baby," she lied. "How do you want to tackle everything today?"

"First, I need a cup of coffee," he said. "And maybe a shot

of Adderall. Then once I can think straight again, I can answer that question."

"Fair enough," she replied, then pointed to the doughnut. "You know, your blood sugar might be a little low. Could be worth it."

The man pursed his lips before finally taking a small bite from the doughnut. Ivy didn't know why she derived such pleasure from giving him a hard time, but she found it hilarious. Not that he let up on her much either.

"Okay, let me grab a cup and give Ayford an update on our progress." He made his way to the kitchen.

"Already took care of it," Ivy said, following him. She could use some more coffee anyway. "Spoke with him when I first got in."

"Thank scott," Jonathan said. "I wasn't looking forward to that conversation."

"Why not?" Ivy asked.

"Because we don't have anything to show for all this effort yet." He reached in the back of the cupboard and grabbed one of the mugs from the back. "And we're no closer to finding Albie Quinn than we were yesterday."

"He wasn't upset," Ivy said. "He believes we can find him. He even said as much." Jonathan gave her an *If you say so* face.

"Hey, would you rather report all this to Nat? That was no better, you know."

"I don't want to report this to anyone," he said. "I want to find this kid before something awful happens to him."

"So do I," Ivy said. "But you have to admit, Ayford is a lot more understanding than—"

"Excuse me, Detectives?"

Ivy and Jonathan turned at the same time to see Officer Jiminez standing at the entrance to the kitchen. She hooked a thumb over her shoulder. "There's a call for you. It's about the Quinn case."

Ivy and Jonathan glanced at each other before rushing back to their desks.

"Did they say who they were?" Ivy asked as Jiminez followed.

"No, just that they would only speak with the detectives on the kidnapping case. It came in from the tip line."

"Thanks, Barb," Jonathan said.

The line was flashing as Ivy got back to her desk. She picked up the receiver and waited for Jonathan to get his as well before she pressed the button.

"This is Detective Bishop, who am I speaking with, please?"

"It doesn't matter," the voice on the other end said. It sounded odd, like someone was speaking through a tin can. "The boy you're looking for, he's at four-six-one-one Westwood Avenue."

"How do you know this?" Ivy asked, but there was no response.

"This is Detective White, please identify yourself," Jonathan said.

"He's there," the voice said again, then hung up.

"What the hell was that?" Ivy asked, replacing the receiver.

"A tip, I assume," Jonathan replied.

"A credible one?"

Jonathan jotted down the address on a notepad. "I guess there's only one way to find out. Do you want to drive or should I?"

Ivy glared at him under hooded eyes.

"Right," he said. "Stupid question."

Chapter Fourteen

"I hate anonymous tips," Ivy said as she drove them west across the interstate and to the other side of town

Jonathan had the same sentiment, though he didn't voice it. Tips of this kind were generally unreliable because they were often pranks— a result of people with too much time on their hands or an axe to grind against the police. Unless they could at least get a name to go along with the tip, it often wasn't investigated.

But something strange had stood out about that phone call. One— the caller had known to ask for their department by name and two— he had provided very specific information. There were instances when a caller would use a tip line like this to dox someone— to share their information without their permission with malicious intent. People had been known to use drug hotlines to call in addresses of family members they were feuding with, which could sometimes lead to very dangerous situations. People didn't often realize that the police only have the information they are given, and have to prepare for every other outcome. That often means going into a situation armed and ready for the worst. And if the call isn't genuine and is instead the result of a spat someone is having with another party— people could be seriously hurt.

Jonathan didn't think that was the case here, at least he hoped not. He hadn't liked how the caller had been using some version of a vocoder— a voice-changer— because it meant not only were they not willing to share their information, but they were actively obfuscating it, leaving him suspicious of their motives. Some people really just didn't want to get involved, but then again, how many people would go to such lengths to obscure their identity?

"Why so quiet?" Ivy asked. "Usually, I can't get you to shut up."

Jonathan smiled. "I was just thinking about the reliability of this tip. We've already had two dead ends. Who's to say this one will be any different?"

"No one, I guess," Ivy replied. "You're thinking about a motive?"

"Just trying to figure out who was on the other end of that call."

"I'm sure Jiminez has traced it by now," Ivy suggested.

"And if the vocoder was any indication, I'm willing to bet it went to an unregistered cell phone, a burner," Jonathan replied. "If they still existed, I wouldn't have been surprised if they'd used a public phone booth."

"Do you want to go back?" she asked.

"No, there was something about the specificity of the call," he replied. "We need to at least check it out. The clock is ticking on Albie."

"You'll get no argument from me."

Jonathan did his best not to stare at Ivy. The change in her over the past few days was noticeable. Since their boss had gone missing, she'd seemed less sullen, more outgoing. Like she'd been relieved of a heavy burden. And he supposed in a way, she had. He couldn't argue with the results; she'd been more amenable at work, more focused. He'd never seen her so… unencumbered.

"Coming up on the neighborhood," Ivy said, pulling the Datsun around a sharp corner. Jonathan had to lean over in his seat so as not to touch shoulders with her. That was the other thing, her phobia revolving around touch had diminished significantly since they'd begun working together. As far as he could tell it hadn't been that way with Wilcox— her last partner. But she hadn't been in such extreme situations then, either. Pulling a perp off a cliff and facing the man who killed her one-time foster mother surely had an effect on Ivy's psyche.

Still, he needed to limit the amount of time he spent thinking about her— otherwise it threatened to overwhelm him. They were partners and he felt they were becoming friends, but that was all. Assuming there could be anything else was an exercise in futility. Plus, Jonathan had his own problems to worry about. His mother had jumped all over his back when she'd found out he'd been up to Portland lately and hadn't come to visit her or his sister. He'd managed to keep her at bay with news that the department was in the middle of a shake-up with the loss of Lieutenant Buckley, but that wouldn't hold forever. He'd have to face her again, eventually.

And then there were the texts.

So far two separate ones, from two separate numbers, both unidentifiable. And both of which had mentioned Ivy by name, and for Jonathan to keep his distance from her. As an officer of the law, Jonathan was used to receiving random messages or threats, but there had been something about the two of these that had seemed more… personal, especially as they pertained to his relationship with Ivy. He hadn't told anyone about them yet, nor did he plan to. As far as he was concerned, they were nothing more than spineless words until he could get to the bottom of them.

Still… they occupied some part of his daily thinking.

"Okay," Ivy said as they pulled up to a row of townhomes nestled into a small community. "Here it is, forty-six-eleven Westwood."

Jonathan stared at the building through the windshield. "Yeah, but which unit?" There were four separate entrances, each, he assumed, leading to a different home. That was a strike against the doxing argument. Someone looking to trip up a nemesis would have given the unit number as well. It also meant the tip itself was now less credible. More than likely someone screwing around.

"Guess we're going to have to do this the old-fashioned way," Ivy said, killing the engine. "Split up?"

"Sure," he replied. "I'll start on the left, you start on the right." Jonathan got out of the car and headed to the leftmost unit which was on the far corner. He made sure his badge was on display as he climbed the single step to the door and knocked. Inside, a dog began barking immediately before scratching on the other side of the door.

"Primrose, *no!*" a woman's voice said from the other side, but the dog continued scratching anyway. "I said no, *madam.* Would you please listen for once in your life?"

Jonathan suppressed a smile as there was a commotion on the other side of the door. He could imagine the homeowner practically dragging the dog away from the door, and from the sounds of claws on the floor, he suspected that was exactly what was happening.

It took a full minute before a shadow appeared in the frosted glass oval of the door, unlatching the lock and throwing the deadbolt. It opened to reveal a woman in her fifties, a mask over her nose and mouth and her dark hair pulled up by what looked like clothespins. She wiped her brow as she took stock of Jonathan, her gaze landing on his badge.

"I'm sorry to disturb you," Jonathan said, holding up his phone with an image of Albie Quinn on it. "But we received a tip that this boy had been seen in this building. Have you seen him before?"

The woman pulled off her mask, revealing red lines where it had pressed into her cheeks. "Sorry, I've been painting all morning and trying to keep my dog out of my hair has been a challenge. My eyes aren't the best, can I take a closer look?"

Jonathan handed over the phone and the woman held it close to her face, squinting. "No, sorry, I don't think I have." She handed the phone back.

"Anyone in this unit with children?" he asked.

"This building? Well, the unit on the other end is empty, or at least it was but I think it sold recently. Other than that, it's just us retirees here."

"You don't work?" Jonathan asked.

"I'm on disability," she replied. "Leg issues."

Jonathan nodded. "Okay, thanks very much. Have a good day."

"You too," she said, closing the door as she replaced her mask.

Jonathan turned to where Ivy stood, speaking with one of the other residents. She was on the second unit from the right, presumably because the first unit was empty or for sale— though Jonathan didn't see a "for sale sign" anywhere in the small yard.

Ivy finished up with the man at the door and they met at the third unit. She pointed back to the first one. "No one home," she said.

"Resident in this unit here says it's empty. That it was up for sale."

Ivy furrowed her brow. "There's furniture inside." They headed back over to the unit which had a large bay window beside the front door. Inside it was easy to spot the furniture that decorated the home.

"Might be a staging company," Jonathan said. "Let's check with the last unit." They headed back to the middle-left unit together, Jonathan opening the screen door and knocking on the inner door before stepping back.

A moment later a man in probably his early sixties opened the door. He wore a tweed sweater and gray slacks and had a pair of glasses perched on his head. "Can I help you?"

"I'm Detective White, this is Detective Bishop. We're responding to an anonymous tip. Have you seen this boy in the area in the past two days?" He held out his phone again.

The man pulled his glasses down and examined the picture before perching them back on his head again. "Is that the boy that just moved in a couple doors down?"

Jonathan exchanged a quick glance with Ivy. "Moved in?"

He nodded. "Just a few days ago. At first I thought it was just the mother, but then I saw her with a kid about his age yesterday. I figured she must have moved in first before bringing him along."

"When exactly did she move in?" Ivy asked.

The man screwed up his face. "Sunday? Saturday? I'm not exactly sure. I teach music from home and on the weekends I like getting out and going out to the coast. All I know is she wasn't here on Friday when I left, but when I got back Sunday afternoon she was moving things into the home. I haven't met her yet, but she seemed friendly."

"Can you describe this woman?" Jonathan asked.

"On the shorter side, maybe five-five, five-four. Dark hair… young. In her twenties or thirties. I'm not really sure."

"Was she Caucasian, Hispanic, Black?"

"Caucasian, definitely. Actually, looked a little pale," he said. "And now that I think about it, she might have been sick."

"Why do you say that?" Ivy asked.

"I'm not sure. Maybe it was something about her eyes. They looked sunken in— you know, like when you haven't slept well for a while? But whatever it was didn't seem to affect her demeanor. She smiled and waved at me yesterday when I saw her and the boy."

Ivy stepped forward. "When did you see them?"

"Around four, I think," he said. "I'd just finished up with a student. She was headed to her car. I was going to stop her and introduce myself but she seemed like she was in a big hurry."

"What kind of car?" Jonathan pulled out his notepad.

"Black Kia," the man replied. "I think it was a Rio. Or maybe a Sorento. I can never keep them straight."

"Did you get a license number?"

"No, sorry. What's this about?"

"This boy was kidnapped from his home on Monday night," Ivy said. "Didn't you see the news?"

"Oh, sorry, I don't have a television," he said. "Seemed redundant these days with the computer and all."

Jonathan showed him the picture again. "Please take a careful look. Are you sure this was the boy you saw yesterday?"

The man pulled his glasses down again and scrutinized the picture carefully. "Yeah, I think it was. He had on a green jacket and jeans."

Ivy handed the man her card as Jonathan dialed the switchboard operator. "Control, this is White. We have a hit on the missing Quinn boy. I need an ABP on a Black Kia, could be a Sorento or Rio. Female driver, dark hair, early thirties, Caucasian."

"Ten-four, unit twelve," Jiminez said on the other end. "Advisory going out immediately." Jonathan hung up and turned back to the man.

"He said she's been here in the mornings but leaves in the afternoons," Ivy said as soon as Jonathan rejoined them.

"Did you see her today?"

The man shook his head. "Haven't seen her yet. But I've been in most of the morning. Didn't have a lesson until one."

"Okay, thank you," Jonathan said. "Will you be here the rest of the day?"

He nodded. "Don't have anywhere else to go."

"We may have more questions." He motioned for Ivy to follow him back to her car after they excused themselves. "We need to get a warrant for that property."

"Do we have enough for that?" she asked.

"Given the circumstances, I think so." But Jonathan wasn't thinking about the warrant. Getting a judge to sign off wouldn't be the issue— not with the situation. He was thinking more about who could have called in the tip, and who this mystery woman could be. Because Mrs. Quinn explicitly stated the person watching their home had been a man.

"What are the odds this is another wild goose chase?" Ivy asked.

"I don't know," he said honestly. "But we have to at least try."

Chapter Fifteen

Forty-five minutes later, Lieutenant Ayford pulled up in his beat-up old Cadillac, right beside the other two patrol vehicles that had arrived on scene to accompany Ivy and Jonathan. They were putting a lot of faith into the neighbor's testimony, and Ivy wasn't sure it was warranted. After all, the gas station attendant had thought he'd seen Albie Quinn too, and look how that turned out. It felt like they were chasing their tails here, and she had a sneaking suspicion this would be no different.

While they were waiting on the warrant, Ivy had done some research into the property records, finding the unit had been purchased by a holding company, not a specific person, last week. There had been no showing, no meeting or negotiation. Someone had essentially just called in and paid cash for the unit, which was suspicious in itself. A moving company had been hired by the same holding company to furnish the unit. They had someone back at the office trying to track down a representative of the holding company to try and get a handle on what was going on here.

But in Ivy's eyes, nothing about this screamed *kidnapping*.

Something strange was going on here, that was for sure, but she wasn't convinced it was related to the Quinn boy.

"Okay, here's your warrant," Ayford said as he approached, holding the piece of paper. "Get in there and find whatever you can."

"No limits?" Jonathan asked.

"Scope is to be limited to anything that points to the boy," Ayford said with an air of dissatisfaction in his voice. "But I don't care what it says. You find something relevant, bag it and tag it."

Ivy nodded as the other officers lined up behind them. "And if there's nothing in there, sir?"

"Then we'll offer our humble apologies and move on."

She had to admit, at least Ayford had their backs. Just being on-site was a big deal.

Ivy motioned to the locksmith who had arrived with one of the patrol units. "We're ready."

The man grabbed his small toolkit and trotted up to the door to get to work. The occupants in the unit beside this one — the Mayfords— were staring out their window at the commotion. They hadn't been able to provide Ivy with any credible information, given they were both in their eighties and barely ever left their house.

Ivy and Jonathan stood close by as the locksmith got to work on the deadbolt. "I'll have to drill it," he said. "I don't have a fob that will work with this model."

"Whatever you have to do," Ivy said. She glanced back at the rest of them watching. If this didn't turn up something substantial, they would have ruined this woman's front door for nothing. But at the same time, if the neighbor was right and Albie *had* been here yesterday, they needed to know immediately.

The locksmith pulled a handheld drill from his case and got to work drilling out the deadbolt lock. It took roughly five minutes, but he finally broke through and managed to pull the front casing of the lock off to get to the bolt inside. Once he'd removed that he unlocked the bottom lock rather easily with nothing more than a spare key and a hammer.

"It's an old locksmith trick," he said once he was done, standing back. "It's all yours."

Ivy motioned to the rest of the team they were ready. Jonathan led the way into the house, which smelled of bleach and cleaner.

"That's not good," Ivy remarked as she took in the home. The furniture was sparse and haphazardly placed, like someone had been more interested with filling the home rather than anything else.

"Albie?" Jonathan called out. "Albie Quinn, are you in here?" The only sound was coming from somewhere in the kitchen. Ivy and Jonathan filed through the townhome to the back to find someone had left a radio on the soft jazz channel.

"Don't like that." Ivy looked around the rest of the kitchen, but it was mostly empty. The cupboards only had the bare minimum of dishes and cutlery, some of which was plastic. "I'll check upstairs."

As she headed back to the stairs at the front of the home, Ivy noticed framed pictures sitting on the end tables and even a few that had been hung on the walls. Except none of them had been changed from the stock photos that had come in the frames. It was as if someone had purchased the frames, brought them here and hung them without even a thought to put an actual picture in them.

All of it left Ivy with a sense of dread. Something was wrong in this home, and she wasn't sure what it was. Maybe the neighbor had seen the boy after all.

She took the stairs carefully, noting how small and tight the corridor was. At the top was one bedroom to her left that was completely empty. Not so much as a pillow was inside anywhere. Immediately to her right was a small bathroom, but likewise it didn't seem used. She made her way further down the hall to the end, finding another small bedroom on her left. This one, at least, had a child-sized bed and a mattress, but no sheets other than what looked like an old quilt. Ivy approached the bed, and the stench of the quilt hit her. It was like someone had rolled it in feces. Lifting up the quilt, she found human excrement underneath.

"Jesus," she said.

"Anything?" Jonathan asked from behind her.

"Someone had an accident," she said, indicating the bed. He covered his mouth with his sleeve as soon as he entered.

The rest of the room was unremarkable and Ivy moved to the last room, what should be the primary bedroom. Another, larger bed was set up in here, but again, no sheets or covers other than a couple of quilts. This bedroom had a very small en-suite with a stand-up shower, sink and toilet. But it was the trash can which drew Ivy's attention. It was full of tissues and paper towels that were soaked in dark red.

"Jonathan," she called out. He appeared behind her, almost too close in the small space. But she could stand it.

"Is that—"

"---blood," she said. "We need to get this to Burns ASAP. Find out if it's the boy's or not."

"Yep," he said. "I need to grab a bag and some gloves."

"In the back of my car."

"I'll be right back." He headed back downstairs as Ivy examined the trash can. It was practically overflowing with blood-soaked tissues and paper towels. More than would be necessary for something innocuous like a nosebleed. She narrowed her gaze and turned back to the bed, pulling the quilts from the mattress. There, on the mattress itself were more spots of blood. Not as much in the trash cans, but it was there.

"She's on her period," Ivy said as soon as Jonathan got back. "I think it's her blood, not his."

"Unless she did something to him on her mattress,"

Jonathan said. "Either way, we need a sample. And we'll want to compare it with Albie's medical records."

Ivy wasn't going to argue; they found blood which meant they had to follow procedure. But at the same time, she didn't think the boy had been injured. "We'll need a sample of the fecal matter too."

"I'll inform Ayford we need Burns and her people over here. If the boy was here, his prints should be all over this place."

Ivy continued to search while Jonathan headed back downstairs. She didn't like the haphazard manner in which this house was presented. Furniture stuck all over the place, no pictures in the frames and yet someone had taken the time to hang them. Beds and mattresses but no sheets. It was like someone wanted the home to seem inhabited, but only from a distance. But why would anyone do that? And what connection could it have to the kidnapping?

None of this was making sense and it was giving Ivy a headache. One thing was for sure, she didn't like this place. It was old, dingy and despite the new furniture, unkempt. Cobwebs hung in the corners and some rooms of the home reeked of mold. Maybe that's what the bleach had been for, she wasn't sure. But someone had gone to a lot of trouble to make this place at least appear from the outside like they lived here— Ivy just couldn't wrap her head around why.

She made a cursory search of the closets of each bedroom, finding little to nothing inside. Back downstairs, Ayford was directing the other officers to search through every drawer or cabinet in the place. They weren't about to leave any stone unturned.

"Lieutenant?" Ivy turned as Officer Touley nodded at an open closet. She and Ayford gathered close to find a duffel bag inside. It was still zipped.

"Do you need a pair of gloves?" Ivy asked her boss.

"No, go ahead," he said. "It's all yours."

Ivy bent down carefully, taking a pair of gloves from Jonathan and pulling them on before unzipping the zipper. Inside were what looked like documents— mostly bank statements.

"Well?" Ayford asked. "What is it?"

Ivy scanned the top statement, which listed a name and the address she was currently standing in. Across the top, the name said *Margaret Weston.*

"I think we might have found the woman we're looking for," she said, holding up the paper for the others to see. "We need to figure out if this woman matches the description the neighbor gave us."

"I'll get right on it," Jonathan said.

"DMV first, county records second," Ayford reminded him, though Ivy saw no need. Jonathan would get everything they needed, including the full make, model and license plate of that car.

"You said this house isn't registered to her, correct?" Ayford asked as Ivy rifled through the rest of the papers. Some were bills and the rest little more than junk.

"Right," Ivy said. "It's owned by *Regional Holdings, LLC.* They're out of Texas."

"Why would this woman be living in a home owned by a Texas company?" he asked.

"That's what we're trying to find out. Whatever the reason, she hasn't been here long."

Ayford looked around the home, as if he were taking it all in for the first time. "Yeah. This place is… weird." He cleared his throat before heading back for the door. "Burns is on her way. Should be here within the hour. But if you and White get solid intel, don't stick around."

Ivy nodded. "Yes, sir."

"Good work so far, Bishop. Let's hope it amounts to something this time." She wasn't sure if that was a backhanded compliment or not, but given what she'd become accustomed to from Nat, she was happy to take it. At least Ayford wasn't running a secret agenda with Ivy at the center.

Stop it.

She needed to stop thinking about Nat. Especially when she was in the middle of an investigation. She needed to keep her head clear and focused to find Albie. That was all that mattered right now. Everything else could wait.

Ivy rejoined Jonathan outside as he tapped his foot, his phone up against his ear. "Yeah. Okay. Thanks." He turned to Ivy. "Nothing on a Margaret Weston in the Oregon DMV."

"Which means she's from out of state," Ivy said.

"Yeah, but which state? I don't want to call fifty DMVs."

She shrugged, looking back at the townhome. "Texas?"

Jonathan sighed. "Sure. Gotta start somewhere."

Chapter Sixteen

A QUIET WHINING woke Oliver from his sleep. He cracked an eye, only to find himself looking in the face of Hero, his nose about four inches from Oliver's.

"Hello," he said, his voice raspy. "What time is it?"

The little dog licked Oliver right in the nose, causing him to try and scoot back, which only sent ribbons of pain through his back, chest and legs. Despite that, he laughed as the gremlin lunged again with his tongue.

"Okay, okay, I get it. I need to get up." Oliver helped Hero off his chest carefully and sat up, though it was a slow process. He grabbed his phone to check the time. As he did, it vibrated in his hand, displaying the one name he definitely didn't want to see today.

"You must have a sixth sense," he told Hero as he debated picking up the call. But he'd already missed one call from her and delaying this any longer would only make things worse.

He hit the accept button and his screen was filled with the image of a bright blue pool set in the middle of a lush, green yard, the view beyond of marble columns with figures atop them overlooking the ocean. The water in the pool was absolutely still. A moment later the image moved as the caller picked up the phone and her face filled the screen.

"I wasn't sure you'd pick up this time." Her self-confident smile dropped as soon as she saw his face. "My God, they really worked you over, didn't they?"

"Hi Cor," Oliver said wincing in pain as he got up.

"Oh no," the woman said with a false sense of concern. "I didn't wake you, did I?"

"Somehow, no," he replied. Though, had Hero not been right in his face he might not have even heard his phone. He'd only meant to close his eyes for fifteen minutes or so, but these pills they had him on weren't conducive to staying conscious. In fact, the only way he could stay awake for more than three hours at a time was to not take them, but then the pain only got worse and the tradeoff didn't seem worth it.

The woman smiled again; this time somehow less genuine than the first. Her sharp and flawless features were the result of years of work to keep her as young-looking as possible and Oliver had to admit, it had worked— to a point. No matter how much someone did to their face, you could always still tell. Her dark hair was pulled back under a sun hat and dark glasses obscured her eyes, but he knew those penetrating green orbs were under there somewhere. "Well," she said, her voice dipping sweeter than before. "I just wanted to call and check on you. I thought it was only right given everything that happened."

"You mean you wanted to make sure I wasn't dead," he replied.

She brought a martini glass into the frame and took a sip. "I admit, Tanaka can be somewhat… heavy handed. Especially when he feels like it's personal. And Oliver, I have to tell you, each of us felt deeply betrayed by what you did."

"Yeah," he said, rubbing his ribs. "I kinda got that."

"And I wanted to tell you that as long as you return the

funds within the next twenty-four hours that all will be forgiven. Okay?"

It wasn't as if he didn't expect this. They weren't going to let him keep it, after all. The beating was just a warning of what would happen if he didn't cooperate. "Of course. You'll have it by the end of the day. I just need to run to the bank."

"Fantastic," she replied and took another sip. "You know, I actually have to admire you a little. It took guts to try and pull something like that. But I guess that's what happens when you're working with a criminal." She laughed as if it were the funniest thing she'd ever heard.

"I guess," Oliver replied, dropping his head.

"Now, I don't want you to get the wrong idea," the woman said. "I'm a forgiving person. Forgive and forget, I say. Which means this won't be affecting any of our plans going forward, right?"

This was not how things were supposed to go. They weren't supposed to find out about his little *transaction*, because it had been the first step in getting out of this business. He had planned to wean himself off of Cor and her *business*, but he couldn't do that without a backup plan. And the money had been step one. But all of that was over now. He had nowhere else to turn, which meant he was right back where he didn't want to be. "I'm good if you are," he said.

"Wonderful. Then I'll be back in touch after those funds transfer. We still have a long way to go." She turned to look at the gleaming pool behind her. "You know, if you can swing it, I'd try to get in with some hydro therapy. It will do wonders for your recovery."

"Yeah," he replied. "I'll look into that."

She gave him one final grin, though this one was different than the others. More threatening— almost predatory. "You do that. Bye bye, Oliver." The call ended and Oliver slumped back against the couch. Hero still sat at his feet, wagging his tail.

He looked at the small creature, feeling a pang of guilt for having put him in harm's way. "C'mon," he said, hoisting himself up and ignoring the sharp stabs as he did so. "Let's go outside for a second." Hero bounded along beside him before rushing for the back sliding glass door. Oliver opened it only for Hero to dart outside and start running laps around the yard.

They'd been cooped up too long. He hadn't had a chance to take Hero on his walks since coming back from the hospital and he knew the dog was bored. Oliver didn't want to admit it, but he was also a little gun shy about going out himself. He hadn't expected Corolene's goons to actually find out where he lived, and yet they had. And they'd destroyed fifty thousand dollars' worth of his equipment, leaving him with a singular laptop. He had to hand it to her: she was serious about her warnings.

He never should have let them in the house. But if he hadn't, they would have just broken in eventually. He thought he could talk them down— that maybe if he just gave them the cash right then and there everything would be okay.

But that Tanaka. He was one mean son of a bitch. And he'd taken great pleasure at going after Oliver. Reeves hadn't been much better. He guessed it didn't matter that Cor was over two thousand miles away. Nothing was out of reach when you had her kind of resources.

How had things gotten so complicated? All he'd wanted to do was make a little money on the side and get a chance to flex his skills. And now he was working for a multi-national crime organization, secretly siphoning off money. The cash that Reeves and Tanaka had come after, that was only the tip of the iceberg. If Corolene knew about his other plans and how much he'd already put into motion… well, he probably wouldn't have woken up at all.

Oliver sighed as he watched Hero run around the yard, not a care in the world. He spotted a squirrel seconds before

Oliver did and set about chasing it all over until it finally found a tree and ran halfway up.

Ivy was right. He *was* still putting Hero's life in danger by keeping him here. But just the fact that he was here and had been a companion for Oliver was such a relief. He'd almost forgotten what it was like to have someone around all the time, even if that someone was just a dog.

Still, it wasn't fair for him to keep Hero if there was even a chance someone could break in and come after him again. They might not be as gentle with him next time. Oliver knew for a fact Tanaka had dogs— he might have been the reason Hero wasn't harmed.

"Hero," Oliver called. The dog turned at the sound of his voice and came rushing back into the house, still doing laps around the kitchen and then down the hall to the living room.

Oliver sighed, making up his mind. He'd call Ivy later and ask her if Carol couldn't take Hero again, just for the short term. No doubt she'd want to know the reason behind his change in mind. He'd try to chalk it up to not feeling well and not being able to take care of Hero, but the odds of her buying that were low. He might actually have to come clean with her— but if he did that, it could put her in danger. And Ivy had more than enough to worry about without adding this to her plate.

Oliver sat down at his desk, pulling out his only remaining working laptop and logging in. The process of uncovering and transferring the money would take a few hours. From here on out, he needed to be completely insulated. He'd consider moving homes, if he wasn't dead sure she'd find a way to track him down again. He needed to show her that there were no hard feelings after what had happened and that he was committed to making the company "whole." She might have acted capricious, but you didn't get to where Cor was without being ruthless. And if she hesitated for even a second, then he'd have to move fast or find himself face-down in a ditch somewhere.

Just as he initiated the first transfer, his phone rang again. Without picking it up he knew it was Ivy— he'd programmed her calls to have a very specific vibrate pattern.

"Hey," he said, picking up. "Good timing. I need to talk to you."

"Is everything okay?"

"Yeah, of course," he replied. "I just… I was thinking about what you said about Hero. I think you may be right. Maybe it's better if he goes to stay with your aunt until I'm a hundred percent."

There was an uncomfortable pause on the other end. "Why?"

"He needs to be walked and in my current condition—"

"That's not the reason," she interrupted.

"No, seriously. He just spent the last fifteen minutes doing laps around my backyard at about fifty miles per hour. He's bored and cooped up here. I can feed him, but I'm not a great companion right now."

"You sure that's why?" she asked.

Damn, why did she have to be so perceptive? It had been the same when they were kids. It was like she could always tell what he was thinking, no matter the situation.

"I'm not saying there's another reason. But out of an abundance of caution, I think it would be best."

"Okay," she finally said. "I'll talk to Carol. I'm sure she'd be happy to have him back for a few weeks."

"Thanks," Oliver said. "That helps a lot. I'll talk to you later."

"Hang on," she said. "I called you, remember? I need a favor."

He rubbed his head. "Oh, right. Sorry, I'm still a little groggy. These meds are kicking my ass. What's up?"

"I need help tracking down a woman in a kidnapping

case. I've got a name, but I need a car and plate number. As soon as possible. The kid may be in danger."

"DMV couldn't help?" he asked.

"Out of state, and we're not sure which one. So far we've checked Oregon, Washington and Texas. But I thought you might be quicker."

"What's the name?" he asked.

"Margaret Weston. Late twenties or early thirties, Caucasian, dark hair."

"Give me a few minutes," he replied, going to work. Using the parameters she'd given him, Oliver managed to narrow down the results through the databases.

"Okay," he said. "Got three close matches. One from Boston, one from Emeryville, Indiana and one from the LA area."

"Do you have cars on any of them?"

"One second." He performed another search, the results populating immediately. "Boston has no current vehicle registered, Emeryville drives a Ford Fiesta, and Los Angeles, a Kia Sorento."

"Los Angeles, that's our one," Ivy said.

"Car is a 2019 Black Sorento, license is VGT88935. According to this she lives north of LA proper, a suburb called Palmdale."

"What's her last listed address?"

"38626 Simpson Avenue," he said. "But the home was foreclosed on last year. Failure to make her mortgage payments. I don't see any other addresses listed since September."

"You mean she's homeless," Ivy said.

"Looks like it."

"What about a work history in the area?"

Oliver searched through the records he could find. "Nothing attached to her social. The last record I can see here is as a waitress twelve years ago. Whatever she's doing now, she's probably getting paid under the table."

"I don't guess she's tried to buy a house in the last week, has she?"

"With what?" Oliver asked. "She's got less than a hundred dollars in her bank account."

"Yeah, I saw that too," Ivy said.

"You saw that? How?"

"Her bank statements here at her house," Ivy replied. "Stuffed in a duffel bag in the closet."

"Really?"

"Yeah, it doesn't make any sense to us either," Ivy said. "Apparently, she's been living in this house the past three days even though she doesn't own it. Can you do another search for me? This one on Regional Holdings, LLC?"

"Sure, what am I looking for?" he asked.

"Anything. Who owns the company, what they do, how they make their money. Literally anything."

Oliver ran through his normal searches, but nothing immediately came up. "Uh, I may have to get back to you on this one. It's not as cut and dry."

"Okay," she said. "Thanks for this at least. It's enough to get us started. I swear, we've been tracking down this kid and it feels like someone just keeps throwing roadblock after roadblock in our way. We even ended up busting a *different* kidnapper in the process."

Oliver chuckled, but he felt it deep in his ribs. "Are you complaining that you stopped a crime?"

"No, I just wish it was the crime I was currently working on, that's all," she said. "I mean, it's good we got the other kid. The guy was taking him north, trying to cross the border. But this… if this really is our kid… for whatever reason she's staying close. In town. And I'm not sure why. Oakhurst isn't that large. Someone was bound to spot him. Again, *if* this is our kid."

"So you're saying she wants to get caught."

"I'm not sure that's the case here," she replied.

"You just said yourself that by staying here, she risked exposure."

"All the more reason I'm not convinced this is the boy we're looking for. Still…" She trailed off in the way that told him she was thinking hard about something. She used to do the same thing when they were kids. "Anyway, thanks. Let me know if you find anything on Regional Holdings."

"It's my first priority," he said with more than a hint of sarcasm in his voice. If she caught it, she didn't say anything.

After getting off the phone, Oliver turned back to the matter at hand. He could look into Regional Holdings later, once his main objective was taken care of. He wanted to make sure everything was copacetic with Cor before he found another pair of goons beating down his door or worse.

As Oliver began the next series of transfers he caught a reflection of himself in the darkness of the screen. But he turned away before he could get a good look.

Chapter Seventeen

"We have her name, her address and her vehicle description. She can't get far," Jonathan said as Ivy drove them back to the Quinn home. Burns and her crew had arrived at the apartment to try to find any evidence Albie Quinn had been there while Ivy and Jonathan were planning to track down Margaret Weston before the day was up.

"That's an assumption," Ivy said. "And you know what happens when you make assumptions."

"Right," Jonathan said. "My point is, if she's in town, we'll track her down sooner rather than later."

Ivy shook her head. "That's not a given. She could be hiding or have driven by her apartment and gotten spooked. We don't know. She could be on the run halfway back to LA by now. We need to find out how Margaret Weston is connected to the Quinns. That's the only way we're going to find her for sure."

"And if she's not connected?" he asked.

"Then we start looking at Quinn's co-workers, their friends. Anyone who knows Albie exists," she replied.

"You still don't think she's the kidnapper, do you?" he asked.

"We're going off the testimony of one elderly neighbor." She caught him staring at her. "Okay, maybe not elderly. But our one witness wears glasses and he may not be the most reliable. Not to mention Mrs. Quinn—"

"—said the stalker was a man, I know," Jonathan finished for her. "But did it occur to you that *her* testimony may be flawed? Maybe she saw a man because that's what she wanted to see. Maybe she didn't get a good look at this person at all. She did say he… or she… was wearing a hoodie."

Ivy hadn't considered that. But he was right. She couldn't make any assumptions if she was accusing him of the same thing. They needed to keep clear heads about all of this. Which meant going all the way back to basics. There was a connection here; she knew it. They just had to find out what it was.

"Do we have a picture for the family?" Ivy asked.

"We can use her driver's license picture from California," Jonathan said.

It wasn't great, but it would work. They hadn't had time to do a deep dive on the woman, but Ayford had someone back at the office searching to see if she had any social media that might give them a clue as to her whereabouts.

"Better than nothing," Ivy said.

As they pulled up to the house, Ivy noticed there was only one vehicle in the driveway. "Shit," she said under her breath.

"Mr. Quinn isn't home," Jonathan replied.

"Don't tell me he went to work," Ivy said more to herself than her partner.

"Guess you'll want me to take the lead on this one."

She shot him a glance. "I mean, I can do it, but I don't think we're going to get very far. Considering the woman would rather gut me than speak to me."

"I don't think it's that dire," Jonathan replied, getting out of the car.

"No? Just watch her try to scratch my eyes out as soon as we get in the house," Ivy replied.

As they approached the front door, Ivy nervously adjusted her jacket, readying herself for what was sure to be a chilly reception.

Before they could knock, the door flung open, revealing Mrs. Quinn, her eyes rimmed red and sunken in. She still had on her robe from the day before— Ivy wasn't sure she'd even changed.

"What's happened?" she demanded. "Did you find him?" Her hand flew to her mouth before Ivy could answer. "Is he dead?"

"Mrs. Quinn, we haven't found him yet," Jonathan said, doing his best to be reproachful. "We came by to ask you a few more questions."

She stared at them for a beat too long. "I've already told you everything I know. What more can you want?"

"I can't imagine how stressful this is for you," Ivy offered. "But we have some new information and thought you might be able to help."

Jonathan handed Mrs. Quinn his phone with the picture of Margaret Weston pulled up. Quinn took it and shook her head. "What's this?"

"Do you know this woman?"

She pinched her features before handing the phone back. "No."

"You're sure?" Ivy asked.

"She doesn't look familiar," Quinn replied. "Who is she?"

They'd already decided not to discuss the specifics of the case until they could be sure Weston was responsible for taking Albie. "She's a person of interest."

"What the hell does that mean?" Mrs. Quinn asked, her tone biting and sharp. "Did she take my son? Does she have Albie?"

Ivy held up a hand. "We don't know. We're still investigating. It would really help us if you could look again. She could be someone you know only in passing. Maybe you've seen her at the grocery store before, or one of your events."

Quinn motioned for the phone back, taking a closer look this time. Ivy wasn't optimistic about this, but it was at least worth a shot.

Mrs. Quinn opened her mouth but closed it again before saying anything. The entire time she stared at the phone. "I don't know if it's the same woman, but there's a lady down at the shelter where I volunteer sometimes. She kind of looks like this, but I can't be sure."

"What shelter?" Jonathan asked, taking the phone back.

"Our Sisters in Arms Mercy," she replied. "I go down there to help out a few times a month."

"And you saw *this* woman there?" Ivy asked.

"I said *maybe*," Mrs. Quinn replied, matching her tone. "I don't know every person that comes in there. Most of the time I don't pay any attention unless someone is causing trouble. But you see some of the same faces over time. Like I said… it *might* be her."

"When was the last time?" Ivy asked.

"I'm not sure, I'd have to check my calendar."

"Did Albie ever go with you?" Jonathan asked.

She nodded. "A few times. Especially during the summer when he's out of school. But that was almost nine months ago. You think this woman, what, waited around for nine months to come abduct my son? Where is she going to take him? She's homeless."

"Did your husband ever go to the shelter with you? Would he recognize her?"

Mrs. Quinn practically laughed, but it was forced. "Jerry? No, I don't think so. I doubt he even knows what the inside of a homeless shelter looks like."

"When will he be home?" Ivy asked.

"I don't know. He's out. He was driving me insane just stomping around the house. I told him to either sit down or go do something about it. He's been gone about four hours. I don't know when he'll be back." She placed her hand over her mouth again, like she was questioning whether he would come home at all.

"What about your daughter?" Ivy asked, thinking about Mr. Quinn's determination to get his hands on a firearm. "She might know—"

"You are not speaking with my daughter," Quinn replied. "She has been through more than enough and is barely holding herself together. I won't have you interrogating her and upsetting her further."

"Even if it could help us find your son?" Ivy asked. She was pushing and she knew it, but she didn't like being told what she could and could not do. What if Jasmine had a crucial piece of information that broke this case open?

"The answer is no," Mrs. Quinn replied, leveling her eyes at Ivy. The mama bear had come out— she wasn't kidding about not letting anyone close to her daughter.

Jonathan cleared his throat. "This is very helpful, thank you. We'll head down to the shelter and see if anyone there recognizes her as well. Thank you."

Quinn nodded before closing the door. "Just… bring my son home."

Once they were back in the car, Ivy exhaled deeply. "That went better than I thought. Not as well as it could have, though."

Jonathan shook his head. "I don't think she would let her best friend near her daughter right now. Plus, she did give us a possible lead. That's more than we came here with."

"True," Ivy said. Maybe they would get lucky with the women's shelter. Then again, maybe all of this was for nothing and Albie was two states away by now. But this was more than they'd had in the past three days and at this point Ivy was willing to try just about anything.

They just needed a break.

Chapter Eighteen

As Ivy drove towards downtown Oakhurst, her mind was filled with the possible connections between Mrs. Quinn and Margaret Weston. Had Weston seen Quinn in passing and just decided that she wanted something of her life? From what Oliver had given her, Weston didn't come from the best of circumstances. It was possible she had some mental issues that might be playing into her thought process.

The problem with that theory was it didn't explain how she'd somehow become a kidnapping ninja— getting into the Quinns' home without being seen or heard and escaping just as silently. Usually, people who were mentally unbalanced didn't have that kind of control. Not unless she was a savant— but even Ivy had to admit she was straying further and further into postulation and moving further away from reality. Was there a possible explanation? Sure, but did it make sense? Not really.

As the streets narrowed and the buildings grew closer together, she resigned herself not to think about it any longer until they'd had a chance to speak with the people at the shelter. She wasn't doing herself any favors by trying to figure this thing out before she had all the facts at hand.

Just as they pulled up to the building, Jonathan's phone buzzed in his pocket. He pulled it out but put it away just as quickly.

"What was that? The APB?" Ivy asked.

"Nothing, just something personal," he replied. She waited for him to elaborate but when it was obvious he wasn't going to, she decided to let it go and got out of the car. The air was still thick with the fog from early that morning, mingling with the less than pleasant smells of exhaust and damp concrete. Our Sisters in Arms Shelter was tucked between a pawn shop and a laundromat, its façade plain but welcoming with a bright, hand-painted murals showcasing groups of people holding hands and smiling against a cartoon background. No doubt the work of one of the local schools as a community project. Ivy had passed by this place a dozen times or more but had never given it much thought. Only now it occurred to her that if Aunt Carol hadn't taken her in, she could have ended up in a place like this when she aged out of the foster system.

Her heart tightened as they stepped inside. Where she had expected a dark and dingy cafeteria-like setting, instead they were met with a warm, bustling hub filled with the low murmur of conversations and the clinking of utensils as lunch was served. A line wrapped around the side of the room, leading to the back where people emerged with trays full of fresh, warm food.

Before they could go any further, Ivy found a young woman in a habit walking up to them, a small fringe of brown hair the only part of her head that wasn't covered. She wore a small silver cross over her robes and greeted them with a welcoming smile.

"Good afternoon, detectives," she said. "How can we be of service?"

"Um, good afternoon," Ivy said. "How did you know we were detectives?"

The woman smiled. "Usually only two types of people come in here. Those looking for refuge and those who are looking for others."

The woman may have looked young, probably no more than Ivy's age, but she was perceptive, and her sharp eyes told Ivy that this woman had more than her fair share of experience with the police. Probably not all of it good.

"We're just looking for a woman who may frequent here, do you know Brooke Quinn?"

The woman's face broke into an even wider smile. "Mrs. Quinn? Oh, yes, she is one of our volunteers. I'm Sister Rena, by the way. Mrs. Quinn has been very generous to this organization."

"Are you in charge here?" Jonathan asked.

"We share the responsibility," Sister Rena replied. "Are you trying to find Mrs. Quinn?"

"No, but we are looking for this woman." He held out his phone with Margaret Weston's picture on it.

Recognition immediately came over Sister Rena's face. "Margaret."

"You know her?" Ivy asked.

She nodded. "I do. She used to come in quite regularly. She'd escaped a tough situation in California and was looking to make a new start. But she had— well, let's just say she had some demons to work through first."

"Demons?" Ivy asked. "Like drugs?"

Sister Rena nodded again.

"Do you remember the last time you saw her?" Jonathan asked. "Was there anything unusual about her behavior?"

"The last time I saw her was maybe a month ago," Rena replied. "Unfortunately, she hasn't been in since then. What do you mean by *unusual?*"

"Erratic, perhaps?" Jonathan asked. "Did she have any interactions with Mrs. Quinn?"

"Not that I can recall," Sister Rena said.

"What about any friends?" Ivy asked. "Anyone she talked to regularly?"

Sister Rena scanned the crowd, pointing out two women sitting side by side chatting. One had a shock of white hair and a rotund face, laughing loudly as her companion, a shockingly thin woman with straight brown hair down to the middle of her back whispered something in her ear.

"Come with me," Rena said. They followed her along the side of the room, passing a wall lined with bulletin boards filled with flyers for job postings, legal aid and mental health resources. Ivy could practically feel the weight of so many lives passing through this space, some fleeting, others hanging on like a raft in a hurricane. Everyone who made their way here was fighting their own battles, often silently. But it was places like this that kept them afloat, gave them a chance to win and move on.

"Elsie, Tanya," Sister Rena said, approaching the two women. The younger of the two with the long hair immediately pulled back from the other woman, sitting on her hands like she'd just been caught doing something she shouldn't have. "These nice detectives would like to ask you about Margaret."

"Margie, Margie, let's go party," the older woman said before cackling again.

"Elsie," Sister Rena scolded. The woman's smile turned into an immediate frown, almost like a child.

"Sorry," she said.

"That's all right," Rena said before turning back to Ivy and Jonathan. "If I can help you further, please let me know."

"Thank you, Sister," Jonathan said before both he and Ivy sat down across from the other two women. They both avoided eye contact, though only Elsie seemed interested in her food. The tray in front of the other one— Tanya— remained untouched.

"Sister Rena told us you know Margaret Weston," Ivy said

gently. "We were hoping you might be able to tell us more about her."

"Margaret was here for nineteen nights," Tanya blurted out. "She last wore a black T-shirt, dark jeans and a green overcoat with stains along the collar. Her shoes were from TJ Maxx, but she didn't buy them. She stole them."

"Hush now," Elsie said. "That's not nice."

"Wait, let's go back," Jonathan said. "You said Margaret was here for nineteen nights? Were those in a row?"

Tanya shook her head. "January fifteenth, sixteenth, eighteenth, twenty-third, twenty-fourth, February first through the sixth, ninth, tenth, twelfth, nineteenth, twentieth, twenty-first, twenty-eighth."

Ivy scrambled to write them all down. "You're sure those were the nights she was here?"

Tanya nodded, pointing to Elsie. "Elsie's been here two-hundred and sixty-four nights. Amanda a hundred and nine nights, Robin sixty-six nights, Beverly eighty-three nights, Lucinda forty-six—"

"Okay, thank you," Ivy said, cutting her off. There was no way to tell if Tanya was telling the truth or just making up numbers, but she certainly seemed to have an affinity for them. "Then February twenty-eighth was the last time she stayed here."

Tanya nodded.

"Did she ever say anything about where she might go if she ever left?" Jonathan asked. "Or what her plans were?"

Both women shook their heads. "Sh-she wanted a house," Elsie stammered. "A f-family."

"I imagine a lot of women want that," Ivy said.

"She was going to get one too," Tanya said. "Bragged about it. Said she was about to move into a nice new home. Didn't need to stay any longer." She turned and whispered in Elsie's ear, causing Elsie to giggle again.

"What's so funny?" Jonathan asked.

"She was gonna invite us over," Tanya said. "For tea." This sent both women into near hysterics. Ivy wasn't sure what to make of it or why it was so funny, but if Tanya was correct, it meant Margaret hadn't been here in almost a month.

"Did she ever talk about any of the volunteers?" Ivy asked. "Or their families?"

Both women shook their heads.

"Do you know Mrs. Quinn?" Jonathan asked. "She volunteers in the kitchen sometimes."

Tanya nodded emphatically. "Brooke Fray Quinn, born on September eighth, nineteen-eighty-five. Five foot six, a hundred and thirty-four pounds. Brown hair, blue eyes, lives at—"

"How do you know all that?" Ivy interrupted, watching the woman carefully. But Tanya turned away from them, almost so she was facing the back wall.

"Sh-she sometimes l-l-lifts wallets," Elsie said. "Sh-she doesn't mean nothing, never takes anything and always gives them b-back. Sh-she just likes doing it."

"Tanya, is that true?" Ivy asked. All of the information she'd rattled off about Mrs. Quinn had been a hundred percent correct. The woman might have an eidetic memory. Which meant her information about Weston was probably accurate.

Tanya nodded, glancing at Ivy out of the corner of her eye. "You're not in trouble," Ivy said. "But did you ever notice Margaret talking to Mrs. Quinn? Did they know each other?"

Tanya shot a glance at Elsie, who was taking a large bite of mashed potatoes. "Once. Margaret spilled her drink. Mrs. Quinn stepped around the counter and helped her get a new one."

"Did Margaret ever have any interactions with Mrs. Quinn's son?" Ivy added.

"Albie, eight years old, four foot-two, seventy-one pounds.

He helps clean up." Tanya's eyes darted all over the room, like she was looking for him.

"And Margaret spoke with him?" Jonathan asked.

"Lots of times. On February second, they exchanged hellos. On the ninth he asked her if she wanted him to take her plate away, and she said yes. On the twentieth she called him over to get her another cup of juice and they smiled at each other. On th—"

"Okay, okay," Ivy said, holding up her hand. "That's good, thank you." It was more than enough to connect Albie to Weston and back again. Weston had begun targeting the boy while he was here volunteering with his mother, possibly luring him into a false sense of security. They could be dealing with a trained predator here, one who used inconspicuous circumstances to find her victims before taking them. They might have been underestimating Weston this entire time.

"Did she ever say anything about ever taking Albie?" Ivy asked. "About them living together?"

"No," Tanya replied. "Never."

That made sense. She would want to keep her cards close to her chest. And she wouldn't have wanted to endanger her operation by speaking about it too much. She could have just been playing everyone here with her *poor me* routine, lulling them all into a false sense of security.

Ivy moved to get up. "Thank you both for your time. If you hear from Margaret again, will you please let Sister Rena know?"

"S-sure," Elsie said. "Whatever you say." She gave them a salute as they walked away and Ivy couldn't tell if it had been genuine or the woman was trying to make fun of them.

Sister Rena met them again at the back of the room. "I hope that was a productive conversation."

"It was," Ivy said, handing her one of her cards. "If anyone hears from or sees Margaret, will you please let us know immediately?"

Rena furrowed her brow as she took the card. "It sounds urgent."

"She's the primary suspect in a child abduction case," Ivy said. "She may have Mrs. Quinn's son. Tanya told us they'd crossed paths."

"Oh," Rena said, placing her hand over her heart. "I didn't realize. Yes, Albie sometimes comes to help his mother. Everyone here loves him; he's a very sweet little boy. I'll let everyone on staff know."

"I think I already know the answer to this, but were you aware Margaret was living in a townhome over on Westwood Ave? We found some of her personal belongings over there."

"No, I had no idea," Rena said. "I'm sorry to say this, but Margaret didn't strike me as the kind of person who could afford to live in a place like that. She was still looking for work the last time she was here."

That was Ivy's assessment as well. But for whatever reason, Margaret Weston had experienced a change in fortunes lately.

They decided to take a quick look around the kitchen and speak to some more of the staff before finally leaving. Heading back to the car, Ivy couldn't quit thinking about her new theory. But it didn't line up.

She looked over the top of the car at her partner as he was about to open the other door. "Tell me something. How does someone with no record of kidnapping manage to pull something like this off? These are not skills someone is just born with."

"You mean how did she get in and out of the house without being seen?" Jonathan asked. "I've been trying to figure that out myself."

"I mean, it's pretty obvious how she targeted him. And hell, Tanya there could have given her the Quinns' address without even realizing it. That much is clear. But what I don't understand is how she got *in*."

Unfortunately, Jonathan seemed to be at as much of a loss as she was. "Maybe Burns will come up with something."

"She better," Ivy said. "Because if this woman is as dangerous as I think she is, we have an icicle's chance in hell of just finding her out in the open. She's on the run and she knows how to hide."

"I know. But we keep working it anyway. Right?"

Ivy sighed before getting in the car. "Right."

Chapter Nineteen

BACK AT THE STATION, Ivy could feel her eyes slipping closed as she listened to the automated music on the other end of the line. With no additional information on Weston and no other leads to follow, they'd headed back to try and track down more about the home itself and the company that had purchased it: *Regional Holdings, LLC.* Ivy had hoped to hear something else from Oliver, but he'd been silent since her call earlier, which left her and Jonathan to try and figure out how a homeless woman from LA had gotten in with a holding company from Texas to live in a barely-furnished townhome.

While Jonathan began looking into Regional Holdings itself, Ivy had focused on the sale of the property, speaking with the listing agent, the mortgage company from the previous owner, even the title insurance company. All of them reported that Regional Holdings took care of everything remotely and they never met anyone from the company. She was currently waiting on a copy of the HUD statement so she could at least see who had signed for the property, but it had been a slow process requiring half a dozen transfers around different departments.

"Hello, Detective Bishop?" a voice finally said, the music cutting off.

"Yes, I'm here," Ivy said, sitting up straight.

"I'm sorry, Monty already left for the day, and he handles all the HUD statements. But he should be in sometime tomorrow."

Ivy cursed the woman in her mind. She'd been on hold for thirty minutes waiting for someone to get back to her. "Can you please let *Monty* know this is of some urgency and he needs to contact me as soon as possible?" There was probably too much frustration in her voice, but Ivy couldn't help it. She felt like she was being dragged around on a leash here.

"I'll be happy to leave him a note on his desk," the woman replied. "Have a good night." She hung up before Ivy could say anything else.

"Yeah, fuck you, too," she said, slamming down the phone.

"That sounded productive," Jonathan remarked.

"It's just these people. They don't understand what's at risk here." But even she had to admit finding out who ran Regional Holdings— or even just who signed for the house— probably wouldn't get them any closer to Margaret Weston and Albie. After their conversation at the homeless shelter, she was beginning to accept that Weston really did have the child, even though all they had was one eyewitness.

The dim light on Ivy's desk cast a long shadow over to Jonathan, whose phone lit his face from below, giving it an almost ghostly quality. "I can't find much either. Whoever runs this company is keeping it close to the chest."

"I don't like this," Ivy said. "Nothing is lining up. It all feels very conspiratorial to me. I mean, how many people would need to be involved to pull something like this off?"

"No way to know," Jonathan admitted. "But more than just Margaret Weston, that's for sure. Maybe we need to go back to friends and family. Maybe there's someone behind the scenes, pulling the strings."

"Jack?" she offered.

"I'm not sure Jack has the capacity for something like this," he said. "It strikes me as very calculated. Someone with an agenda. Someone dangerous."

"Like who?"

He smiled. "If I could tell you that, this thing would be solved already." He snapped off his phone and shoved it into his pocket. "Let's call it. I don't think we're going to get much else done here and I want to get a good night's rest."

Ivy stood, gathering her things. "You rest. I still want another crack at Regional Holdings."

"What does that mean?" he asked but she didn't answer. It was no secret he and Oliver had never really seen eye to eye, and Ivy didn't want to make things worse.

"How is he, by the way?" Jonathan finally added.

"Getting better," she admitted. "One day at a time."

"You know you can't bring him in on this," Jonathan said, that edge creeping into his voice.

"I already did, when I asked him for help with Weston's vehicle," she replied. "Nothing is going on the record. He said he'd do some work on *Regional.* That's all I want to check on."

Her partner sighed. "Just… don't—you know what? Never mind. I'm not getting into it." He switched off his light and headed for the door. "Have a good night."

"You too," she called after him. Shit. Jonathan wasn't the kind of man who telegraphed when he was angry, but she'd learned how to tell. It was in the abrupt way he ended conversations, walked away before he said something he'd regret. And she knew she could only push him so far. He had always been a straight shooter, so she couldn't really blame him for not wanting Oliver's input. Even Ivy didn't know exactly what Oliver was into. But considering the treatment he'd received by his so-called "clients," it was probably illegal.

Still, she needed to go over to check on him anyway, and to pick up Hero for Aunt Carol, who was thrilled she'd get to take care of the little dog awhile longer. Maybe he'd found something useful by now and was just waiting to gather a few more bits of data before contacting Ivy.

When she reached the parking lot, all the other vehicles were gone, save for two patrol cars that were always on the lot. They belonged to the on-call officers who would cover the night shift. But as she fumbled with the keys to her car, Ivy felt someone's eyes on her. She turned, scanning the darkness, only to find there was no one out there. Still, she couldn't shake the feeling. She got into her car quickly and locked the doors, mad at herself for getting spooked. She wasn't the kind of person who normally let that kind of thing bother her. And she didn't want to start now.

Fifteen minutes later she pulled up in front of Oliver's place. One of the lights on the side of the house was on, a halo glowing in the faint fog that had settled back on Oakhurst. Ivy made her way to the door, half expecting Hero to come running around the corner. When he didn't she couldn't help but think about the last time she'd stopped by like this and had found Oliver nearly dead. The image was so strong in her mind she forwent knocking and just used the key he had given her in case of an emergency to let herself in the house.

"Hello?" she called out, stepping one foot inside. The home was dark and quiet and a shiver ran up Ivy's spine. *Not again.*

A second later, Hero bounded around the corner, heading straight for her. Ivy bent down and picked up the little dog before he could attack her with licks as she made her way through the house. "Oliver?"

Reaching the back room, her mind's eye immediately went to the scene she'd seen last time of Oliver splayed out on the ground, bleeding and bruised. But this time, he was still at his desk, his head laying on the desk itself and soft snores coming from him. Ivy let out a breath of relief, noticing his laptop was still open. She couldn't help but notice what was still on the screen: a bank transfer of almost a hundred thousand dollars to an account in the Cayman Islands— a country known as a lucrative tax shelter.

An ear-splitting alarm shot through the air, nearly causing Ivy to drop Hero as she covered her ears. Oliver sat straight up, turned to see Ivy, then inputted a series of commands on the laptop. The alarm silenced immediately.

"Hey, Vee," he said, breathing hard. "You forgot—"

"—the alarm, right," she said, setting Hero back down and trying to pop her ears. "I think I'm deaf."

"You'll be okay in a few minutes," he said, rubbing the back of his neck. "These pills, man. I'll be glad when I don't have to take them anymore."

"You should be in bed," she said. "Resting. That's the whole point."

"I was just trying to get some work done," he said, closing the laptop. Whether he realized Ivy had seen what was on his screen or not didn't seem to matter in his still-groggy state. "What are you doing here?"

"Checking on you and picking up Hero, remember? You wanted Carol to take care of him?"

He nodded. "Right. Sorry. Here, let me help you get his stuff together."

"You stay right there," she said. "I know where everything is. I'll get it." She spent the next few minutes gathering the dog's food, toys, bed and medicines. There was no telling how long Carol might need to take care of him. She loaded it all into the car before heading back to the bedroom where Oliver had resumed typing.

"My God, it's like pulling teeth," she said, reaching over him and closing his laptop.

"Hey!"

"Don't piss me off or I'll put it somewhere you can't reach it," she said. "You have two choices. Bed or couch. Pick one."

"Couch," he said, pushing himself up with some effort.

"Do you need help?"

He shook his head. "No, I got it. It's getting easier."

But from the grimace on his face, she wasn't sure that was true. She knew he was forcing himself to do it on his own because of her aversions, but she was sure she could push through for a few minutes to help him. Touch with some people was still hard, but if Ivy was ever going to figure a way around this, she needed to practice.

Gingerly, she took Oliver by his good arm and allowed him to put his weight on her.

Her entire body tensed as the sensation of pulsing electricity ran through her, urging her to let go, but she held fast until he was in the doorway to the living room, the couch in sight. As soon as he was down on the couch she let go, the sensations ceasing immediately.

"Wow," he replied. "I guess all I needed to do was almost die to finally get you to touch me."

Ivy frowned, stepping back.

"I'm sorry," Oliver said almost immediately. "That was low. I don't know why I said that."

"It's okay," she said. "Forget about it." Hero had jumped up on the couch and was trying to get into Oliver's lap. "Do you need anything else?"

He hesitated for a moment. Had he realized she'd seen his screen? Or was it just the medicine and injuries that were making him slower to respond than normal?

"No, I'm good. Thanks, Vee, for doing this. I just… can't keep up with him right now."

She nodded, taking Hero into her arms. "He'll be in good hands with Carol. She lets him sleep on the bed."

"That's just great," he replied. "What was the point of a crate then?"

Ivy could only give him a satisfied shrug. She'd gotten what she'd wanted— the dog wouldn't be in danger anymore. So why did she still feel so uncertain? Was it because she knew for a fact Oliver was into something shady and there was nothing she could do about it? Or was it that he was in effect lying to her about all this?

Whatever the reason, she couldn't force him, just like he couldn't force her to tell him about the cabin and that entire shitshow. And while she'd come here to get more information on the case, it was obvious Oliver was in no condition to help. He needed rest, and she wasn't going to sacrifice his health for her personal benefit.

Ivy made her way to the door. "Let me know if you need something, okay?"

He waved her off. "I'll be fine. Just make sure he's okay."

"I will." Why did it feel like she was saying goodbye forever? She would be back tomorrow to check on him again. And yet, something felt off.

Ivy carried the little dog to her car, unable to stop thinking about it the entire way.

Chapter Twenty

This is so stupid, why am I even doing this?

As he waited for the elevator, Jonathan thought about turning around for the tenth time. He'd been on his way home, trying not to think about how he'd left things with Ivy when he realized he didn't want to be that person. He didn't want to be the guy who just walked away mad. And yet, that's exactly what he'd done.

They needed to be a team on this, and he didn't want his own personal hang-ups to get in the way of the case or anything else.

Finally, the doors to the elevator opened and Jonathan stepped inside, his phone buzzing as he did. He pulled it out, glanced at the message from the unknown sender and grimaced. This was the fourth one of these he'd received. Each of them cryptic in their own way. And this one was no different.

Keep your distance from Bishop. And watch your back.

When he'd received the first text he'd thought it had been a joke, maybe from Ivy herself. But when she didn't mention it or even allude to it, Jonathan began to grow suspicious. And then the others came. Each time he tried responding and each time it came back as undeliverable. This was the final straw. He tapped the number and waited for the ringtone.

"Sorry, this number cannot be reached as dialed. Please check the number and dial again."

Jonathan clenched his fists in frustration. Someone was messing with him and he didn't know why. If they were going to keep coming— and there was no indication they weren't— he was determined to figure out who was behind them. The undeliverable number meant someone was sending them from a burner phone or a ghost account and deactivating it before he could respond. Which meant they didn't want to have a discussion. All they wanted to do was send him ambiguous "warnings" for no apparent reason. Why would he need to worry about anything with Ivy? He should check with tech services in the morning.

The elevator doors opened on her floor, and he stepped out, headed for her door. He checked the time: almost eight. Not late enough to be rude but getting close. He just needed to get this off his chest tonight otherwise there was no chance he'd sleep well.

As he reached the door, Jonathan hesitated. What if she got the wrong idea? Or what if she just slammed the door in his face? He supposed that was a risk he'd have to take. But Ivy was a reasonable person most of the time. He didn't think this was crossing a line.

At least, he hoped not.

He knocked, taking a few steps back so she could easily see him in the peephole. A moment later the door opened. She was still in her work clothes, though her leather jacket was missing. He caught sight of it on the hook behind her.

"Hey," she said. "Is everything okay?"

Jonathan took a deep breath. "I just wanted to… apologize for earlier. I shouldn't have been so… dismissive. I know you and Oliver have a… unique relationship. And it's not my business."

"You didn't have to come all the way over here to say that," she said, watching him carefully.

"I felt bad," he admitted.

"I get it," she said. "It's not an optimal situation."

"Did he at least find anything on Regional?"

Her lips twisted into a frown. "I didn't even ask. He's still recovering, and I had to take Hero back over to Carol's house. I figure if he has something to update, he'll reach out. He's never been shy about it in the past."

Jonathan nodded. "Okay. I won't keep you. I just wanted to— I guess I just needed to make myself feel better. Sorry if I intruded on your night."

"I just got home not too long ago," she said. "Do you— want to come in?"

His eyebrows shot up. "You're not sick of me?"

"Apparently not," she replied. "I don't have much other than beer in the fridge, though."

Jonathan glanced down the other end of the hallway. "I should probably get back home," he said. This was veering into an area he wasn't comfortable with. He'd known partners who had become more than that, and most of the time it ended in disaster. He didn't want that to happen with Ivy, or even entertain the possibility. She was a good cop and they made a good team. Maybe in time they would get to the point where he felt comfortable coming over to hang out at her place without any kind of expectation beyond friendship. But they'd only been partners for a couple of months. And after everything that had happened with the Lieutenant... it was too much, too soon.

"Yeah," she said. "I'm pretty tired too. I guess we should get some rest. Gotta run the gauntlet again tomorrow." She clung to the door like it was a lifeline. Even though she didn't seem like she was in distress, there was something off about her posture.

"Are you...okay?" he asked.

"Fine," she replied a little too quickly. Had he just made this whole thing worse by not accepting her invitation?

"On second thought, I could stay for a bit. It'd be good to see your place when we're not in the middle of planning some kind of sting." He thought back to the last time he'd been here when Ivy had her brilliant plan to get thrown in jail in order to pump Kieran Woodward for information. A plan that had worked for the most part, even though the cost was Woodward's sanity… what remained of it.

She smiled, holding the door open for him and he found himself in a large, expansive studio apartment. "So what'll it be? Beer or beer?"

"Just water," he replied.

"Whatever the gentlemen wants." She headed over to the kitchen and poured him a glass before handing it to him and returning to the living room where she sat down on the couch, a bottle in her hand. Jonathan took up one of the chairs opposite her.

"You sure you're okay?" he finally asked. She was acting… strange.

Her eyebrow shot up. "Using those detective skills on me?"

"Just an observation."

She hesitated a moment, looking at her bottle. "I saw something tonight," she finally said. "And I'm not sure what to do with it."

"Something…" he waited for her to fill in the gaps, but she remained silent. "Okay, so you can't talk about it. How can I help?"

Again, she hesitated a second longer than he expected. "Let's say you received information about someone you knew — someone close to you. And the information was… troubling. Or at least, suspect. Would you confront that person? Or just leave it alone?"

Jonathan swallowed, thinking about the texts. She couldn't know about those, could she? No, this had to be about something else. "Well, how important is this person to you?"

"Important enough," she replied.

"Without specifics it's hard to say," Jonathan replied. "Will this information potentially hurt someone? Either the person in question or someone else?" Again he thought of the texts. Should he just tell her?

"Probably."

"Then I don't think you can keep it to yourself. That's not going to do you or them any good."

She took a draw from the bottle. "Of course you'd say that. If it's against the rules…"

"It's not that, it's a matter of safety," he argued. "If this person is planning to hurt someone or through their actions someone will be harmed, then we have a responsibility to try and prevent that from happening."

"I thought the police didn't prevent crimes; we only respond to them."

"I'm not a policeman in this situation. And even if I were, that's not how I operate. There's already enough suffering out there in this world. I don't want there to be more because I was too afraid to take action."

"So if I don't do anything it's because I'm afraid," she shot back.

"No, that's not… I'm just saying—" He set down the glass of water. They were clearly talking about two very different things here. She had seen or maybe witnessed something at Oliver's that had given her pause. He was receiving strange text messages about her and had decided not to tell her. "I can't tell you what you should or shouldn't do about Oliver. And honestly, I don't have any room to speak anyway."

If she was surprised that he knew they were talking about Oliver, she didn't show it. "Why not?"

Jonathan sighed, pulling out his phone. "Because of

these." He handed his phone over to her, the most recent text message pulled up.

She stared at it for a moment. "What the hell?"

"I started getting them four days ago. Once per day since. You can see I tried texting back, but it's undeliverable. I tried calling, just a few minutes ago. Nothing. I have no idea who they're from or why." He took the phone back. "I was waiting until I had more information to tell you. And after what happened the other night, I thought…" he paused. "Well, I guess I thought I was protecting you."

She didn't reply, instead just stared at him in the way he'd seen her stare at suspects in the interrogation room. Now he was the one under the microscope. He could see why some of those guys cracked so easily.

"I don't need you to protect me," she finally said.

"I know, I should have told you immediately. But it came in on Sunday night and after everything with the cabin…"

Her expression softened. "Yeah… I guess I can see why you waited."

"I've been meaning to look into it, but we've been so bogged down with this kidnapping case I haven't had a chance."

Ivy swung back the rest of her beer before getting up and heading to the fridge. "You think Burns's people might be able to figure out who sent it?" She pulled another bottle out and popped the cap before returning to the couch.

"Doubt it. My bet is a burner phone that's been destroyed by now. But whoever it is, they're going to a lot of trouble to warn me about you for whatever reason."

"Better watch out," Ivy said, tapping her finger against the bottle. "I'm dangerous." She smiled. "Talk about cowardly, right? If someone is trying to warn you, they should at least tell you who they are. Otherwise it's just like our anonymous tipster. The warning doesn't matter if they're not willing to back it up."

Jonathan relaxed his shoulders. He was glad she was taking this well. Better than he'd expected her to, anyway. He hadn't been sure *how* she'd react. But at least now he wasn't keeping anything from her anymore.

"I saw a money transfer," Ivy said. "On Oliver's computer. Almost a hundred grand. To an account in the Cayman Islands."

Jonathan took a minute to process what she'd said. "I wasn't aware Oliver had that kind of money."

"He doesn't. At least, I didn't know about it," she replied. "You can understand why I'm concerned."

"Do you think it had something to do with why he was attacked?"

She studied the bottle a minute before setting it to the side. "I'm almost certain of it."

"You said you took Hero from his house. Was that because you were afraid of what might happen to him?"

She shook her head. "He was the one who suggested it. I think *he's* afraid of what might happen. Which means he's not out of danger."

"And he won't tell you anything about it?" Jonathan leaned forward, his elbows on his knees. Whatever Oliver was into was bad news and there were only two options. "I guess you can either confront him, head-on. Or you can threaten him."

"Threaten him?" she asked.

"Charge him."

Her face turned into one of comical expression. "With what?"

"Something to scare him into getting out of whatever he's into."

She took a deep breath. "That's just it. I don't think he *can* get out. If you were beat within an inch of your life, wouldn't that be all you needed to convince you to quit whatever you were doing?" She tapped on the glass bottle with her finger-

nail. "I think he's trapped. Whatever he's into— they've got him by the jugular."

"Then he's going to need all the help he can get," Jonathan said. "But first he has to come clean with you. He has to be willing to take that step."

"How can I ask him to do that when I can't do it myself?" she asked.

"What do you mean?"

She didn't reply, and didn't meet his eye either. Then he understood. "The cabin. You haven't told him either."

"I haven't told anyone."

"It sounds like you're both in the same situation," he said gently.

A silence descended upon the room and for a few moments, Jonathan thought he'd overstayed his welcome. He clearly wasn't helping with the situation. Had that been why she'd wanted him to come in, to ask his advice about Oliver? If so, he didn't feel like he'd been much help.

"It was the strangest sensation," she said, breaking the silence. "As soon as I stepped into that place I knew something bad had happened there. I could feel it." He looked up, surprise on his face, but he didn't dare interrupt.

"And then it was like I wasn't in control of my own body anymore. I wanted to continue. At least part of me did. But my feet wouldn't move forward. They were stuck to the floor. I remember Alice ahead of me, her flashlight and gun out as she moved deeper into the cabin while I just stood at the door, barely able to move, barely able to look around. It was like something had frozen me to the spot. *I* should have been the one out in front. I should have been taking the risks. But I just couldn't move."

"What did you feel?" he asked.

"Terror. Fear. Like if I took one more step into that place I would die, right then and there. I… I couldn't stay. I had to get out of there. And I left her." Ivy shifted in her seat, unable to get comfortable. "She came running out after me and I said something to her, but I don't even know what. I just got into the car and drove off, leaving her alone."

"Alice is a big girl," Jonathan said. "She'll get over it."

"But it could have been so much worse," Ivy said. "Someone could have been there, waiting for us. And if they'd come for her, I wouldn't have been able to do anything about it."

"What do you mean *someone*?" he asked.

"I felt… a presence there," she said.

"Like a ghost?"

"Like an aura," she said. "It wasn't tangible, but I sensed eyes on us. Or, I thought I did."

"You're thinking about that guy you confronted. The one who met with Lieutenant Buckley."

She squeezed her features together. "I'm… not sure. It felt more malicious than that. I didn't feel threatened by the guy on the side of the road. This was something else."

Jonathan sat back. He had hoped Ivy would share what happened with him, but now that she had, he wasn't sure what to make of it. Whatever had happened, it was clear Ivy had some experience with that cabin.

"I ended up at Aunt Carol's," she continued. "In some kind of trance. It took me a while to come out of it."

"And how do you feel, now that it's been a few days?" he asked.

"Confused. Frustrated with myself." She paused. "Angry."

"I know this might be a little 'out there' but have you considered hypnotism or therapy?" She shot him a look. "I know. Police officers don't make the best patients. But I had a therapist when I was younger, when we learned about my sister's illness. I didn't want to go— I was an angry teenager. But I have to admit it really helped."

"I dunno," she said. "I'm not certain a therapist could

help in this situation. And hypnotherapy? I'm not a good candidate. I don't like to relinquish control."

He chuckled. "No, I guess not. At any rate, thank you for telling me. I know that couldn't have been easy."

"I'm not sure I can tell anyone else," she said. "Oliver… whatever he's got going on… it's not good. And I'm not sure I trust him right now."

"Would you like me to speak to him?"

She laughed. "God, no. Can you imagine how that would go?"

Jonathan chuckled. "I suppose it wouldn't be a good idea. So then what do you do?"

Ivy shrugged. "I guess… just leave him alone until he's ready to open up. It's like you said, there's not much else I can do."

He agreed. She'd have to let him come to her. In the meantime, Jonathan kept turning over what she'd said about the cabin in his mind. Obviously, it was the location of some kind of trauma for her. And she'd have to face it again eventually. But not until she was ready. Finally, as the pauses between their words grew, he decided not to overstay his welcome.

"Try to get some rest," he said as he headed for the door. "Know that you've done everything you can for him right now."

"I guess," she replied. "Thanks for… listening."

"Anytime," he said. "It's what I'm here for. See you tomorrow?"

"Bright and early." She hesitated a moment before closing the door. And for some reason, he hesitated as well.

"Night, Ivy." He turned and headed back down the hall.

"Night, Jonathan."

Chapter Twenty-One

Ivy sipped on the coffee that she held in one hand as she kept the other on the wheel, the morning sun breaking through the clouds and painting the sky in a bright blue this morning. She'd slept better last night than she had in the past three days, and she couldn't help but wonder if that was because of her discussion with Jonathan.

When he'd shown up last night it was like a pressure valve had been released. She hadn't realized how badly she'd needed to just talk to someone who wouldn't judge her. Not that Aunt Carol would do it on purpose, but sometimes Ivy could feel the woman's silent criticism coming through no matter what. Oliver was obviously out of the question, and if the other night proved anything, it was that she didn't know Alice well enough to be honest with her.

Jonathan had been the perfect person to work some things out with. It wasn't something they could do during the day, when they were working. But when they were off the clock, she found him incredibly easy to talk to. She hadn't meant to open up about the cabin but was glad she had. It gave her the chance to go back over it in her own mind with something of a "net" to work with. All the other times when she'd thought about it, she'd almost started shaking— unable to really relive it in her mind. But with Jonathan there, she'd felt safe.

And part of her had to admit she hadn't wanted him to leave.

She just hoped it didn't make today awkward. They had a lot of work to go through and were still no closer on this kidnapping case. Albie Quinn was going on day four and with each passing hour the chances of finding him were dwindling.

Just as Ivy was about to make her way into the building, Jonathan came rushing out to meet her. "Good timing. Just got a hit on the APB," he said.

"Where?"

"Bluebird motel," he said, hurrying back to her car. "Clerk recognized Weston from the news. Called it in. She was trying to book a room with a fake ID."

"Is she still there?" Ivy asked, rushing to the driver's side.

"No, he said she ran."

"What about the kid?" she tossed the rest of her coffee and slid back into the driver's seat, revving the engine.

"Clerk didn't see one."

"Damnit." Ivy backed the car out and hit the accelerator. Yesterday's wild goose chase crossed her mind. They still didn't know who dropped the anonymous tip, but she hoped this would be more productive. The drive over was intense, Ivy weaving through the traffic as Jonathan filled her in on the additional details and made sure backup was on the way. The fact that Quinn wasn't with the woman was a bad sign, indicating that they might have been looking for the wrong person this entire time.

They arrived at the Bluebird motel— a nondescript one-story building with a busted sign out front. A cruiser was already on the scene and officers were cordoning off the area. Ivy pulled up, recognizing Officer Toombs as the one pulling the police tape.

"The suspect's vehicle is over there," Toombs said,

pointing to the parking area. "But there's no sign of the woman. Clerk said she headed east, on foot."

"Why wouldn't she just get back in her car?" Jonathan asked.

"Because she knows we have the plates," Ivy said, running over to the car to confirm it was the right vehicle. The color and plates matched what Oliver had given her. "I've got the clerk."

"Go," Jonathan said. "I'll take care of this. Toombs, get me a crowbar."

Ivy rushed to the front entrance of the motel as Jonathan and Toombs went to work on the vehicle. If Albie was in the trunk or stashed in the footwell somewhere, they needed to get him out of there as soon as possible. There was no telling what condition he was in.

The clerk stood outside the front of the motel, looking visibly shaken. Ivy held up her badge to him. "Detective Bishop. You saw this woman?" She pulled up a picture of Margaret Weston on her phone.

The clerk nodded. "She was looking very jittery when she came in. Otherwise, I might not have noticed. But I remembered the report on TV last night."

"And you said she left here on foot?"

He nodded again. "Sure did. That way." He pointed in the direction of a derelict park that sat close to the motel which ran beside the river.

"What was she wearing?" Ivy asked.

"Black jacket, jeans. Pullover hat… purple, I think."

"Thanks," Ivy said. "Stay here. The officers will finish getting your statement." She rushed back over to the car where Jonathan had pried open the trunk.

"Just clothes," he said as she ran up. "Nothing else in the car."

"Clerk said she headed off into the park. We need to go after her," Ivy replied.

Jonathan waved Toombs and the other officer over as another police cruiser pulled up. "Our suspect headed in the direction of the park."

"Clerk reports she was wearing a black jacket, jeans and a purple pullover hat," Ivy added. "We don't know what kind of condition she's in, so if you find her, approach with caution. Inform the others, we're headed out now."

"Yes, ma'am," Toombs said. Ivy hadn't been a detective long enough to feel like she had any authority over anyone, but the way they were all intently listening to her and Jonathan was a small bolster to her self-esteem. Was this what it could be like all the time?

They headed in the direction the clerk had indicated, their strides quick and purposeful. The park was only a few blocks away, a stretch of green and brown amongst the buildings and businesses out here. As far as Ivy could tell, the park was abandoned. The only sound were a few birdsongs and the squeak of an abandoned playground swing. The park itself was large and sprawling, giving Margaret Weston plenty of places to hide.

"You take east, I'll head west?" Ivy suggested. She glanced behind her to see two more officers headed in the direction of the park, all of them fanning out to cover different areas. That was good— it increased the chances of finding her fast. The realization that she might have abandoned Albie somewhere made Ivy sick to her stomach. If she was scared and, on the run, there was no telling what she might have done.

"Good luck," Jonathan said as he headed off.

Ivy's eyes darted from one bush to the other, looking for signs that someone may be hiding amongst them, or maybe near one of the maintenance buildings. She rushed over to the closest one, checking to make sure the locks on the doors hadn't been broken. When she determined there was no way they had, she continued, until the park opened up to a footbridge that arched over the flowing river below.

That's when Ivy saw her— Weston, her figure unmistakable even from a distance, standing on the edge of the bridge, looking down.

Ivy's heart raced as she approached. "Margaret!" she called, her voice steady despite the adrenaline surging through her veins.

The woman turned, her eyes wide and terrified. Ivy thought for a second she might actually jump, but she stayed where she was. "I can't do this anymore," she said, her voice barely audible over the roar of the river.

"Where's Albie, Margaret?" Ivy asked, approaching slowly. "All we want to know is that he's safe."

"I don't know," she replied, her eyes flickering with a mix of fear and relief. "I couldn't take it anymore. The voices… they just wouldn't *shut up*."

"Why don't you come down and we can talk about it," Ivy said. "You don't have to listen to the voices anymore." The woman was practically trembling, her face pale and sallow. She barely resembled the picture they had on file— no wonder the clerk had hesitated. Her skin was so pale it was practically translucent and she looked like she hadn't eaten in days. Her skin clung to her bones like that of a mummy. She could see how this woman would have easily fit into the women's shelter in this state.

But item one was finding Albie. And they needed to get Weston into custody so they could question her and figure out just how she managed to kidnap him. Not to mention this business with the townhome. Ivy had about a million questions and only one person could answer them. "We can help you," she added.

"No, he won't stop," she said. "He keeps telling me things. Terrible things. He's never quiet." She looked down at the water again.

"It's okay," Ivy said, taking a step closer. She could feel another presence behind her. Whether it was Jonathan or one of the other officers she didn't know, but she didn't dare take her eyes off Margaret. "Just tell me where Albie is, okay? Then this can all be over. We'll get you some help."

"I left him… I let him out of the car on… on Slauster. Near that Chinese grocery store. I thought if I let him go, the voices would stop."

"That's good, Margaret, that's very good. Thank you for telling me," Ivy said. Hopefully whoever was behind her would relay the information and they could find the boy immediately. "Now take a step back from there, okay? We don't want you to get hurt."

But the woman shook her head. "No. Don't you get it?" She slammed her fist into the side of her head. "He. Won't. Shut. Up." She looked back at the water. "There's only one way."

"That's not true," Ivy said, stepping forward again. "I know what it's like…to feel despair, like there's no way out. It feels like the world is closing in on you and you don't have any other choices. But I promise you do. There *is* another way. *Please* let us help you."

The woman's eyes softened and a smile came across her face. Her entire posture relaxed and in one deft move, she stepped off the bridge.

Ivy lunged forward, but she wasn't close enough and the woman's jacket slipped through her hands as she plunged into the freezing water below. Ivy almost went over after her, were it not for a pair of strong hands holding her back. Jonathan helped her back over the railing.

"Do you see her?" Ivy asked. But the current was moving quickly due to the recent rains, the river higher than normal, almost bursting at the banks.

"No," Jonathan replied. He motioned to the other two officers who had gathered close. "Get downstream, watch the riverbanks."

"She had him, and she let him go," Ivy said, watching the

water, hoping to see the woman's head bob up somewhere. But there was nothing.

"Then we need to find him," Jonathan said. Ivy felt his hand still on her arm, but she didn't feel the normal shock. Just a little bit of warmth. "Ivy, c'mon. We can't do anything from here."

She watched the water a moment longer, then turned and followed him back to the car.

Chapter Twenty-Two

"WHY WOULD she just let him out of the car?" Ivy asked as she tightened her grip on the wheel. Jonathan was certain she was either going to crush the steering wheel or break her fingers as the knuckles were a bright white. "What sense does that make?"

"Maybe her conscience got the better of her," he suggested as Ivy took the next turn at almost fifty miles per hour, tires screaming down the street.

"So she just lets him out in the middle of a busy intersection? That's a good way to get him killed. I'm surprised we haven't had a hit and run call."

They'd been monitoring the radio chatter ever since they'd relayed the information about Albie Quinn to Central as they sent out the information to all available units. Toombs and Kilgore had stayed behind at the motel until they could find a spare minute to investigate the car and anything else Weston had left behind.

The radio crackled to life. "Unit Twelve, be advised. Unit one-zero-nine at 222 Lovett Boulevard is responding to a 10-32. Stand by."

Code 10-32 was the one they used for a drowning. And

222 Lovett was about a mile downriver from where they'd been in the park. It had been almost fifteen minutes since Margaret Weston had gone into the water. Unless she'd managed to stay above the current for most of that way, the odds were she was already dead.

"Damn," Ivy whispered to herself, somehow gripping the wheel even tighter.

Jonathan lamented the loss, but he wasn't going to spill any tears over the woman. She'd abducted a small child and left him in danger. And she'd just made their job harder by removing the only person who could answer their questions. He was sure Ivy wanted answers as badly as Jonathan did. The townhome, Regional Holdings, the kidnapping itself… none of it made much sense. Especially for an out-of-work transient who had come up from Southern California. Jonathan wanted to go back and investigate the motel further, try to figure out what she'd been doing there. He needed to get into her head. Why drop the kid off and then drive to a motel if you're just going to kill yourself anyway? She knew she couldn't go back to her place… and had been on the run for more than a day. Maybe she'd been exhausted and when the clerk refused her, she figured she had no more options and had just given up.

Whatever the reason, it was unlikely they'd ever really know. All they could do at this point was make supposition.

"Slauster and Independence, coming up," Ivy said. That was the corner where the Chinese food market sat. As she pulled up to the building, Jonathan saw no sign of the boy anywhere. He got out of the car, calling the kid's name, but there was no answer. Just a few patrons of some of the nearby businesses looking at him strangely.

The market sat in the middle of a strip mall with businesses on either side. "You take that way?" Jonathan asked, pointing to their left, since Ivy was on that side. She nodded and trotted off for the first door.

Jonathan stepped into the market, its crowded shelves closing in on him like food caverns. He had to turn sideways to fit through the aisles to get to the back of the store. There was so much product in here it might be easy for a kid to get lost. At the back was a middle-aged man with concern etched on his face. "Help you?" he asked.

"I'm looking for a young boy, he was dropped off outside here earlier today. He's eight, about this high," Jonathan said, holding his hand up to his abdomen. "And he would have been alone."

"No, no children alone today," the man replied. "Very busy, hard to see everyone."

"Ok, thanks," Jonathan said and made his way back out to the next business next door— a bakery. Inside he repeated the information and again the woman behind the counter said she hadn't seen him.

As he stepped back outside, he caught Ivy speaking with a group of teenagers near the bus stop on the other side of the businesses. She was speaking animatedly as she showed them a picture of Albie on her phone.

"Anything?" Jonathan asked as he approached.

She shook her head in frustration. "It's like he's vanished into thin air. How can a kid be out here all alone and no one sees him?"

"We need to widen the search," Jonathan said. "Talk to more people. He can't have gone *that* far on his own." He was being optimistic, but at this point what choice did he have? Declare the kid lost and give up?

"Okay," Ivy said. "Let's split up again. Block by block." There was an undercurrent of worry in her voice and for good reason. Jonathan glanced at the busy intersection with cars coming and going in all directions. All it would have taken was an errant step in the wrong direction…

He didn't let his mind finish the thought. Plus, if someone had hit the kid they would have heard about it. A bystander would have called something like that in. No, he hadn't wandered out into traffic. But he had gone *somewhere*. Jonathan tried to think. If he was eight, where would he try to go? Home, right? The question was, did Albie Quinn know this area well enough to know which direction home was in? Even Jonathan wasn't sure. They weren't anywhere near Albie's part of town, which meant the kid probably didn't know where to go.

Jonathan trotted down to the next block, which had a laundromat tucked between a café and a bookstore. He chose the bookstore first, the little bell over the door jingling as he entered.

"Excuse me," he said, showing his badge. "I'm looking for a boy, eight years old. Brown hair, fair skin. He would have been by himself earlier today."

The woman behind the counter, a college student from the looks of it with black hair and eyeliner to match, as well as two nose rings and half a dozen piercings in her ear, looked up. "Actually, I think I saw him… a few hours ago, maybe. Right as we were opening. He looked around for a minute and left. I was going to go after him, but he seemed determined, like he was looking for someone. I figured he had just misplaced one of his parents for a second." She paused, putting her book down. "I went back out to check like five minutes later and didn't see him."

Hope surged in Jonathan's chest. "Did you see which way he went when he left?"

"Maybe in the direction of the gas station? I'm not a hundred percent sure. But I know he wasn't out there an hour ago. I just took out the trash and there was no one in the alley."

"Thank you," Jonathan said, pulling out his phone as he left the shop. He shot Ivy a quick text.

. . .

POSSIBLE SIGHTING. BOOKSHOP ON THE BLOCK PAST IVERSON. Meet me over here.

HE SHOVED THE PHONE BACK IN HIS POCKET AND HEADED IN the direction given to him by the bookshop lady. That side of the building led to an alleyway open on both ends. Jonathan worked his way all the way down the alley, checking every pile of trash and small hole for the child, but finding nothing. As he emerged on the other end, he met up with Ivy, who was breathing hard having run from a couple blocks down.

"He's here?" she asked through labored breaths.

"A few hours ago. Bookshop owner said he wasn't hanging around."

"Probably didn't want to get picked up again," Ivy offered. "That was the big thing at the foster home. If you ran away, first order of business was to figure out how *not* to end back up in the home again. Which meant you had to stay away from roads or anywhere busy where you might be spotted."

That made sense. Considering what the kid had been through, he was probably scared to death of someone else kidnapping him, or Margaret coming back. He'd be laying low, in the lowest-traffic area possible.

Ivy scanned the area on the other side of the alley as Jonathan looked for any other hiding spots where the kid might be. There wasn't much back here other than the backs of some businesses and dumpsters.

"Wait," Ivy said, looking off to the east. "I think I might know where he went." She began jogging down the back alley with Jonathan close behind her. They emerged back onto the main street, but this time turned left and headed down a few more blocks until they came to a low building on a large plot of land with parking lots on either side. The sign on the front of the building said *COUNTY LIBRARY*.

"You think he's in here?"

"He'd go someplace familiar," she said. "And what kid doesn't like the library?"

"This kid," Jonathan said.

"What, you never read?" she asked, trotting for the building with him close behind.

"Only what was required," he replied.

The doors of the library slid open for them, opening the cool and quiet place. A couple of librarians stood behind the counter and Jonathan went over to them as Ivy began searching the stacks of books.

"Excuse me," he said, showing them his badge. "I'm looking for an eight-year-old boy. He may have come in here in the past few hours. About four feet tall, brown hair, Caucasian."

The librarians exchanged a look. "You'll have to be more specific than that. That's half the kids that have been in here today."

Unfortunately Jonathan didn't know what Albie had been wearing when Weston had let him go.

Out of the corner of his eye he caught Ivy motioning for him. He followed her over to the children's section to find her staring at a small boy, his back up against the stack, his nose practically touching the pages of the book he was holding.

It was Albie Quinn. And other than being a little dirty, he didn't look like he was worse for wear.

I'll go around, Ivy motioned with her lips. Jonathan nodded, not taking his eyes off the kid as he sent a quick message to central to let them know the kid had been found. As soon as Ivy was on the other side of the room and at the other end of the row, Albie must have seen her out of the corner of his eye, because he dropped the book and ran in Jonathan's direction. He tried to squirm past Jonathan, but he managed to snag the boy.

"Hey, it's okay," Jonathan said as the boy squirmed in his

arms. "I'm a police officer, okay? I'm gonna get you back to your mom."

"*No*," the kid yelled. "Let me go!"

"Look," Jonathan said, managing to pull out his badge with one hand. "See?"

As soon as the kid saw the shiny silver badge he stopped squirming, though they'd already attracted the attention of the rest of the library patrons.

"It's okay," Ivy called out, her badge on display for everyone. "We're taking him back to his parents."

Albie looked up at Jonathan. "I can go home?"

He nodded.

"Ambulance is on its way," Ivy said, joining them. Jonathan noticed that Albie shied away from Ivy, almost hiding behind him. She seemed to notice as well and backed up enough to make the boy feel comfortable.

"Here," one of the librarians said, coming over to them. "Would you like this?" She held out a red sucker for Albie. He took it tentatively, but Jonathan could tell he was still apprehensive of her. The only one he didn't seem to be afraid of was him.

"Don't worry," Jonathan said. "Everything's going to be okay now."

Chapter Twenty-Three

Ivy sat at her desk, attempting to fill out the bevy of reports this case had already required. Her eyes drooped and she could already feel herself nodding off, but she needed to get these done before she called it a day because she didn't think she had the strength to deal with them tomorrow. Even though Albie had been found, there were still so many questions to be answered. Thankfully, the frenzied pace that had become the norm over the past two days in the precinct had finally died down, giving her some mental solace.

"Here," Jonathan said, setting a mug of coffee on her desk as he came around before taking a seat across from her. The smell from the mug was enough on its own to snap her back awake.

"Oh, you are a godsend," she said, taking the mug in both hands before relishing a sip.

"I was afraid of what might happen if I didn't," he said, grinning. With the kid out of danger, it was like a weight had been lifted from her shoulders. And thankfully, he hadn't mentioned last night. Ivy wasn't sure she wanted to get into it. In the cold light of the morning, she'd begun questioning the wisdom of inviting him in like that. Should she bring it up now? Was there anything *to* bring up? It didn't feel like there was a proverbial elephant between them, but at the same time, maybe they needed to at least have a discussion about it. But before she could make a decision, Ayford appeared at the heads of both their desks.

"Okay, you two. Let's get it over with." He motioned for them to follow. Ivy took a longing look at her mug before she followed Jonathan to his office. No doubt it would be room temperature by the time she got back.

"Take a seat," their boss said once they were in his office. Ivy was barely in the chair before he began going into the specifics of the case.

"I just heard from the hospital. They're treating Albie Quinn for a stomach bug of some kind. Something he picked up while he was with the Weston woman. But other than that, he seems to be fine, physically, at least. Mentally— that's going to take longer."

"What does that mean?" Ivy asked. "We need to speak with him about the experience."

Their boss shook his head. "Not until the family gives us permission and right now, I'm lucky if they'll take my calls. The mother especially. Seems she doesn't have the best opinion of us." His gaze lingered on Ivy for a second too long. "Regardless, the kid has gone mute. Hasn't said a word since arriving at the hospital. They just want some time for him to get back to normal before we come to ask any questions."

Ivy was about to argue, but what was the point? Weston was dead, the kid had been found, where was the urgency? The only risk was him forgetting or blocking something important out. If they had to wait a few days or even weeks, she figured she could deal with that. After everything he'd been through, she didn't want to make it any worse for him.

"At any rate, good work, both of you," he said. "You really hustled on this one."

"Thank you, sir," they both said.

"Especially you, Bishop," Ayford said. "To hear Buckley tell it, you were something of a wet blanket. But I don't think she was giving you your due. Clearly you know how to hold your own out there."

The reminder of Nat's low opinion of her was like a sting to the arm, but Ivy ignored it. The woman was out of her life now, and if it took another five years to rebuild a tattered reputation, she'd be happy to do it.

"If we can't interview the kid, how should we follow up?" Jonathan asked. "There are still a lot of unanswered questions on this one."

"Par for the course, White," Ayford said. "Now that the kid is back safe and sound, I want your time to be dedicated to your other cases. As far as I'm concerned, this one is no longer your priority, understood?"

"What about Weston, sir?" Ivy asked. It had been her body retrieved from the river after all. She'd been transported down to Burns's office for examination.

"What about her?" he replied. "We can't very well charge a dead woman, now can we?" He leaned forward. "Look, do what's necessary to wrap this one up. Get me the reports in the next day or two, then move on, understood? In the meantime, I'll speak to Armstrong about your work here. I'm sure he'll be pleased to learn you're fitting in well after Buckley's desertion."

"Is that how it's being treated?" Ivy asked.

The man tilted his head. "She's been gone nearly a week with no word, no contact. All attempts to reach the woman have gone unanswered. Armstrong won't hold her job forever. I'd expect to see an announcement in the next few days regarding the matter." He leaned back. "That's it. Get back to it and we'll close this one up in the morning."

Ivy and Jonathan stood, heading back to their desks. "Do you really think Armstrong will say something?" he asked her as they took their seats again. Ivy found her mug wasn't as cool as she'd thought.

"He'll have to eventually, won't he?" she asked. "Nat just up and left."

"I suppose," he replied. "I guess I just couldn't believe she would do something like that."

"Trust me," Ivy said. "She'll do *anything* if it fits her agenda." The phone on her desk rang just as she was about to take a sip from the mug. *Son of a...* "This is Bishop."

"It's Burns, down at the morgue. I need you and White down here. Immediately."

AS THEY REACHED THE MORGUE, DR. BURNS MET THEM outside the examination room, snapping her gloves off. "I know you two aren't squeamish, so I won't spare you the details. But this is going to be a little jarring. You may want to hold your noses."

"Why?" Ivy asked. She couldn't imagine what Burns had found in the few hours since Margaret Weston had been pulled from the river.

"Come with me," she replied." They followed her through the double doors into the room, where Weston's body lay on a metal tray. She'd been stripped and her body cavity lay open, with various organs having already been removed. But it was the smell that hit Ivy the hardest. She began to tear up it was so strong.

"Jesus, what is that?" It was as if someone had mixed up a bowl of fish and rotten eggs, then left them out for a week.

"Stomach cancer," Burns replied. "Weston was in the advanced stages of it, though I'm not sure she knew it. The blood we found at the townhome was hers. Not from her period, but from internal hemorrhaging."

"Hemorrhaging from what? The cancer?" Jonathan asked.

"From this," Burns said, pointing to various purple spots all over her body.

"Bruises?" Ivy asked. Burns nodded. "I'm guessing those aren't from the fall or the river?"

"Her lungs were full of water, she drowned almost immediately," Burns said. "But some of these bruises are days, even weeks old," she replied. "Someone was working this poor woman over like a body bag and it was killing her."

"I don't guess they could be self-inflicted?" Ivy asked. She recalled how Weston had hit her head over and over on the bridge, surely a symptom of her mental instability.

"Some, but not all. Like the ones on her back," Burns replied. "It would have taken someone who was really determined to create bruise patterns like this by themselves. The more likely explanation is someone was doing this *to* her."

Ivy exchanged a quick glance with Jonathan. This complicated things. "Can you tell us how recently she may have sustained some of these?"

"I'd say within the last three days or so," Burns replied. "Also, given the advanced state of her disease, she probably would have been dead within a few weeks. She had to have been feeling the effects, though she may not have understood exactly how serious it was."

This complicated the case. It meant Weston wasn't just a kidnapper, she was a victim too. But how did that play into what they already knew? "What would have been her symptoms? From the cancer, I mean."

"Persistent abdominal pain, nausea, fatigue," Burns said, pulling a sheet back over Weston, which, thankfully, curbed the smell a bit. "Maybe vomiting, trouble swallowing. I noticed her esophagus was calloused. She may have thought she had a fever or the flu."

Ivy didn't like where this was going. "Do you think someone in this condition could have climbed up the outside of a home? Gotten in through a second-story window?" One look at Jonathan told her he was thinking the exact same thing.

Burns's lips formed a line. "I'd say it would have been highly unlikely. She probably wouldn't have had the strength or the stamina. It would have been a challenge for this woman to get up a flight of stairs."

"Shit," Ivy said.

"Accomplice," Jonathan said.

"Or tormentor," Ivy added. "Someone else was running her. And someone else got into that house to take Albie. But why go to the trouble? Why kidnap the kid, then pawn him off on someone else? That doesn't make sense."

"It does if you want to obscure your identity," Jonathan suggested. "We've maintained that the kidnapper had to know the family in some way or another. It doesn't make perfect sense, but it would be a good way to throw us off the trail."

"To what end, though?" Ivy asked. "The kid is back home. Weston didn't do anything other than maybe get him sick."

Burns nodded. "The excrement we found belonged to the boy. We found traces of bacteria in the sample, indicating he may have eaten something rotten. I don't think it's anything to worry about and I understand he's at the hospital now."

Ivy nodded. "I'm sure they're doing a full workup on him."

"Then they'll provide the necessary treatment if they find anything dangerous," Burns replied. "I don't think that was anything malicious. If she'd wanted to hurt the boy, she could have just poured bleach down his throat."

"We need to interview him," Ivy said. "There's more going on here than just a kidnapping."

"You heard Ayford," Jonathan said. "I don't think Mrs. Quinn is going to let us anywhere near him right now."

Ivy turned to Burns. "Thanks, Doc. We appreciate the update."

"There's something else. Weston's fingerprints don't match

those we pulled from the Quinn home. Not that it's saying much, but I thought you should know."

"Not surprising," Ivy said. Those prints could belong to any number of people— even friends of the family.

She turned back to the body. "I'll keep working, see if I can't pull anything else useful from her. But that dip in the river eliminated a lot. Still, I might be able to uncover something."

"We appreciate it," Jonathan said, shaking Burns's hand before they headed out. What had looked like a slow night had just done a complete one-eighty. Burns's revelations meant there was another player in this case; one they hadn't even known was there. But the more Ivy thought about it as they made their way back to the office, the more it made sense. Mrs. Quinn had identified a male figure watching the house. And *someone* had to have purchased that townhome for Margaret Weston, setting it up like that. And now they had evidence she had been abused. Ivy wanted to go back to Our Sisters in Arms and speak with the residents there again. Maybe one of them knew something about a boyfriend or an acquaintance.

"Dibs on not telling Ayford," Jonathan said as they got back to their desks.

Ivy wrapped her hand around the mug of coffee again. Sure enough, it was cold.

"Perfect," she said. "Just perfect."

Chapter Twenty-Four

Ivy leaned back in her chair; it felt like she'd been glued to the thing ever since coming back from the morgue. She'd had to inform Ayford that there was probably another perpetrator still out there and that the case wasn't as closed as they had assumed. And while he hadn't said it, she could feel the disappointment in his voice, almost like he'd expected it. Reluctantly, he told them to keep on it and keep him updated with their progress.

After that it had been back to building a list of possible suspects from the Quinns' contact lists. Ivy wasn't about to miss anything a second time and was building a comprehensive list of everyone from estranged family members to past co-workers. They couldn't leave any stone unturned if they wanted to find out who was really behind Albie's kidnapping. The report on Weston's car hadn't come back yet, but she hoped to get down to the impound garage sometime tomorrow to see it. There might be a trace of evidence left behind belonging to someone other than Weston which could point them in the right direction.

She also planned to return to the Rescue Mission, but couldn't go back until tomorrow. It was already closing in on eight-thirty and she figured that was something better left for the daytime. Someone had been abusing Margaret Weston, maybe even coercing her. Ivy's thoughts kept going back to what the woman had said on the bridge. She'd said "he'd never stop" and Ivy had assumed at the time she'd been speaking metaphorically— tormented by some unseen mental ailment that wouldn't go away. But now she considered that Weston had actually been talking about a real person— someone who had used and abused her for their own means. And Ivy had a pretty good indication that someone was a man.

As she rubbed her eyes, Jonathan's phone across from her rang. He'd been pulling the same number of hours she had— unwilling to leave her to work on this alone. She supposed it was good neither of them had families they needed to get home to.

"This is White," Jonathan said, picking up the receiver. Concern fell over his face as he listened to the other end. "Put her through immediately." He reached over and put the phone on speaker, laying the handle back in the cradle. "Dispatch. They have a call from Mrs. Quinn saying it's an emergency."

Ivy barely had time to process what he'd said before the line roared to life. "Detective?" Mrs. Quinn practically yelped. Her voice was high-pitched and it wasn't hard to hear that she'd been crying. Ivy's first thought was something had happened to Albie— that the infection had been worse than they thought.

"Mrs. Quinn," Jonathan said. "Is everything all right?"

"She's missing, she's *missing*," the woman practically screamed.

"Who, Mrs. Quinn?" Ivy asked.

"My *daughter*, who else?" the woman snapped back. "*Jesus fucking Christ!* You people are supposed to protect us. To protect *her*. You said the kidnapper was dead!"

"Tell us everything that's happened," Ivy said.

The woman took a few deep breaths on the other end of the line, steadying herself. "We left Jasmine at the Moore's... two doors down while we went to the hospital to be with Albie. She didn't want to go— Jasmine hates hospitals, so we told her she could stay with them. But just as we're ready to come home with Albie, I get a call from Juliette telling me she can't find Jasmine anywhere, that Regan last saw her outside. They thought maybe she'd gone back home without telling them, but when we got here, the doors were locked and no one was in the house."

"Are you at home right now?" Ivy asked, motioning for Jonathan to start notifying patrol units.

"Where else would I be?" the woman snapped.

"Stay there, we have units on their way to you," she said.

"I just spoke with 911," Mrs. Quinn replied. "They said the same thing. But *you* need to find her. *You* need to fix this."

"We'll be there in fifteen minutes," Ivy said. "Just hang tight." She hung up before the woman could say anything else.

"Coincidence?" Jonathan asked as he pulled on his coat.

She scoffed. "Not in a million years." She grabbed her coat as well, following him as they passed Ayford's office. It was dark— he'd already gone home for the night. She'd have to call him on the way.

"So then what? The girl was the target all along?" Jonathan suggested as they burst through the doors and headed for Ivy's car.

"Then why not just take her that first night instead of the boy? Whoever did it obviously had the capability," Ivy said. "*And* her window had been open. It would have been easier than grabbing the boy." Nothing about this made any sense. Just what the hell was going on here? Just when she thought they were in the clear, now they were facing yet another missing child. And while there wasn't any definite proof the kid had been taken by someone, if Ivy had been in Vegas, her entire bet would have been on black. There was just no way it was some kind of mix-up.

Less than ten minutes later they pulled into the Quinn's neighborhood, a sick sense of deja-vu settling over Ivy. Just like last time neighbors were out watching the commotion as two other patrol units had arrived before they had, this time their lights flashing in the dark, lighting up the neighborhood. One of the units was in front of the house two doors down from the Quinn place.

"Wanna start there?" Ivy asked, pointing at the house. "They'll be able to tell us more about what happened."

"Actually, we need to approach this from both sides at once," Jonathan said. "You speak with the neighbors; I'll go speak with the Quinns again."

Ivy nodded and pulled up to the home that sat between the two houses. She headed back while Jonathan went forward to the Quinn home. At the Moore house, her old partner Wilcox was standing out front, giving her a quick wave.

"Ivy," he said.

"Hey, Alan. How've you been?"

"Better," he replied. "They're kind of a mess in there. I don't know how much you'll get out of them."

"You guys set up a perimeter?" she asked.

He nodded. "Fuller's in the back right now and Lieutenant Drummond is on his way. He's coordinating with traffic to try and set up a two-mile perimeter around the house."

"Does he suspect the perp is on foot?" Ivy asked.

"Unknown. We're still looking for anything that could tell us how he nabbed her."

Ivy nodded. "Okay, thanks. I'm going to speak with the family, then take a look around."

"Good luck," Wilcox said. Even though Ivy loved working with Jonathan, sometimes she missed her old partner. He'd been the best kind— one who doesn't ask too many questions or get too personal. Just the right kind of partner she'd needed when she'd been on patrol.

"Hey," she said. "Can you back me up on this? I don't want to interview them alone." It was always better to have two officers present when speaking with witnesses, just because one person couldn't keep track of it all.

"Of course," he said, hooking his hands into his belt and following her into the house. "I believe they're in the kitchen."

Ivy headed into the home, which in many ways was like the Quinn house. It was a large, Craftsman-style home with upscale furnishings and an open floor plan, allowing Ivy to see all the way across the house. A woman and her daughter sat in the kitchen, both of them looking up as Ivy entered.

Ivy held out her badge for them to see. "I'm Detective Bishop. I think you know Officer Wilcox here. You're Juliette Moore?"

The woman nodded, holding out her hand. Ivy took it briefly and gave it a quick shake as she felt the ripple of current through her arm. It took everything she had not to wince.

"And you must be Regan," Ivy said to the girl sitting at the table playing with her phone. She looked to be thirteen or fourteen and barely acknowledged Ivy.

"*Regan*," her mother hissed. "Don't be rude." But the girl didn't respond. Mrs. Moore turned to Ivy. "I'm sorry about her. This has been— a tough day."

Ivy took a seat at the kitchen table as Wilcox stood at the end of the kitchen. "Tell me what happened."

Moore took a deep breath. "Jasmine came over about three. Brooke told me that the police— you— had found Albie and they needed to meet you at the ambulance or something before going to the hospital. Jasmine comes over here all the time so I didn't think anything of it. The girls are friends and I thought it would be better for her if she didn't go, so I said yes."

Ivy tried to keep an eye on Regan while her mother talked, but it was hard to split her attention. She hoped Wilcox was keeping an eye on her. "Okay, then what happened?" Ivy asked.

"I was doing laundry and Regan came in. Apparently the girls had a spat of some kind. So I assumed Jasmine was still outside on the deck. But when I went out there, I couldn't find her anywhere. Regan and I looked all over the house and at first I assumed she had gone back home. I called Brooke as they were on their way home and when they got there, she told me Jasmine wasn't there either. I think that's when she called you."

"About what time did you come back in the house?" Ivy asked Regan.

"It was around seven," Juliette said. "They'd been out there most of the afternoon."

Ivy nodded. "Can I ask what happened? You two had a fight?"

"It wasn't a fight," Regan said without looking up.

"Then why did you come back in?" Ivy asked.

"Because she wouldn't stop talking about her brother," Regan replied. "Yeah, it sucks. But he's fine. They found him."

"*Regan*," her mother admonished. "That's enough."

"You don't seem very upset," Ivy said. "Aren't you worried about your friend?"

The girl didn't reply. She barely even looked at Ivy. Ivy glanced back at Wilcox who seemed to be appraising the girl. There was more going on here than she was saying. Ivy stood and walked around the table to take the seat right beside Regan. "Regan, Jasmine is *missing.* She could be hurt. I need you to tell me what you know right now. No more bullshit, got it?"

"Detective, could you please not—" Mrs. Moore stopped speaking when Ivy held up her hand.

For the first time Regan actually met her eyes.

"I need you to be honest with me," Ivy said.

Regan bunched up her features. It made her look five years younger, just like a little kid. "It's not fair," she said. "He was my boyfriend first."

"Who was?" Ivy asked.

"Connor Trace," she replied.

"You and Connor broke up months ago," Mrs. Moore replied.

"He broke up with *me*," Regan said. "I thought it was just a temporary thing. I didn't know he and Jasmine had started going together."

Ivy sat back in her chair. "And Jasmine told you this afternoon."

"She didn't mean to, it slipped out," Regan said, her anger growing. "She's been lying to my face for weeks."

"Listen," Ivy said, leaning down. "Sometimes people lie to us because they don't want to hurt our feelings. Because they care for us."

"If she cared about me, she wouldn't have gone behind my back," Regan said.

"People also make mistakes," Ivy replied. "Have you ever done something you wished you could take back?"

The girl crossed her arms and lay her head on them on the table, but she seemed more amenable than she had a few moments ago.

"Did Jasmine say anything before you came back inside?" Ivy asked.

The girl shook her head. "I… I called her a bitch."

"That's it, you are grounded," Mrs. Moore replied.

Ivy held out her hand again, though the girl seemed unaffected by the punishment. Maybe it was a common occurrence. Regan seemed to be a brash kind of kid— she reminded Ivy of herself at that age. "Did anything else happen while you were out there? Anything strange?"

Regan squeezed her features together. "Like what?"

"You tell me."

"I dunno. We were on our phones most of the time," she said. "But I guess… I think I remember hearing lots of animals in the woods."

"Animals?"

She nodded. "Yeah, we get lots of animals through here all the time. Deer, foxes, you know." Ivy looked out the back door and could just barely see the tops of the trees of the forest that backed up to the house in the dying light. Of course, the house shared the same back border as the Quinn home. It backed up to the woods in the exact same way. The lights in the back were on and she could see Fuller out there, looking around.

"Thank you, Regan. I appreciate you talking with me," Ivy said before getting up. She motioned for Mrs. Moore to follow her back into the hall.

"I'm really sorry, Detective. She's picked up this rebellious streak ever since—"

"Don't worry about it," Ivy replied. "Has Mrs. Quinn told you about what she's seen in her backyard?"

Juliette turned and looked back towards Regan before lowering her voice. "She mentioned she thought she saw someone out there once or twice. But I've never seen anyone. And I've been looking carefully."

"I notice you have a fence around your yard," Ivy said. "Is there a gate in the back?"

"No, we didn't see a need for one," the woman replied. "Why… is that— is that how they took Albie? They came in through the backyard?"

"We're still piecing that together," Ivy said. "But for now, I'd stay inside. And keep a close eye on your daughter. I don't want to alarm you, but you need to be vigilant. Do you have security cameras?"

She nodded. "In the front. We didn't see a need for any in the backyard."

"Keep them on and running. We'll be leaving a patrol unit in the neighborhood, okay?"

"Thank you," she replied. "And please let us know if there's anything else we can do. Jasmine is such a sweet girl."

Once they were back outside, Ivy turned to Wilcox. "Anything?"

"The girl is obviously upset and doing everything she can to hide it," he said.

"Yeah. Unfortunately, I don't think it helps us find Jasmine. Thanks for backing me up in there. It was nice working together again." She caught the hint of a smile on his lips. "What?"

"That badge looks good on you. You've changed a lot since your patrol days."

"Changed?" Ivy asked.

"Matured," he said. "It's good to see. They were right to promote you."

Ivy tried not to blush. "I'm sure if you spoke to Drummond or Armstrong, that—"

He waved her off. "Nah, I don't have any desire to be a detective. I like working the streets. And I like sleep." He gave her a wink.

She nodded. This job wasn't for everyone. "I'm going to check on Fuller. If anything else comes up—"

"—you'll be the first to know," he replied.

As Ivy made her way to the Moore's backyard, she only hoped Jonathan was making more progress with the Quinns.

Chapter Twenty-Five

JONATHAN HAD SPENT the better part of twenty minutes trying to speak with Mr. and Mrs. Quinn, but most of the conversation had been one-sided, with Mrs. Quinn dominating everyone's time. She was practically frantic, pacing back and forth through the house as Mr. Quinn sat on the couch with their son, who was covered up under a blanket. He wore a pair of noise-cancelling headphones. Whether they were pumping in any music or just white noise, Jonathan didn't know, but his eyes were closed even though he wasn't asleep. Whatever he was listening to, it was probably better than witnessing the near-shouting match Jonathan had been a part of for almost half an hour.

"My partner is speaking with the Moores now," Jonathan said for what felt like the third time. "And we have units setting up on all the surrounding streets to create a perimeter. Our hope is to catch this person before they can get very far."

"It took you *four days* to track down the woman who stole Albie from us," Mrs. Quinn yelled. "And now we're just supposed to trust that you'll get Jasmine back in no time?"

"I didn't say that," Jonathan replied. "And I didn't mean

to imply that this would be easy, but we are doing our best to—"

"Oh, well as long as you're doing your best then that's all that matters," Mrs. Quinn sniped back.

"Brooke, sit down," Mr. Quinn said, his voice heavy with resignation.

"Our children are under attack, Jerry. I will *not* sit down," the woman replied, practically stamping her feet as she paced the room. One of Albie's eyes cracked open before his father ran a supportive hand over his head.

"I know this isn't what you want to hear," Jonathan said. "But our best chance at finding Jasmine is by speaking with your son. He may have seen or heard something that could be important to the investigation."

"How?" Mrs. Quinn said. "You said the woman who captured him was dead."

Jonathan nodded. "Yes, she committed suicide this morning."

"Then how—"

"We believe there was another party involved. And the woman who had Albie may have met up with this other person. A man. I believe you said it was a man you saw watching your house, is that correct?"

The woman stopped pacing. "Yes."

Jonathan nodded. "We were originally operating under the assumption this was all being done by one person, because that's what the evidence suggested. But now we believe there may have been at least two people involved. Maybe more, we don't know. But if Albie saw or overheard something…" He let the unfinished words hang in the air, hoping they would finally come to their senses and at least let him try with Albie.

The kid had barely looked at him when he'd come into the house. Jonathan had to remember he'd had a terribly hard day. Clearly the kid was traumatized, and if it was up to him, they would wait a solid week before asking him anything. But time was of the essence, and they couldn't afford to wait any longer.

Mr. and Mrs. Quinn exchanged looks for a moment before he finally nodded. Mrs. Quinn, to her credit, managed to calm herself for her child, getting down on her knees as she leaned up beside him on the couch. "Albie, honey?" she asked, gently removing the headphones.

The boy squirmed and squeezed his eyes shut tighter.

"Son, you remember Detective White from earlier, right? He's helping us find your sister. Can you sit up and speak with him a moment, please?" his father asked. The boy remained where he was. "C'mon." Mr. Quinn ran a strong arm under the boy and lifted him up into a sitting position where he finally opened his eyes.

"Sweetie, all you have to do is answer a few questions then you can go back to sleep, okay?" Mrs. Quinn said. The boy didn't respond, verbally or otherwise. She turned back to Jonathan. "This is how he's been since the hospital. They say he's still in shock— that it will wear off. I don't know how you're supposed to get him to answer questions if he won't even talk."

"I have some experience with this," Jonathan said, sitting on the floor in front of Albie, crossing his legs in front of him. "I have a sister, who was a little younger than you when she got lost. She was on a field trip with her school and they went to a park. The teachers lost sight of her and she went into the woods, because the park connected to our grandmother's house on the other side. And my sister... well, let's just say she didn't like school very much." Jonathan smiled at the memory. "In fact, she would rather be just about anywhere else other than school. And she actually made it— all the way to our Nana's place. The only problem was no one was home, because no one knew she'd be coming. And when she went back to the park, there were all these police around, just like here. But my sister was scared. Do you know why?"

Albie, who had been rapt with attention on Jonathan, nodded.

"*Oh,*" Mrs. Quinn whispered, covering her hand with her mouth as her eyes teared up.

"Because she thought she'd get in trouble," Jonathan said, causing Albie to nod even more. "But that's not what happened. When she finally came out, everyone was relieved. They were just happy she wasn't hurt. Like your parents here, who are just happy to have you back. So I don't want you to feel like you'll be in trouble for anything you tell me, okay? None of this is your fault. And I just want to ask you a few questions so we can find your sister, okay?"

He nodded again.

"Great. And you can just nod yes or shake your head no, you don't have to say anything," Jonathan said. "First question, you ready?" Albie nodded. "Did the woman who you stayed with have a friend with her?"

A shake of the head.

"Did she talk to anyone on the phone a lot?"

A nod. *Yes.*

"Could you hear what they were saying?"

No.

"Did she ever mention this person's name?"

No.

"Could you tell if it was a man or a woman?" *Yes.* "Nod once for man, twice for woman." He nodded once. "When you were with her, did she make any regular stops, or take you to the same place twice?"

No.

Jonathan sat back. So Albie could confirm there was another party— a man— but he hadn't seen him. He decided to try another approach. "Albie, do you remember Monday night?" He nodded. "Do you remember going to sleep in your bed?" *Yes.* "Do you remember anything after that?"

"What are you getting at?" Mr. Quinn asked.

"I'm just curious if he remembers what happened that night," Jonathan said. He knew he was straying into dangerous territory here. By making Albie relive the events, he could retraumatize the child.

Albie didn't move, but his eyes were wide. Jonathan was afraid he might have strayed too far. He'd hoped to determine if Weston had been the person to abduct Albie— and try to figure out why he didn't cry for help. Maybe he had just been too scared. It had to have been terrifying.

"You know what, nevermind," Jonathan said. "You did great, Albie. Thank you for your help. I think your parents should let you watch whatever movie you'd like, don't you?"

He gave Jonathan only a small nod, though his eyes were still wide.

"Albie, sweetie?" Mrs. Quinn asked. "Can you nod for Mommy?" But Albie's eyes remained glued on Jonathan. Oh, man. He might have really screwed up. "Albie?"

Finally, the boy opened his mouth. "Vents," he said.

"Vents?" Mrs. Quinn said. "What does that mean?" She turned to Jonathan. He shrugged— at a loss for what the boy meant.

"At least he's speaking again," Mr. Quinn replied.

"Honey, can you tell us what you mean?" Mrs. Quinn wrapped her arm around her son, but he just stared up at Jonathan. Apparently, that was all they were going to get out of him.

His phone buzzed with a message from Ivy. "Excuse me, I'll be back in a moment," he said. "If he says anything else, please let me know." He left the three of them with Officer Suarez as he made his way back outside to where Ivy was waiting.

"How's it going in there?" she asked.

"Kid's starting to talk. He confirmed Weston spoke with a man on the phone more than once while he was with her. He never saw the man though."

Ivy sighed. "Not as helpful as I'd hoped."

"He also said something peculiar. *Vents*."

Ivy's face twisted. "Okay. Like… dryer vents?"

He shook his head. "I have no idea. And I don't see how it helps us find Jasmine. Any luck on your end?"

She pointed to the back of the Moore house. "Jasmine was alone for at least thirty minutes in their backyard. Someone could have scaled the fence and snatched her from there. Or she could have made her way back over here and he could have grabbed her. There are a dozen and one ways she could have been taken and so far, no one has seen anything."

"Neighbors?" he asked.

She pointed to one of the other units. "Perry and Ellis are already working both sides of the street. But if he grabbed her from the woods, no one would have seen it. These houses are perfectly positioned so no one can see the backs. It makes staying concealed very easy."

Jonathan looked at the officers moving from home to home, while another held back the crowd that had formed. This neighborhood was getting quite the show this week. He scanned the faces of the onlookers, hoping to see one that might be out of place, but still there was nothing.

He dropped his head. "I'm at a loss. Why take the girl now? Was he upset because Weston let the boy go? Was this a backup plan, or the idea all along?"

"Albie is the key," Ivy said. "He's the only one who can tell us anything at this point. Because I can guarantee you there won't be a ransom note."

She was right. Weston hadn't taken Albie because she wanted to squeeze the Quinns for money. The problem was they didn't know *why* she had taken him at all. It seemed like she was trying to raise him in some strange way— providing a place for him to live. And yet, she hadn't been the one who had bankrolled any of it.

"I can't believe I'm saying this, but I think you need to

bring Oliver back in on this," Jonathan said. "Neither of us can find anything about this Regional Holdings operation and with Weston gone and the kid having been through enough, I think he's our best option."

She hesitated. "I'm not sure he's in the headspace to help right now."

"Look, I know you two are on uncharted ground here. But you know I wouldn't be saying this unless I was desperate."

She scoffed. "Yeah, I guess that's true."

"We've been running in circles since we got this case. He might actually be able to break it open."

"And if he can't?" she asked.

Jonathan turned to look back at the house. "Then we'll have to rely on luck."

Chapter Twenty-Six

Ivy stood at the door, taking deep breaths. She'd worked
the scene with Jonathan until it was late, trying to gather any
evidence from either the Moore's backyard or the Quinns'.
But just as before, the evidence left behind was thin. They
couldn't tell how Jasmine had been abducted, just that she'd
been outside on the Moores' deck when Regan had come
back inside around six-thirty. By seven, she was gone.

It was now closing in on eleven. Ivy had three text
messages from Aunt Carol she needed to answer, though when
she checked, two of them were pictures of Hero chewing on
toys. Leaving Hero with Aunt Carol gave Ivy some comfort.
She didn't like the thought of her aunt alone all the time and
the little dog gave her a distraction all day.

And at the same time, it meant he couldn't be here with
Oliver. And Ivy was more worried about him than she was her
own aunt. Because whatever Oliver was doing, it was dangerous. It had nearly gotten him killed.

And now, here she was, about to ask for another favor.

She was about to knock on the door when another text
came through. This one from Oliver.

. . .

Just use your key.

She looked up to the camera on the front door, smiling. But the smile faded as she realized that the camera had failed to capture Oliver's attackers. At least… she had assumed it had. She'd thought— given the state of his one-time server room— that any footage from the security cameras would have been destroyed along with Oliver's equipment. But he hadn't replaced any of that equipment yet. And if he could see her right now…

She fished out her key and opened the door, part of her expecting Hero at her feet. Oliver sat on the couch in the nearby living room, his laptop on his lap.

"That thing works?" she asked, pointing back to the door.

"What?"

"The security camera," she replied. He hesitated. "*Oliver.*"

"It uses cloud storage," he replied. "And before you ask, I can't show you the footage. I already erased it."

She came all the way into the living room. "*Why?* We could have used that footage to charge the people who attacked you. Do you want this to happen again?"

"It's not going to happen again," he said, though he winced as he sat up and set the laptop on the nearby table.

"Answer my question," Ivy demanded. "Why did you erase the footage?"

He sighed. "Because these are not the kind of people you arrest," he replied. "And even if you did, there would just be two more right behind them. And two more after that. And on and on and on."

She took a seat across from him. "Will you please tell me what's going on? I promise, I won't judge."

"I *can't,*" Oliver insisted as Ivy glared at him. "You're out late. Still working the kidnapping case?"

It was clear he wasn't going to tell her what was going on.

For whatever reason, he'd decided that she couldn't handle it. She'd told Jonathan she wasn't sure she could trust Oliver, but now she didn't even want to try. Weren't they supposed to be best friends? Besides Aunt Carol, Oliver was pretty much the only family Ivy had.

"We need to find some way past this," she said. "I get if you're not comfortable talking—"

"That's not it," he interrupted before sighing. "I just can't. Things would only be worse."

"Why?"

He didn't answer.

"What if I promised not to do anything? Not to pursue it any further? Is that the problem? You think I'll go after them?"

He chuckled. "I know you would. But that's not the problem."

"Then what?"

He met her eye. "Don't you get it? If I tell you, everything between us will change. And I don't know how to handle that."

She sat back. "You think I'll turn on you."

"I'm just trying to do the right thing here, Vee. This all started before you came back into my life, okay?"

As much as she hated to admit it, Ivy didn't really know all that much about Oliver. She hadn't seen him in years and had been suddenly thrust back into his life. For a while she'd been able to pretend like they could just pick right back up where they'd left off as kids. But that had been naïve, and stupid. Oliver had lived his life, just like Ivy had. She couldn't come in here and expect him to just spill his guts to her. But the bigger problem was whatever he was involved in was dangerous and no doubt illegal. This created a unique problem for her, being in law enforcement. If she had knowledge of his activities and didn't take action, it could cost her the job she'd worked so hard for, maybe even her freedom. Right now, she still had plausible deniability.

"Okay," she finally said. She was out of options. There was no other choice but to let it go and hope Oliver could handle himself.

"Okay?" he asked, looking up.

She nodded. "Yeah. I understand."

"Thank you," he finally said, smiling.

"I just hope you know what you're doing."

"Me too." He moved to get up, and she went to help him. "No," he said. "I need to be able to do it on my own. I start physical therapy next week and I don't want to be stiff as a board going in there."

She watched him struggle until he was on his feet where he took a deep breath before heading around her and towards the kitchen. "Can I get you anything?"

"No. The reason I came by was because I need some help. Did you ever find anything on Regional Holdings, LLC? We've got another missing kid."

He stopped, leaning on his crutch before turning to her. "*Another* one?"

She nodded. "Same family. The sister. Abducted this evening, not ten hours after we'd recovered the boy."

"That can't be a coincidence," he said, hobbling into the kitchen. He grabbed a wine cooler from the fridge, holding it out for Ivy. She reluctantly took it as he grabbed one for himself and popped the cap before taking a sip. "Ugh, these things are terrible."

Ivy just stared at hers. "Why do you have these?"

"They were a gift from Carol, actually," he replied. "She came by earlier to check on me. And she brought Hero. She's really thoughtful."

"Oh," Ivy said. She hadn't realized Aunt Carol had done that. Maybe that's what that other text to call her had been about. But she was glad for it. "She's a thoughtful person."

"I couldn't find anything on Regional Holdings," he said as he hobbled past again, headed back for the living room. "Other than it's a shell company with ties to a business in Guatemala."

"And what is a company in Guatemala doing buying townhomes in western Oregon?" Ivy asked, following him.

"No idea. I managed to uncover a couple of other holdings by similar shell companies. It looks like they were all set up to purchase single properties. I doubt the owners are even Guatemalan. More than likely it's some kind of racketeering outfit. At least, that's my guess. Because otherwise it's just bleeding money."

"But no way to trace who owns the company? No contact?"

"Other than a PO Box in Central America, no."

"What about the housing contract?" Ivy asked. "Someone had to sign for the purchase."

"Electronic signature, made by a J.E. Zimmerman," he replied. "But surprise, surprise, I can't find any record of a J.E. Zimmerman in conjunction with a Regional Holdings anywhere." He took a seat on the couch again. "How was the girl taken? If it were my kids, I wouldn't have let them out of my sight."

"She was staying with a friend while the parents were at the hospital with the boy," Ivy said. "Somehow he picked her up from either her own backyard or the friend's."

Oliver took another sip of the wine cooler. "That's messed up."

"The family has already been through so much trauma," Ivy said. "I'm not sure how much more they can take. Jonathan thinks maybe the girl was always the original target. That maybe this was an elaborate ruse to get her alone."

"But then why not just take her to begin with?" Oliver asked.

"That's what I said." Ivy slumped into one of the chairs. This was beginning to feel hopeless.

"What about the boy? Did you talk to him?"

She shook her head. "Jonathan tried. He's been through a lot and isn't talking very much. He mentioned something about vents but that's it."

"Vents?" Oliver asked.

"Why? Does that mean something to you?" she looked up.

He furrowed his brow. "That's a weird thing for a kid to say." Oliver grabbed his laptop and began typing away.

"He's been through a lot," she replied. "I was surprised Jonathan managed to get anything out of him at all."

"Do you remember that time when we planned to sneak out of the Bakers' house at like two in the morning?" he asked, still typing.

"Yeah," she said.

"And we thought the only way we could get away with it was by making sure everyone was asleep? Because no matter how you moved through that house, someone *always* heard you. And with a dozen people there—"

"Someone would always wake up and tell on us," she said, remembering. "We thought the only way we could get away with it was to pump gas into the house, knocking everyone out."

"Exactly," he said. "And the only way to do that would have been through the air vents." He turned his computer around to show her. "Octamethyleneimine Dioxide, better known as Vapoxil."

She leaned closer, looking at the webpage. "It says it's available for commercial use."

He nodded. "It's a chemical oxidizer. But it was found to have the ability to render users unconscious for short times, which is why you need to wear N-95 masks when using it."

"You're not thinking someone used this on the Quinns, are you?"

"I mean…"

Ivy considered the possibility. Whoever got inside the house would have needed to get past the parents in their own bedroom. And if Mr. Quinn really was a light sleeper, the only way to do that would have been to make sure they were knocked out. Now that Ivy thought about it, using a gas to incapacitate the family would have made abducting Albie a lot easier. Except… "The parents kept their windows open. Wouldn't it have just gone right out the window?"

"Not if they were only cracked," he said. "Though, I admit, it would have taken a shit ton of the stuff to pump in there. There would have had to have been a tank somewhere, connected to the HVAC system."

Ivy recalled Officer Kilgore mentioning there had been a HVAC truck near the Quinn's the day Albie went missing. "Do me a favor," she said, standing up. "See if you can find any purchase orders of that stuff that were shipped to Oakhurst or anywhere around here."

"On it," Oliver said. "Are you going back to the house?"

She nodded. "I need to see if there's any evidence of this tank anywhere." She made her way towards the door.

"Ivy," he called just as she reached the handle. "The gas leaves a very light residue. It'll be light blue in color if you find it."

"Got it," she said. "Thanks."

"Anytime," he said. "Good luck."

Chapter Twenty-Seven

JONATHAN HAD BEEN HALF-ASLEEP when the call came in from Ivy. But by the time she pulled up to his place, he'd yanked another suit on and was combing his hair as he ran out the door.

"You look gorgeous, now come on!" she yelled at him through the open window.

"Ivy, it's almost midnight," he said. "I don't think the Quinns—"

"They will if they want their daughter back," she said. "If Oliver is right and the kidnapper pumped this gas into the house, we need to get a sample of it."

"It sounds like something out of a cartoon," he protested as she peeled away from his place, forcing him back into the seat as she swerved around obstacles to get back on the main road. "Someone pumping knockout gas into the house."

"It's not stupid if it works," she said. "Think about it. The only way into the house without breaking a door or window were the upstairs windows. Oliver said if they were only cracked, then the gas had enough viscosity to remain in the house. The kidnapper, the *real* kidnapper could have scaled the wall, gotten in through the bedroom and made his way down to Albie's room, taking the boy without him even realizing it. He didn't cry out because he was unconscious!"

"And Jasmine?" Jonathan asked. "Why not take her then too?"

"Because her window was wide open, remember?" Ivy said. "So the gas wouldn't have affected her— at least not as much. The kidnapper may not have been able to get her as planned, so he did the next best thing and took Albie."

"And then pawned him off on Margaret Weston?" Jonathan asked.

"Maybe he wasn't prepared to take care of Albie— maybe he just wanted to get back to Jasmine. And he figured he could use the confusion around Albie's kidnapping to do that. He knew the parents would be staying close to Jasmine after what happened to their son, so he'd need a way to get her alone if he was going to grab her."

He had to admit, it made sense. But that didn't make it the correct theory. "I still don't understand what he wants with Jasmine, though," Jonathan said. "Why *her*?"

Ivy shook her head as she drove. "No idea. But we're going to find out. Radio the patrol car that's still on site. Let them know we're coming in."

TEN MINUTES LATER, IVY PULLED UP BEHIND THE PATROL CAR in front of the Quinn home. Most of the lights in the house were still on. As Ivy and Jonathan got out of her car, they were met by Kilgore and Toombs.

"I'm going to need a full description of that HVAC van the neighbor reported the other day," Ivy said to Kilgore.

"Now?" he asked.

"Right now," she replied. "Find the neighbor, double check the info and get it down to Central. I need to know where that business is located and who's running it."

"Have you notified the family we'd be coming?" Jonathan asked Toombs, who had hooked his thumbs in his belt, watching Ivy and Kilgore's exchange.

Toombs nodded. "Just informed them a few minutes ago. But I can tell you the wife isn't too happy."

"What else is new?" Ivy asked as she jogged up the stairs to the house with Jonathan close behind. She knocked on the door twice before stepping back.

The door opened to reveal Mr. Quinn, his eyes sunken in deep to his sockets. "Any news on Jasmine?"

"Not yet, but we may have a lead. We need to inspect your HVAC unit," Ivy said.

The man's face twisted into concern. "Why?"

"We think someone may have sabotaged it," Ivy said. "In order to incapacitate your family. Where is the main unit for the home?"

"It's up in the attic," he said.

"Have you had any HVAC maintenance done lately?" Jonathan asked.

"A couple of weeks ago, just normal maintenance, nothing wrong," he said.

"Show us," Ivy instructed. Quinn led them back up the stairs and to the access cover with a small string to pull it down.

"Jesus, what now?" Mrs. Quinn had appeared at the corner of the hallway in her robe, her arms wrapped around herself. Ivy climbed the ladder to get up into the attic as Jonathan squeezed around it to speak with Mrs. Quinn.

"Do you mind if I take a look at your bedroom again?"

The woman looked like she wanted to argue, but the fight had gone out of her. "Go ahead," she said, motioning behind her. Jonathan entered the large, expansive room, and for the first time, examined how many vents provided the room with air and heat. There was one directly over the bed. He returned to the hallway.

"Do you have a ladder I can borrow?"

"There's a stepladder in the hall closet," Mr. Quinn said. "Why?"

Jonathan didn't bother answering. He went to the closet, retrieved the ladder and set it up beside the bed. Once he was up to eye-level with the vent, he pulled out his keys and used one of the smaller ones to unscrew the vent cover on both sides. It was slow, but once he finally got it off, he pulled out a nitrile glove, snapping it on.

"What are you doing up there?" Mrs. Quinn asked from behind him.

Jonathan ran his finger inside the vent and when he pulled it back to inspect it, the beige glove had a slight blue tint to it. "Residue," he said.

He could hear Ivy climbing back down the ladder in the hallway and slowly got down so he could join her.

A bead of sweat prickled across her forehead before she wiped it away with her sleeve. "It's up there. A small tank connected to the unit. The sticker's been torn off, but there was a corner of it left. I'm going to send it to Oliver to see if he can get an ID on it."

Jonathan pulled out his phone. "I'll call Burns. We'll need to take the tank for evidence."

"What tank?" Mrs. Quinn demanded.

"It looks like someone— presumably your HVAC company— installed a canister of Vapoxil on your unit," Ivy said. "There's a little time-release device on there, which means they could probably trigger the release of the gas any time they liked. We think they waited until you were asleep, triggered it, then broke into your home to take Albie."

"You can't—is that what really—" Mr. Quinn seemed to be at a loss for words. Finally, though, he managed to recover. "Ok. How does that help you find Jasmine?"

"Because if we can find out who installed this unit, and how it came to be in their possession, then we can find who went to all this trouble to abduct your daughter," Jonathan said. Ivy had been right. Worse than that, *Oliver* had been right.

"He's got the picture," Ivy said. "How long will it take to get Burns over here?"

Jonathan shook his head. "Maybe an hour."

She turned to the Quinns. "I know this is a lot. But scrubbing this house down for evidence may help us in locating Jasmine."

"Whatever you need to do, do it," Mrs. Quinn replied with a stern look on her face. "I don't care what it is."

Ivy turned to Jonathan. "Okay. Let's wake everyone up."

Chapter Twenty-Eight

Ivy glanced at her phone, noting the time. Her foot tapped impatiently as she waited in her car, sitting in front of Landon's Plumbing and HVAC. She and Jonathan had spent the better part of the night piecing everything together as Burns grumpily worked to pull anything she could off the tank attached to the Quinns' HVAC. To say that Burns was not happy about being woken up in the middle of the night and dragged back down to the crime scene was an understatement. The woman had practically torn Ivy's head off, but had gone about doing her work regardless. Ivy figured she should probably get her a gift card to a nice restaurant somewhere as a thank you.

Burns had managed to snag a pair of fingerprints from the canister that had been attached to the unit— fingerprints that didn't match any others from the house, including those she'd obtained when they'd first searched the home.

Oliver, meanwhile, had tracked down the Vapoxil manufacturer from what remained of the sticker on the canister. It was a company based out of Seattle, which was next on Ivy's hit list. However, the biggest bombshell had been that according to its website, Landon Plumbling and HVAC employed a Jason Zimmerman. A picture was missing from the website, but the name and all his technical expertise was there, along with an explanation of how long he'd been in the business. And considering they were looking for a *J.E. Zimmerman* who had signed the townhome contract, Ivy wasn't about to chalk it up to coincidence. In fact, after waking Ayford and explaining the situation, they had determined they had enough to arrest Mr. Zimmerman.

Which was why Ivy was now sitting outside the company's address, waiting on Jonathan to show up with the warrant. It wasn't even eight o'clock yet, but Ivy had already seen a number of employees head into Landon Plumbing to start their day. She'd been looking for anyone who might fit the bill for Jason Zimmerman, but couldn't tell based on looks alone. There were plenty of tough-looking guys though. If she spent her days crawling around attics and basements to get to hard-to-reach ductwork she would probably look pretty rough herself.

As Ivy waited, watching the building, her phone buzzed in the seat next to her. Thinking it was Jonathan, she picked it up, but frowned when she saw the number. "Hello?"

"Ivy?"

"Hi, Samantha," Ivy replied. It had been months, maybe even a year since she'd spoken with Nat's ex-wife. She hadn't realized the woman still had her number. "Is everything okay?"

The woman hesitated on the other end. "Have you heard from Natasha?"

"No," Ivy admitted. "Not in a few days." She wasn't sure how much she should reveal about what had happened. Nat and Samantha had been split up for a while now; Ivy wasn't sure how involved they still were with each other's lives.

"Oh," the woman replied. "I had hoped… well, I thought maybe she was screening my calls."

"Is something the matter?" Ivy asked.

"Nothing serious. But Audrey called me asking why she couldn't get in contact with her. Nat and I... well, you know. We haven't gotten along well since the divorce. But she's never ignored calls from our daughter."

Ivy paused. Nat hadn't even let her *family* know what was going on? As angry as Ivy was with the woman at the moment, that was inexcusable. "I really wish I could tell you what's going on. She just left work the other day and hasn't been back since," Ivy said.

"You don't think... I mean... something hasn't happened to her, has it?"

"I'm sure we would have heard," Ivy said. "She always kept her emergency contact information updated. If there had been an accident or something, we would have been notified immediately."

Silence on the other end.

"I can try calling her again," Ivy said, knowing full well Nat wouldn't pick up. According to Oliver, she was somewhere outside San Francisco right now. But giving Samantha that information wouldn't do her any good. Ivy didn't have an exact location on Nat and didn't want to try to explain why she'd been tracking the woman's phone.

"No, that's okay," Samantha said. "I just thought... well, I guess she's screening everyone's calls. It's probably nothing to worry about. She used to do this sometimes when we were still married. In fact, her lack of communication is one of the reasons... well, I don't need to go into all of that with you. I'm sorry if I disrupted your morning. I know it's early."

"No, that's fine," Ivy said. "I'm sure she'll be in touch in a few days."

"Yes, of course. Thank you, Ivy."

Ivy hung up. And even though her eyes were on the HVAC building, she couldn't help but think about what Nat was doing. She was destroying every relationship in her life and for what? To hide from the truth? Ivy wasn't surprised she'd run when things had gotten a little too real, but to cut off her only family because of it? That was low.

Finally, Jonathan's car pulled up beside hers, across the street from the business. She hopped out of the car, her adrenaline pumping. Now was not the time to worry about what Nat was or wasn't doing. She needed to be sharp if they were going to nail this guy. "Did you get it?"

He held up the document. "As well as an order for them to comply and hand over all their records regarding Zimmerman and Vapoxil."

"Perfect," Ivy said. "Let's kick ass."

Stepping into the chilly office, Ivy noticed a palpable change in the atmosphere among the people who were already at work. A young woman with a headset on sat at the desk facing the door while everyone watched Ivy and Jonathan carefully.

"We need to speak with someone about an employee of yours— Jason Zimmerman," Ivy said, showing the woman her badge.

"I'm the manager, Dave Landon." a middle-aged man wearing a polo shirt emerged from a back room, apparently having overheard her. "Who are you?"

"Oakhurst Police," Jonathan said. "Is Zimmerman here?"

"Jason quit four days ago," the man replied. "Well, I say *quit* when really he just didn't show up for work. We tried calling, but no answer. I had to terminate his employment. We have a no-tolerance policy around here, and that was made clear to him when he took the job."

"How long has he been working for you?" Ivy asked.

"About three months," Landon replied.

Jonathan handed Landon the warrant. "We have a warrant to gather any information related to his employment as well as any and all records you have of the usage of Vapoxil."

The man furrowed his brow. "Vapoxil?"

"It's an aerosol, a chemical cleaner," Ivy explained. "You don't use it?"

"Not to my knowledge." He turned to the receptionist. "Check the records for this stuff. How do you spell it?"

"V-A-P-O-X-I-L," Ivy explained.

"I don't see that anywhere in the system," the woman replied.

"Zimmerman used it. On one of your client's homes. The Quinns," Jonathan said.

"Then he did it without our knowledge," Landon replied. "But we'll cooperate however we can. Amanda, pull all the records on Zimmerman for these people." The receptionist nodded and headed into the back office.

"Did you run a background check on Zimmerman when you hired him?" Ivy asked.

"Of course. We're required to by state law. Can't be hiring a known thief and then give them access to someone's home. What did he do?"

"I'm assuming that check came back clean."

Landon nodded. "Wouldn't have hired him otherwise." Given Zimmerman managed to purchase a townhome using a Guatemalan shell company, Ivy wasn't surprised he could fake a background check. Zimmerman might not even be the man's real name.

"Here you go," Amanda said, handing over a file folder with Zimmerman's name on it. Inside was his application, the reference checks as well as the results of his aptitude test.

"He scored high," Ivy said, reading the document.

"Sure did. One of the highest scores we've had. He was a good installer. We thought we were lucky to get him. Guess not, huh?"

She turned to the back of the folder which showed a picture of the man, presumably for his security badge. "He's older than I expected." The picture was of a man in his mid to late fifties, a gray moustache and goatee decorating his face.

"We try not to be ageist around here. I admit, installing these kinds of units is a young man's game, but Zimmerman never had trouble keeping up. In fact, he had the stamina to keep working after a lot of my other guys quit for the day."

"Hey," Ivy said. "Look at this." She pointed to the address he had listed on file.

"It's the townhome address," Jonathan said.

That made sense. Why use a different address when you have a perfectly good townhome you can use? Ivy was almost certain now that Zimmerman wasn't his real name. "How long have the Quinns been clients of yours?"

Landon looked to the receptionist, who pulled it up on the computer. "Three years," she said.

"And how often do they receive maintenance on their systems?"

"They pay for the quarterly service," she said.

Ivy tucked the folder under her arm. "Thank you, we'll be in touch if we need anything else."

"If you find him, let him know we'll mail his paycheck to him," Landon called after them as they headed back outside.

"Three months," Ivy said as they headed back to the cars. "So Zimmerman probably figured he could weasel his way into the Quinns' home eventually. He just had to wait for their maintenance appointment."

"We need to show his picture to the Quinns, see if they recognize him."

Ivy handed him the file. "You do that, I'm going to contact the Vapoxil supplier. See if they have anything else that might help." She hopped back in her car and pulled up the information Oliver had given her regarding KHS Chemicals. Now that it was after eight, she figured someone would probably be there to answer. As the phone rang, she couldn't help but glance over at Jonathan, who was on his own phone in the warmth of his own car. There finally seemed to be some light at the end of this tunnel. They just needed to see it through.

The line connected. "KHS, how can I help you?"

"This is Detective Bishop with the Oakhurst Police, down here in Oregon," she said. "I'm investigating a case that involves the purchase of Vapoxil. Can you help me find some purchase records?"

"Of course," the man on the other end said. "What can I help with?"

"I'm looking for a purchase by a J. Zimmerman or Jason Zimmerman within the past six months," she said.

Thankfully, he was cooperative, pulling up the information quickly. "One twelve-ounce canister Vapoxil, shipped to 4611 Westwood Ave. on February nineteenth of this year," he said. "Retail price was one-thousand, four hundred and sixty dollars."

Ivy's eyes went wide. "Why so much?"

"It's not something that's ordered in huge amounts, so we don't keep a lot in stock. It's more of a specialty item." February nineteenth. That more or less confirmed that Zimmerman was planning on infiltrating the Quinn's house at some point in the future and he just had to wait for the right time. Unfortunately, it didn't give her an indication of where he might be. The townhome had been sealed up, though there wasn't anyone keeping an eye on it. Could Zimmerman have fled back there? She didn't think so. There wasn't any reason to. He probably had other options. She needed to get in touch with the DMV, see if she could pull any records on him. Maybe another address.

"Okay, thank you," she said.

"Ma'am, I don't know if it helps, but there's another order here," the man said.

Ivy furrowed her brow. "He made a second order?"

"There's another order under his name, but it's much older. It came up under his purchase history."

"How old?" Ivy asked. She shot a glance at Jonathan in his

car. He was talking animatedly— probably with Mrs. Quinn about the picture of Zimmerman.

"Looks to be about fifteen years or so. Hang on." She could hear him typing in the background. "Yes, okay. Sorry, I was confused for a second. This was back before Vapoxil was reformulated. Due to how it was manufactured, we could only deliver it in fifty-gallon tanks. That all changed around 2015 when the company redesigned the formula from the ground up, which thankfully made it much easier to transport."

"You're saying Zimmerman bought a fifty-gallon tank of this stuff fifteen years ago?"

"Yes, ma'am," the man on the other line said. "Hang on, let me get the purchase details. Looks like… yep, purchased in June of two-thousand-seven. Shipped on July ninth. Ground freight."

Ivy's heart jumped. Zimmerman couldn't have owned the townhome back then. This might give her a clue as to his current location. "Where was it shipped?"

"The address I have here on the order is 1113 Winding Way Rd. Oakhurst."

Ivy's stomach bottomed out. She found it impossible to speak. That couldn't be right.

That was the address of the cabin.

The same cabin she and Alice had entered not more than five days ago, determined to uncover something about what had happened to Ivy's family.

The same cabin where she'd lost her nerve, leaving Alice all on her own.

"Ma'am, are you still there?" the man on the other end asked.

"I am," Ivy said, her mouth dry. It was almost like she was speaking through a trance. That same feeling from before was back— the one she'd felt back at Aunt Carol's, the one where her mind had shut down— refused to take in any new information.

"Are you okay?" he asked.

Ivy *willed* herself to pull it together. There was a missing girl out there for fuck's sake; she couldn't be worried about herself. So what if it was the same location? That cabin could have been used by dozens of people over the years. Maybe it was just a coincidence that Zimmerman had decided to ship something there only a few months before Ivy's family disappeared.

But in her heart, she knew that wasn't true. Somehow, this all connected back to *her*. "That's all I need, thank you." She hung up, glancing back over at Jonathan. He was still engaged in his conversation, which didn't look like it was making any progress. She needed to get to the bottom of this. But she wasn't sure if she could bring Jonathan along with her. The last time she'd been in the cabin, she'd put Alice's life at risk. What if Zimmerman had been there then? It had been pure luck that the cabin was empty at the time.

Then again, going it alone wasn't smart either. What if it wasn't empty? What if he was there, waiting? And what if he was keeping Jasmine there? Or it might not have anything to do with the current case at all. But it was a lead, no matter how small. And Ivy needed to figure out what it meant.

She waved to Jonathan to get his attention. He turned; his brows knitted. Ivy mouthed: *Phone's dead. Headed back to the station.* He nodded, motioning that he would catch up. She turned the engine over and pulled out of the lot, headed in the direction of the station, but as soon as she was out of his sight, Ivy took a detour.

She couldn't put this off any longer. She'd already let herself down once by not facing the one thing that could give her an answer as to what had happened to her family. And now, somehow, it was connected to this missing girl. This time, Ivy wouldn't freeze. She wouldn't chicken out.

She couldn't.

Chapter Twenty-Nine

Jonathan pulled his car into the precinct parking lot, expecting to see Ivy's car there, but it was nowhere to be found. He yawned as he got out of the vehicle. Maybe she'd decided to head back home for a few hours to catch up on sleep— though, given they were on the trail of Zimmerman, that was unlikely. Ivy wasn't the kind of person to just drop out of a case in the middle because she was *tired*. There was a reason they worked on a steady diet of coffee, after all.

But, Jonathan had to admit, he was beginning to feel it. They'd been pulling a lot of late nights lately and it was catching up to him… especially after last night.

He headed into the building and up the stairs to Ayford's office, where the man sat, reading the morning paper. He looked up as Jonathan poked his head in.

"Is Zimmerman in custody?"

Jonathan shook his head. "Disappeared four days ago. They haven't seen him since. I spoke with the Quinns; they recognized him as the man who came and worked on their HVAC, but otherwise they don't know him. We couldn't find any connection between him and anyone in the family. It's almost like he targeted the Quinns at random."

Ayford put the paper down. "That's not good news. Where's Bishop?"

"Said she was on her way back here, but I haven't seen her yet."

"As soon as she gets in, tell her to check with me," he said.

Jonathan nodded. "I'm going to feed his picture and prints into ViCAP. See if we can get a hit. And I'll contact the DMV. Maybe we can pull another address. Or at least a vehicle."

Ayford regarded him. "You need rest, White. You and Bishop have been running nonstop on this thing. *I'll* run his info. Leave me what you have. You get a few hours and you can get back to it this afternoon."

"Sir, that's really not—"

"Or you can stand here and argue with me about it," Ayford said. "I don't need you falling asleep on the job. Go home. Get two hours of rest and come back since you can't seem to stay away from this place."

Jonathan smiled. "Yes, sir." He handed over everything he had on Zimmerman and headed back to his car. He shot Ivy a text letting her know he was headed back home for a few hours to rest and to make sure to call Ayford whenever her phone came back on. It was funny; she'd been charging her phone on and off all night as they'd worked. It wasn't like her to use it so much that it died completely. Then again, maybe something had happened to the phone itself. They did tend to use them a lot and it wouldn't be out of the ordinary for it to just give up.

As he got to his car, Jonathan decided not to give it another thought. He wasn't even sure why he was thinking about it anyway. Just as he got to his car, his phone buzzed and he figured it was Ivy responding. But when he looked at the device he grimaced.

YOU HAVE ONE DAY. STAY AS FAR AWAY FROM BISHOP AS POSSIBLE.

. . .

He knew if he tried to text or call the number it would be futile. But there had to be something he could do to find out who was behind this. Jonathan had never been technically savvy— at least no more than the average person. He could work a computer, figure out GPS, all the normal stuff. But when it came to the advanced side of things, he tended to lose interest quickly. He thought about taking his phone into technical services and having them try to determine if they knew who could be doing this. But if he did t hat, it would only raise more questions than it would answer. And he'd have to report it to Ayford or Armstrong. Until he knew who was behind this and why, he wasn't opening his mouth to anyone.

Putting his exhaustion to the side, Jonathan sat behind the wheel of his car. There was *another* option, though he didn't relish the idea. But if he wanted to get to the bottom of this, he needed some help. And he was pretty sure he'd be able to get it.

It just meant swallowing his pride first.

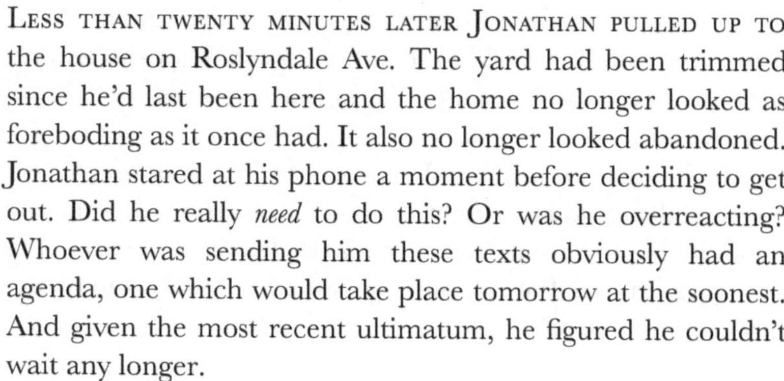

Less than twenty minutes later Jonathan pulled up to the house on Roslyndale Ave. The yard had been trimmed since he'd last been here and the home no longer looked as foreboding as it once had. It also no longer looked abandoned. Jonathan stared at his phone a moment before deciding to get out. Did he really *need* to do this? Or was he overreacting? Whoever was sending him these texts obviously had an agenda, one which would take place tomorrow at the soonest. And given the most recent ultimatum, he figured he couldn't wait any longer.

He stepped out of the car, straightened his tie and made his way through the gate, up the sidewalk and onto the porch, walking quickly and purposefully. He glanced up to the camera above the door, staring at it and not bothering to knock. A few moments later, the bolt on the door unlatched and it opened to reveal Oliver, his weight on one crutch.

"What the hell are you doing here?" he asked.

Jonathan had to take a second to compose himself. He hadn't realized how badly Oliver had been hurt. Even now, five days later, he was still very swollen and half his face was still purple. But the steely-eyed glint that had always been there remained. He might have had the crap kicked out of him, but it hadn't changed his personality.

"I need some help."

"Not interested," Oliver said and moved to close the door.

"It's about Ivy," Jonathan said before he could get it all the way closed. Oliver slowly pulled the door back open. "I've been receiving a series of cryptic texts about her. Every time I try to text back or call the number; it returns as undeliverable. Someone is baiting me, and I want to know why."

"What kind of texts?" Oliver asked.

Jonathan pulled out his phone and showed him the list of all five. Each from a different number.

The man sighed and moved out of the doorway. "Come in."

Jonathan followed him inside and closed the door behind them. "Where's your dog?"

"With Carol," he said over his shoulder as he hobbled back to the living room and gingerly set himself down on the couch. He held out his hand. "Let me see your phone."

Jonathan handed it over and Oliver plugged it into the laptop sitting on the table in the room beside a couple of food wrappers and discarded wine cooler bottles. Funny, he wouldn't have taken Oliver as a wine cooler kind of person.

"First one came across on Sunday," Jonathan said.

"I see the data," Oliver said, typing away on his screen. "They all came from burner phones."

"I figured as much," Jonathan said.

Oliver furrowed his brow as he read over the texts. "These are… strange."

"That's why I'm here," he said.

"No, I mean their digital signature. It's strange. It doesn't correspond with what I'd normally see with a burner phone."

"You think they were sent some other way?" Jonathan asked.

"Hang on." Oliver continued to work, which left Jonathan standing there with his hands in his pockets. He took the place in, not that it looked much different than the last time he'd been here. Though then Oliver had been working out of his back room, a room filled with server equipment. A room that had been destroyed, according to Ivy.

Jonathan wandered down the hall casually, taking his time. Eventually he came upon the kitchen, where one of the windows had been boarded up with plywood. That must have been the route the men took to get out of the house after the assault. He took a second to peek into what had once been the server room. Sure enough, shattered equipment covered the floor and nothing was running.

"Yo! Flatfoot, where'd you go?"

Jonathan returned to the living room. "Flatfoot?"

"I saw it in a movie once," Oliver said. "Okay, looks like these didn't come from a burner phone after all. They're all from the same phone."

"But they're different numbers," Jonathan said.

"They're masking their real number, using a couple of sophisticated techniques. It also prevents any call backs or the ability to respond in any way. *But*, I'm just good enough that I managed to uncover the real number."

"Do you know who it belongs to?"

He shook his head. "But I can tell you approximately where they are. I just pinged the phone. Pulled up about ten miles south of the California border, moving north, it looks like."

"I-5?" Jonathan asked.

"That would be my guess."

That meant they would be in Oakhurst by nightfall. But who would want to come after Ivy? And why?

"Okay, so that's one question answered. But I need to find out who is behind these texts. I can't prepare if I don't know what's coming."

Oliver shrugged. "I could always set up a mask of my own. Give it a call and see if we can't get someone to answer."

Jonathan nodded as Oliver handed his phone back to him. "How long will that take?"

"Maybe ten, fifteen minutes," Oliver said. "Does Ivy know about this?"

"Not the most recent one, but I told her about the others. Her phone is dead, I think she went home to rest. We've been pulling a late shift on this kidnapping case."

"Right," Oliver said. "Did she ever figure out what was going on with the Vapoxil?"

"We're still working on it," Jonathan replied. He wasn't comfortable with a civilian being so involved with their cases. But Ivy had made it clear that was the deal, and Oliver *had* been a help; he couldn't deny that.

"Uh-huh. I feel like we should rope her in on this. Shouldn't she know who's threatening her, even if they're doing it through you?"

Jonathan sighed. "I guess." He hated to wake her, knowing she was probably as exhausted as he was. But Oliver was right. She would want to know. He dialed her number, but it went straight to voicemail. "Her phone must still be dead. It's going to voicemail."

Oliver screwed up his features. "Ivy's phone is never dead." He typed out a few keystrokes. "Nope, it's pinging. It's on, she just sent you to voicemail manually for some reason."

"Why would she do that?" Jonathan asked, unease bubbling up in his stomach. "Where did it ping?"

"Somewhere north of town. I can't get an exact location, but I can triangulate to within about a mile or two." He grabbed his phone. "Let me try. Maybe she's just screening your calls." He shot Jonathan a smarmy grin. But a second later that grin turned into a frown.

"Maybe she's screening your calls as well."

"At least she didn't lie to me," he replied, going to work again. A second later he turned the screen to face Jonathan. On it was a map with a large red circle around it. "She's somewhere in here."

Jonathan examined the map. It wasn't anywhere close to her apartment, or Carol's house. And she definitely wasn't at the station. He thought for a second maybe she had decided to return to the Quinn home, but she wasn't near there either. "Wait a second," he said as he realized what part of town she was in. "Correct me if I'm wrong, but that's Winding Way right there, isn't it?"

Oliver turned the computer back towards him. "Shit. She went back to the cabin?"

Why on earth would she do that? They were in the middle of an investigation. There was no doubt she was upset about what had happened on Sunday— but as far as Jonathan could tell, she hadn't been chomping at the bit to get back there. In fact, she didn't seem like she wanted to go back at all. So why now?

"I need to go up there," he said. "Something about this doesn't feel right."

"She obviously doesn't want to be bothered," Oliver said. "You should just leave her alone."

"After what happened last time, I don't think so," Jonathan said. He looked to Oliver for support, but only saw suspicion instead.

"She told you what happened?"

Jonathan steeled himself. "Look, I don't have time to deal with bruised egos. I can't help it if your relationship is in a weird place. And frankly, we're all dealing with our own shit right now." He hadn't meant to curse, it had just come out. But he was tired of Oliver's *hurt puppy* routine.

"Hey, asshole," Oliver said. "You were the one who came to *me* for help. Not the other way around."

"I did, and I appreciate what you've done. But it isn't my fault if Ivy shares things with me and not with you. From what I understand, you both have secrets you're keeping close to the chest."

He recoiled. "That's different."

"If you say so. But something about this doesn't feel right to me. And if she's back in that cabin, it means something is wrong. She shouldn't be there alone."

Oliver just stared at him as Jonathan headed for the door. They would have to resolve whatever was going on between them at some point and Jonathan wasn't going to get in the middle of it. All he knew was Ivy had been in a precarious position regarding this cabin and for her to just up and go there now was very strange and not like her at all. Even worse, she was screening her calls from everyone, not just him. And a cop only did that in the field if they were at risk of being discovered.

But what really bothered him was that she had *lied*. And he didn't know why.

They were partners— whatever she was dealing with must have been so personal she thought she had to take care of it herself. Still, it wasn't like her to drop a case like this. To just abandon Jasmine Quinn for her own pursuits? That wasn't like Ivy at all.

Which meant he needed to be prepared for anything going in.

Chapter Thirty

Ivy STARED out the windshield at the cabin. Even though it was daylight, the low clouds blanketed the area in a darkness that almost seemed to emanate from the cabin itself. Somehow, it seemed even more ominous in the daytime. When she'd been here with Alice, they'd barely been able to see anything; it had been raining so hard. But now, she had a clear view of the building, and took it all in.

She'd been sitting in her car for a solid twenty minutes, trying to convince herself to go inside. But that same terror that had seized her before kept her glued to her seat. How was she supposed to go in there now? She could barely get through the door last time and she'd had someone with her. Now she was alone, and whatever was in there was far worse than she could even imagine. She didn't know how she knew that, but she could *feel* it in her soul.

"C'mon, get out of the car. You can do this, just get out," she mumbled to herself. She half expected someone to come bursting through the front door, guns blazing. But the place was quiet. There were no other cars that she could see and there had been no movement at the windows the entire time she'd been here.

Her phone buzzed and she immediately cancelled the call. When she looked at the phone she cursed. *Jonathan.* Maybe he'd still think her phone was dead. At least, that's what she hoped would happen. But it reminded her she was on limited time here. If she didn't want to put him in harm's way, she needed to do this, and to do it fast. Jasmine could be inside and here she was, sitting outside, too afraid to go in.

Like a child.

Ivy opened her door and stepped out, pulling out her weapon and checking to make sure the safety was still on. She closed her door gently, not making a sound as her phone buzzed again. She practically fumbled to kill the call again, this time from Oliver.

Oh *no.* What were the odds Jonathan *and* Oliver would call her within mere seconds of each other if they weren't together? But that was ludicrous, wasn't it? Why would they be within a mile of each other if they could help it?

She might have less time than she thought. This time, she made sure her phone was on silent before she headed up the gravel driveway to the building, her heart hammering in her chest. Except this time, she didn't go straight for the front door. Instead, she circled around the building, keeping her weapon pointed at the ground, but also watching for anything out of the ordinary. It was something she and Alice should have done when they were here last time, securing the perimeter. But Ivy had been so on edge that she'd neglected to do it, and Alice— being a reporter— hadn't known any better.

As Ivy came all the way around to the back of the building, she spotted a large oil tank that provided heating oil to the cabin. But it was the smaller blue container beside the tank that attracted more of her attention.

She approached gingerly, watching her steps. It was only little in comparison to the massive oil tank beside it, and time had stripped away most of its color and begun to rust the edges of the tank itself, but there was no denying it. It was a

Vapoxil tank. Most of the lettering was so faded she could barely read it, but she could still make out the manufacture date, which matched up exactly with what the customer service rep on the phone had given her.

It was true. Zimmerman *had* been here fifteen years ago. And he'd hooked the fifty-gallon tank up to the cabin as well, just like he had at the Quinn's house. Had Nat known about this? Did this tank have something to do with Ivy's family? If Zimmerman had used the gas on the Quinns…no, that was insane. But the evidence was staring her in the face. Had he used it on Ivy's family as well?

She found an anger boiling up in her chest, burning away the fear she'd felt before. It was almost like a rage deep within her, forcing her to move, focusing her mind to a sharp point. She moved with purpose around the rest of the structure, checking for anything else that might be out of the ordinary. But everything else looked to be in order.

Without hesitation, Ivy climbed the stairs to the porch, flipping off the safety on her sidearm. She sidled up to the front door, much in the same way she'd done with Alice, only this time, she was the one who reached out for the handle. She could see in her mind's eye Alice taking the action of opening the door quickly as she stood on the other side of the doorway before shining her light inside the place and proceeding in. Ivy had been right behind her and made it three steps in before stopping.

Grimacing at how *stupid* she'd been, Ivy focused her anger and forced the door open. If there had been a lock, it was long gone. She peeked inside for a brief second before returning to cover. Like before, there hadn't been much to note at first. No furniture, and what little light made it into the cabin only highlighted the specs of dust in the air.

"This is the police," Ivy announced. "Show yourselves!" But there was no response. She checked the corner again, and sure she didn't see any forms in the darkness, turned the corner and made her way into the cabin.

She found her feet slowing after two steps, but Ivy thought again about that Vapoxil tank outside and the anger surrounding what it could mean. When Alice had first found this cabin, Ivy had thought it might have been nothing more than a meeting place where Nat had coordinated some kind of coverup about Ivy's family. But the second she stepped foot in here, Ivy had *felt* something. Something familiar, like *she* had been in here before, even though she had no memory of the place. And now that she was in here again, she could remember. *That's* what had freaked her out so badly. Some part of her had recalled being here, and it had stopped Ivy in her tracks.

Not again. Not *ever* again.

Ivy took another step forward, and another. Until she was standing fully in the large room. There were five windows in the great room itself, which was attached to a small kitchen off to the right. The appliances were old, from the eighties or nineties and covered in dust. Ivy tried a nearby light switch, but the power was off. No surprise, who would be paying the bill?

The only room that wasn't part of the combined space was a bedroom, which was on the other side of the kitchen. Ivy didn't know how she knew that, but she did. The door to the room was closed. She crossed the space in a few short steps, opening the door and finding only an empty room behind. All the furniture from the cabin had been removed. Though… this place had a basement. It had to, because the garage had been cut into the hill, a single door that was on the floor below the home, while the hill beside it led up to the cabin itself.

Ivy searched around for an access point or some way to reach it, finally realizing the bedroom wasn't as big as she thought. Back in the great room, there was another door on the other side of the closed-off bedroom. It was recessed back into the wall a bit so it was harder to see, but the door was still there.

Ivy pulled out her phone and shone her light on the door and the floor leading up to it. There were prints in the dust. Prints that looked too large to belong to Alice's dainty feet. She hadn't mentioned going into the basement. Maybe she'd been too afraid or maybe Ivy's freakout had distracted her. But whoever had gone down there had done it recently and Ivy was relatively sure she knew what she'd find when she followed.

The smart thing to do would be to go back outside and wait for backup. To call Jonathan, Ayford and everyone else to come out here and storm this place. But at the same time, she may have already alerted Zimmerman to her presence. And if he had Jasmine here, there was no telling what he would do with her now that he'd been found out. Ivy could wait, but waiting might cost Jasmine her life.

Plus, she wanted answers. Starting with what the tank that had been installed here was being used for.

Ivy took a deep breath, and opened the door.

The stairwell was dark; she couldn't see any light at the bottom. If Zimmerman was down there, he was standing in complete darkness. She didn't have a choice, she shone her light down the stairs, finding they curved at the bottom before reaching the floor below.

Carefully, but still with purpose, Ivy made her way down the stairs. Zimmerman could be lying in wait, but if he was, he'd already know she was coming. He would have heard her on the floor above. At the bottom, she kept her back to the wall, then flipped the light around the corner at the same time she looked before pulling back quickly.

There was no one there.

Ivy checked a second time, and a third, before finally

coming all the way around the wall and shining the light all over the room. It was dingy, dusty and smelled faintly of mold, but there was no one down here. The basement was just concrete walls, though there were some calcite lines on one of them, indicating water had permeated the basement at some point. The garage door sat against one wall, though Ivy wasn't sure a full-sized vehicle could even fit in the space. The room was tiny.

She let out a frustrated breath as she holstered her gun. How could she have been so wrong? Maybe the trail leading here hadn't been ironclad, but she'd *felt* it was right in her gut. Then again, maybe she was just letting her emotions run away with her. This cabin had some connection to her past, yes. But that didn't mean it was connected to *everything*. She'd wasted valuable time following a dead lead and now she had zero idea where Jasmine Quinn could be.

What was worse, that feeling deep in the pit of her stomach was gone. It was like as soon as she'd explored the cabin, it had all gone away, like it had never been there to begin with. There was nothing special about this place. Nothing unique.

Nothing…

Something caused Ivy to turn her head. Not a sound, more like a faint echo. She wasn't even sure she'd heard something. On the back wall stood a shelf full of old paint cans full of nails and screws, all of them rusted from time. Without knowing why, Ivy reached out and tugged on the shelf, finding it was affixed to the wall itself. She pulled a little harder, and instead of the shelf coming off the wall, the wall came with it. The whole unit swung on a hidden hinge, which revealed another hidden room.

No, a hidden *tunnel*.

Ivy shone her light down the passageway. It had been dug out of the earth, supported with wooden beams. And it looked like it had been there a while. Lights hung on the beams to her left, connected by a long extension cord to each individual light. But they remained off.

Had she known this place was here? Or had she just guessed? She couldn't be sure, but that dark pit in her gut had returned, stronger than ever. She was on the right track now. What it would lead her to, she had no clue. But she had no choice but to follow it.

Ivy took a deep breath, steeled herself and walked into the tunnel.

Chapter Thirty-One

Ivy kept the light on the wall as she followed the long corridor. The entire way she kept thinking about how someone could have done this. It must have taken forever to dig out, or at least someone with some special equipment. Surely this tunnel couldn't have been excavated by hand. The ceiling was low, but it was tall enough for her to stand up fully and wide enough that she had plenty of room on either side of her.

The beams also suggested that whoever did this had planned it in advance, and it hadn't just been a whim. Had Nat known about this place? Had she been in here as well? She must have— otherwise why leave when Ivy mentioned the cabin? Because she was afraid of Ivy finding this place… *that* had been the secret she'd been so terrified of Ivy discovering. Whatever was at the end of this tunnel, it might answer all of Ivy's questions. It might reveal answers she'd been pursuing for the past fifteen years.

As Ivy walked, she stepped carefully, unsure what could be at the end. Her weapon was back out and she swept the light back and forth in front of her. She still wasn't sure she'd actually heard anything that might have revealed this place. But then how else could she have known it was there? Nothing about it felt familiar, other than that nagging pain in her gut. But she pressed on, noting there were impressions in the dirt floor. Not enough to determine the kind of shoe being worn, but enough of an impression that Ivy could make out two separate sets of tracks, one smaller than the other. It was the first clear indication that Jasmine might be here after all.

But the further Ivy walked, the more worried she became. She was well beyond the confines of the cabin by now, and even though she hadn't been tracking how far she'd walked, she must have been at least fifty yards or more. She tried pulling up her location on her phone, but she was either too deep or she was out of range because she didn't have a signal down here.

At least the flashlight still worked.

Finally, the hallway ended at another door, similar to the others in the cabin. It was old and made of wood, affixed into a solid frame. And it looked heavy. Its only other feature was a large handle on one side which looked ancient. But it didn't appear the door was locked. She figured the subterfuge of hiding it at the end of a tunnel underneath an abandoned cabin was probably more than enough security. Still, she didn't like the idea of opening that door. Her heart pounded as she reached for the handle, unsure what she'd find.

As soon as her hand touched the handle, it was like she had been electrocuted. She yanked it back, thinking for a brief second that someone had wired the door as a booby trap. But then she realized it was the exact same feeling she had when someone touched her. That same oppressive feeling of being crushed and fried at the same time. There wasn't anything wrong with the door. It was *her*. She was having a physical reaction to this place, and she didn't know why.

Ivy took a deep breath. She could do this. Jasmine was counting on her. Even though a million questions flooded her mind, Ivy couldn't stop. Not until the girl was safe.

She put her phone away, leaving herself in complete darkness as she gripped her handgun tighter. She thought about Jonathan, about how it didn't affect her when he touched her or vice versa. There had to be a way to channel that. Her focus was on how she felt when there was contact between the two of them. And with that image in her head, she grasped the handle of the door again. It still hurt, but not enough to make her pull away. Instead, she turned the handle, the door swinging open towards her. A dim light emanated from inside the room, but she stayed on the far side of the door until she could check the room for threats.

But nothing happened.

Ivy released the handle, standing on the other side of the door with both hands on her weapon as she took three deep breaths. She then peeked around the corner quickly for an assessment. The room beyond resembled those in the cabin, though there was little else inside other than a table and a single lightbulb hanging from the ceiling. There was also another door beyond, but it was closed as well.

Ivy checked the room again, just to make sure, before coming around the doorway and into the space. It wasn't much larger than a bedroom, the walls made of stacked logs just like the cabin had been. But there were no windows. It bothered her that the light above the table was on, however. It meant someone had been— or still was— here.

The table had been pushed up against one of the walls and Ivy inspected it quickly. A smattering of mechanical drawings and designs covered the table, the scraps of old paper ripped and deteriorating. And given the amount of dust everywhere, she suspected no one had used this table for a long time. But when she began examining the drawings, something tugged at the back of her mind. Something... terrible. Something she didn't want to think about. She didn't recognize the images; they were for some kind of device, but it was difficult to tell what. And the more she tried to grab hold of it, the less tangible it became, like smoke through her fingers.

There was something very familiar about this place, and it was clearly having an effect on her. What that effect was, she didn't know.

Leaving the table, she approached the second door. This one didn't seem as heavy as the first and seemed to act more like a divider than a barrier. Light leaked out from above and below the door. Ivy placed her head next to the wood, listening for any sounds on the other side, but there was nothing.

Slowly she reached for the handle again, keeping in mind her lesson from the last door. This one was easier, and didn't provide as much of a shock to her. As before, she opened it, keeping the door between her and whatever was inside.

But this time, when Ivy checked the other side of the door, she froze.

This room was bigger than the other one, about twice as large. Inside the room were three chairs, all lined up in a row. But they looked more like the kinds of chairs that were used for electrocutions than anything else. They all had straps on the arms and the legs, and they tilted back at a forty-five-degree angle on some kind of hinge. Above them, hanging from the ceiling by a chain, was a large metal scythe that was attached to some kind of winch on the other end of the room. The whole place resembled a medieval torture chamber straight out of a horror movie.

Worst of all, Jasmine Quinn had been strapped in the nearest chair, tears streaming down her face.

"Oh my God," Ivy whispered, causing Jasmine to turn her head, her eyes pleading.

"Help me," the girl whimpered.

Ivy surveyed the rest of the room, which was empty as far as she could tell. Did Zimmerman build all this himself? If so, who were the other two chairs for?

"Are you alone?" Ivy asked.

"I… I don't know where he went," Jasmine admitted. "He was here a second ago."

"Did he say anything? Why did he kidnap you?"

"I don't know," she reiterated. "All I heard him say was he was waiting for something."

"Did he say what?"

"I don't *know*, okay?" Jasmine pleaded. "Can you please get me out of here?"

She didn't have time to lose. Ivy stowed her weapon and went to work on the binds holding Jasmine to the chair. They were thick nylon rope that had been tied tight enough to cut off the poor girl's circulation. Her hands were beginning to go purple and they clutched the handles of the chair like she might fly off any second.

Likewise, her feet were bound in a similar way, the ropes cutting right across her ankles above her tennis shoes. What was even stranger was the chair seemed to be designed to hold someone against their will as it had places for the ropes to go, binding the subject to the chair efficiently. Ivy's first thought had been maybe it was someone's bad idea of a sex dungeon, but that blade hanging precariously from the ceiling killed that idea.

This really was a torture chamber. And she needed to get Jasmine out of here as soon as possible. She could deal with Zimmerman later.

Ivy began tugging on the ropes, but found they had been tied so incredibly tight she would need a knife to cut them off. Looking around the room, the only sharp object was the scythe above her. If she could somehow figure out how to get it down without cutting herself in two…

Movement behind her caused Ivy to spin, her weapon back out and pointed at Jason Zimmerman.

"Well," he said. "Aren't you curious." His voice was deep and resonant through the room and if he showed any anxiety at having a weapon pointed at his head, he didn't show it.

"Don't move," Ivy said, keeping her gun trained on the man. He was about ten feet away from her, having come through the same door. There must have been an antechamber in that other room she hadn't noticed, or another passageway in the tunnel. Either way, there was only one way in and one way out of this place.

Zimmerman held up his hands. "I'd like to congratulate you, Detective," he said. "I honestly didn't think you'd be able to find this place." Ivy watched in horror as one of his hands moved ever so slightly to the lever that was attached via a winch to the blade. "However, you are not in control here."

"Move another inch and I blow your head off," Ivy said.

"And my hand falls on this lever, killing poor Jasmine," he replied. Jasmine whimpered behind Ivy. "You need to remember to be aware of your surroundings."

"You need to shut the fuck up," Ivy said, looking down the barrel of the gun. "Step away from the wall."

"No."

Ivy tensed. His hand hovered precariously over the lever. How likely was it he was right? That if Ivy shot him he'd end up hitting it one way or another? She should have just shot him the second he'd come into the room. "What do you want?"

"For you to put down your weapon, of course," he replied.

"Not going to happen," Ivy replied.

"Then I guess you'll just have to deal with the conse-quences." He moved ever so slightly towards the lever.

"*No!*" Ivy yelled. She grimaced. She'd painted herself into a corner here. Nothing else mattered other than Jasmine's life. But first she needed to get Zimmerman away from the wall. "You step back and I'll put down my weapon."

"You first," he said, grinning.

Sweat dripped down Ivy's temple. There was no way she

could trust him. If she put down her gun, he was just as likely to pull the lever anyway.

"Put me in her place," Ivy said.

"Excuse me?"

"Let her go, and you can put me in the chair," Ivy said. "I'll do it… willingly."

"Well, now," he said. "That's an interesting proposition. But how do you suggest we go about such a thing? The second I move away from this wall you're just as likely to kill me as cooperate."

Ivy didn't have an answer for him. Any movement on either party's part required the trust of the other, and right now she didn't trust Zimmerman for one second. "Why Jasmine? Why all this?"

He smiled. "That is the question, isn't it?" He glanced up at the blade, just barely moving above them, the tension on the ropes holding it to the ceiling taut. "I must say, I would *love* to have you in that chair. But I just don't think it's going to happen."

Before Ivy could move his hand fell on the lever and immediately the scythe swung down on an arc. Ivy had to drop to the floor to keep it from slicing through her head as Jasmine's scream abruptly cut off. Ivy turned just in time to see her eyes go glassy, before her head separated from her body, falling neatly into the bucket below. Blood poured out of the wound, soaking the wall behind her as her heart continued to pump its final beats.

A sharp kick to the face sent Ivy flailing to on her back as she tried to process what had just happened.

"Let me ask you something, Detective," Zimmerman said, picking up Ivy's gun as stars swam in her vision. She was on her back, next to the wall that was not covered in crimson blood pouring from the poor girl's neck.

Zimmerman stood close, examining her weapon. "Does this place seem… *familiar* to you at all?"

"You… you killed her…" Ivy managed to whisper. She couldn't believe it. It had been so quick, and she hadn't stopped him. He'd just…done it.

And Ivy had stood there and watched.

Something deep in her gut pulled at a memory, but it was lost in the disgust and horror Ivy felt at allowing such a thing to happen. She glanced over at Jasmine's dead eyes, staring at her from the bucket on the floor.

She couldn't help it. Ivy turned to the side and retched.

"That's it, let it all out," Zimmerman said, pointing the gun at Ivy.

Flecks of blood covered Ivy's jacket and she could feel the moisture on her cheek from the splatter that had finally begun to subside as Jasmine's body ran out of blood to pump. The entire room really did look like something out of Texas Chainsaw Massacre. The scythe, once clean, now had a thin coating of blood on the edge as Zimmerman flipped the handle back up. The wench went to work and the blade began to slide back into place, slowly ratcheting back up to the ceiling.

"You know," he said. "I think I will take you up on your offer. Feel free to get in the seat next to her."

Ivy watched as the scythe slowly ticked back up towards the ceiling. She had failed Jasmine, and the Quinns. But she couldn't let Zimmerman do this to someone else. She couldn't let him get away with it.

Ivy didn't believe in Hell, but still she said a silent prayer that what she was about to do wouldn't send her there regardless. In one swift move, she grabbed the bucket with Jasmine's head and chucked it at Zimmerman, surprising the man as he tried to catch it, and knocking him off kilter. As he fumbled with the bucket and the head, Ivy rushed him, plowing into the man and driving them both to the ground with an *oof* from him. Jasmine's blood covered him from the chest up, having spilled all over his neck and face as he fell backwards and he found himself gargling as he tried to keep breathing as he was overcome by a wave of viscous liquid.

Ivy drove her fists into the man's ribs over and over, until she heard a satisfying *crack* as Zimmerman yelled out, though the sound was wet and muffled. He'd dropped the gun when they fell back, and Ivy scrambled for it as Zimmerman fought to breathe. Finally, she got her hands on the weapon and leveled it at him.

"Don't move or I will put one right through your skull," she said.

Zimmerman continued to gargle before finally coughing, blood hitting the floor as he tried to clear his lungs. When he could finally get a breath, Ivy was surprised to find it was a laugh. "Go ahead," he snarled. "Do it."

"No," she replied. "You're going to pay for what you did to her," Ivy said.

But Zimmerman only shook his head. "*I* didn't do it. *You* did."

Ivy had heard enough. But she had no way to restrain the man. He was temporarily incapacitated, but how long would that last? And would anyone really begrudge her for putting a bullet in him? She'd be able argue self-defense— that it had been him or her.

"You're thinking about it, aren't you?" he said, chuckling. "My little killer."

Ivy didn't know what the fuck he was talking about, and she didn't want to. She stood, keeping the weapon on the man as she stood over him. Her finger hovered precariously over the trigger, the intrusive thought threatening to win.

"No," she finally said. "That's not justice." Instead, she raised the weapon and struck Zimmerman across the skull, sending him sprawling to the ground.

She took a deep breath before letting it out. "And you don't deserve an easy out."

Chapter Thirty-Two

As soon as he'd arrived at the cabin, Jonathan had made his way inside, sure he'd find Ivy dead— the victim of someone's foul actions. The entire drive over he couldn't help but think about the cryptic texts, and that there was a possibility they could have meant something even more sinister than they suggested. They obviously were talking about Ivy— but to what end he didn't know. All he did know was he didn't like the idea of her going off on her own, no matter her reasons.

After securing the scene, he'd spent the better part of twenty minutes searching the cabin. When he'd pulled up, Ivy's car had been down at the end of the driveway, but the engine had been cold and there was no sign of her inside. But when he didn't find her anywhere in the cabin, he'd immediately called for backup, assuming she had to be somewhere in the surrounding woods. It was an area much too large for Jonathan to search on his own, and he was only growing more nervous by the second. While he waited, he'd returned inside only to find some footprints in the dust. The house had been completely empty, including the basement. Ivy was nowhere to be found.

By the time the patrol car pulled up, Jonathan was back outside, searching around the house. She had to be here *somewhere*. Maybe she'd run into trouble and had pursued someone through the woods and had gotten hurt. Or maybe someone had gotten the drop on her and had already taken her somewhere else. The calls to her cell phone were going straight to voicemail which meant she was out of range or didn't have service. It also didn't give Jonathan a very good feeling.

Wilcox came trotting up, having just returned from searching a grid south of the house. "Nothing," he said. "No sign of footprints, human or animal. She wasn't out there."

"This is all very wrong," Jonathan said as Officer Perry joined them, having just searched the north side. But the look in his eyes told Jonathan he hadn't made any more progress than Wilcox had. "I think we need to operate under the assumption she's been abducted. I don't see another explanation."

"I'll radio it in," Wilcox replied. "We should check with—"

Before he could finish, Jonathan's cell phone rang. He pulled it out to see it was his partner. "Ivy? What's going on? Where are you?"

"Too much to explain," she said, though her voice crackled with the effect of a bad signal. Jonathan noted he only had two bars out here. "I need backup to the Winding Way cabin."

Jonathan reflexively looked around. "We're here," he said. "Where are you?"

"Wait?" she said, the word breaking in half over the static. "You're here?"

"We're outside, where are you?" he asked.

"Come to the basement," she said before ending the call.

What the hell? Jonathan didn't like this. He'd already been in the basement. Twice. There was nothing down there. Could someone have gotten hold of Ivy's phone? Made her say something that could draw them into a trap?

No, he was being overly paranoid. Ivy needed his help. "She said she's in the basement," he told the other two officers. "Let's move. Keep on your guard." He could tell neither Wilcox nor Perry were enthusiastic about heading into the cabin, but he didn't care. Ivy needed their help. He just couldn't imagine what she could have gotten into out here. Whatever it was, they needed to get back on the Quinn case. He knew the cabin was important to Ivy, but it shouldn't take precedence over the case— not right now.

He pulled out his weapon as they headed back into the cabin again, this time moving methodically as a group, double checking every inch of the place before descending into the dark basement. Jonathan held a small flashlight out along with his weapon, sweeping the stairs in front of him. As they came around the corner, he exhaled. The room was still empty.

"Um," Wilcox said behind him.

Before he could respond, there was a creaking sound and the shuffling of what sounded like a broom being dragged across the floor. He shone the light in the direction of the noise to see one of the walls of the basement, the one with a shelf full of paints and discarded tools *opening*. Behind what was apparently a *door*, was Ivy, her hair a mess and half covered in blood.

Jonathan's stomach immediately dropped out.

"I need some help," Ivy said, looking directly into the light. "He's... down the tunnel."

"Who?" Jonathan asked, rushing over.

"Zimmerman," she replied as she collapsed against the open doorway, sliding to the ground.

Jonathan knelt beside her. She had a massive bruise on her head and her face was splattered with dried blood, though he didn't think it was hers. The opening had revealed a dark tunnel that led who knew where.

"Are you hurt?" he asked.

"Yeah, but… we need to get him into custody," she said, breathing heavily.

"I think you have a concussion," Jonathan said. He turned to Wilcox. "You and Perry head down there. Let me know what you find."

Wilcox nodded as he and Perry headed down the dark tunnel, each of them switching on their lights.

Jonathan turned back to Ivy, examining her head again. Her cheeks were wet, but not with the blood. In fact, it looked as though tears had cut through the blood on her face, almost giving her the look of wearing sad clown makeup.

"Ivy," Jonathan said gently. "What happened?"

"Detective?" Wilcox called from somewhere deep in the tunnel. "You need to see this."

"He… he killed her," Ivy said, her breaths becoming more ragged. "He did it right in front of me. I tried to stop him, but I… I shouldn't have let him get close. It was my fault."

Jonathan didn't understand just what on earth was going on. How could Zimmerman be here? And who had made this tunnel with a secret entrance?

"Just hang on, I'll be right back," he said, placing his palm against Ivy's cheek. She didn't pull away, which worried him. "Don't go to sleep."

Jonathan trotted down the claustrophobic tunnel, only a small amount of light ahead to guide him. When he passed through the doorway into a room that looked like it could have been in the cabin itself— log walls, dirt floor, ceiling beams above holding only a few dangling light bulbs, he realized whoever must have built the cabin probably built this place at the same time.

But when he entered the second room where Wilcox and Perry stood, his stomach bottomed out.

It was like something out of a slasher movie.

The body of a young girl sat in a chair that had been tilted back, positioned underneath a large swinging blade that hung precariously from the ceiling. Horrifically, he realized it was the body of Jasmine Quinn when he spotted her head about ten feet away, near a bucket that was still covered in the girl's blood. Beside both her head and the bucket lay the body of Jason Zimmerman, his entire torso and face absolutely coated in crimson. It looked as if he had almost tried to drink the blood and… what? Passed out? One thing was for sure, he was still alive, given how his chest rose and fell with each breath.

"Get him into custody," Jonathan said. "Don't touch anything else. I need to get in contact with Burns."

He headed back down the tunnel, arriving in the basement again where Ivy sat, staring into the darkness.

He leaned down in front of her. "Ivy. I need you to tell me exactly what happened in there."

"I need to get out of here," she said, her voice sounding old and ragged, like it had been pulled through a series of blades itself.

Jonathan glanced over to the garage door. It was bolted from this side, but he threw the bolt and raised the door up, allowing the cool air from outside in. He then helped Ivy to her feet and escorted her outside, where she collapsed on the ground again, her head between her knees.

"Ivy, don't fall asleep, okay?" he said, sitting down beside her.

"I'll be lucky if I ever get to sleep again," she said. She turned to him. "You saw?"

He nodded.

"I should have stopped him. I shouldn't have come here alone. If you'd been here maybe we could have——"

"I'm sure you did the best you could," he interrupted before she started in on the heavy guilt. "How did you even find that place?"

"I don't know," she said. "I thought… maybe I heard something. It all felt… familiar."

"Like you'd been there before?" he asked.

She shook her head. "I'm pretty sure I'd remember if I'd ever been there before. That's not the kind of place you forget."

"No, I suppose not," he said.

"I got the information from KHS Chemicals. They had a record of Zimmerman buying a canister of Vapoxil back in the early aughts. Delivered it to this address."

"I don't understand," Jonathan said.

"Neither do I," she replied. "The canister— it's hooked up to the back of the home. Still there. Zimmerman must have been using this place for years. He could just pump the stuff in there whenever he wanted, take down whoever was staying inside."

"So why didn't he do that with you?" Jonathan asked.

She shrugged. "Maybe it's empty."

A few moments later, Wilcox and Perry emerged from the basement, each of them with an arm under Zimmerman as they got him outside. The man still looked to be unconscious as they lowered him into the grass and bound his hands with zip ties.

"He's been here a long time," Ivy said. "He's known about this place. He must have." More tears streamed down her face. Jonathan thought back to the body of Jasmine Quinn as the sounds of sirens arose in the distance. "And I walked right into his trap."

"You made it out," Jonathan said. "You got the bastard."

Ivy made no notice of his choice of words. She just stared straight ahead. "Doesn't matter. Jasmine is dead. Mrs. Quinn was right. We couldn't protect her family."

"That's *not* your fault," he reiterated.

"If you say so," she replied, but he could tell she wasn't buying it. Not for a second.

As the lights became visible in the distance, Zimmerman began to stir. Jonathan exchanged a look with Perry and

Wilcox. He could tell both had been shaken by what they'd all seen down there. They might not have been able to save Jasmine Quinn, but he was going to make sure Zimmerman paid for what he'd done.

If it were up to Jonathan, he'd make the man fry for it.

Chapter Thirty-Three

It had been a harrowing nine hours. Jason Zimmerman had been transported to Oakhurst Hospital to receive medical care for his ribs and to receive any additional treatment. Burns and technical services had arrived on the scene to process everything, while Ivy had also been taken to the hospital for observation regarding her injury. Everyone kept telling her not to fall asleep, but she didn't think that would be very difficult. Every time she closed her eyes she kept seeing the terrified face of Jasmine Quinn. Even in the split second when she would blink and her vision would black out for the briefest of moments, Jasmine was there. Ivy would never sleep again if she could help it.

She'd undergone a few tests as well as long periods of observation at the hospital. Apparently she had what was known as a Grade 1 concussion which could come with dizziness, nausea or a sensitivity to light and noise. But to her, most of the world felt like someone had muffled everything. If she put a lot of effort into it, she could bring everything back into focus, but as soon as she let go, it would all get muffled again. When she asked the doctor about it, he attributed it more to the trauma she'd endured rather than any actual physical ailment.

Aunt Carol had come by for a few hours to sit with her, but Ivy had barely registered the woman's presence. She appreciated Carol coming by to check on her, but it didn't really matter. She'd already been told she'd be released later that evening after her last round of tests came back with positive results.

Carol tried to talk to her about what happened, but Ivy found herself just going through the motions, trying to persuade the woman she didn't need a babysitter. Eventually, she managed to convince her she was okay and that she should go back home to take care of Hero.

Jonathan had also stopped by for a short time to let her know about the fallout that was about to rain down on the department. Apparently, Armstrong wasn't happy and Ayford was doing all he could to contain the situation, but at the end of the day they still had a dead girl and it wouldn't be long before the media got wind of the circumstances. There was also going to be a formal inquiry into Ivy's activities— none of which surprised her. She hadn't followed protocol, and as a result, a girl had died. The best she could hope for was losing her job. The worst— probably jail time.

But what really stuck in her craw was Zimmerman. The man had been so flippant, so arrogant and even more inexplicably, he acted like he knew Ivy. Though she was sure she'd never met the man before in his life. Of course, it was possible he was just crazy. After all, he'd probably been the one who had built that torture chamber down there. The question was, who else had he killed? He hadn't gone to all that trouble for Jasmine Quinn... there had to be more to it.

But the odds of Ivy finding out those kinds of details were slim to none. Jonathan had already been removed from the case and Ivy was on temporary suspension, having turned in her weapon and badge to Jonathan so he could deliver them to Ayford— at least until the conclusion of her inquiry.

"Ms. Bishop?"

Ivy looked up to see a doctor coming into the room. It didn't escape her that only a few days ago she and Jonathan had been running around this very hospital, trying to track down and capture Doctor Brachman for killing Father Rouge. It was a strange twist of fate.

"Good news, your vitals have all remained stable. We're going to go ahead and discharge you, okay?"

"Sure," Ivy said.

The man smiled. "Great. Just give us a few minutes to finish up the paperwork and we'll get you out of here." He paused. "You'll probably be sore for a few days, but an ice compress is all you should need. Twenty minutes, three times a day. I'll also prescribe some painkillers."

"That's okay," Ivy said. "I don't want them."

"Well, let me give you the script anyway. In case you change your mind," he said as he headed out of the room.

Ivy didn't want painkillers. In fact, she didn't want anything more to do with this room. She'd been poked and prodded more than she'd ever been in her life and it had been practically impossible not to shake everyone off her and tell them to leave her alone. She'd had to endure more physical contact than she had in *years* and it had taken all her willpower not to fold into an anxiety-ridden mess. But if she had, they would have recommended a psych evaluation and she wasn't about to go through that again. All she wanted to do was to go home, climb under the covers and never come out again.

She threw off the flimsy bedsheet and grabbed the stack of clothes Carol had brought for her. Her other clothes had been seized and entered into evidence considering they'd been covered with Jasmine Quinn's blood.

Once she was dressed, she grabbed her phone and what other effects she had and headed out of the room. They had her address; they could mail her any forms she needed to sign. Right now, she just wanted to get out of here.

But as she reached the elevator, she stopped. Instead of pushing the *down* button, she pressed *up* instead and stepped into the car when it arrived. On the fourth floor, she headed down the hallway until she reached the recovery unit, where Officer Suarez sat in a chair, reading a paperback.

As soon as he saw Ivy he stood. "Detective. You're not supposed to be here."

"I need to speak with him."

"Ayford said no one goes in there until tomorrow. He wants this done by the book. The public defender is supposed to be here in the morning."

"I don't care," Ivy replied. "Five minutes."

Suarez hesitated.

"You know what he did, right?"

The man exhaled. "Yeah. I heard about it from Perry."

"They've pulled me from the case," she said. "So I won't get to interrogate him. But I need answers. I may never get another chance."

Suarez sighed. "Fine. But if you end up strangling him with a bedsheet or something I'm telling Ayford you incapacitated me to get in there."

Ivy grimaced. "Fair enough."

"I'll be back in a few," Suarez said, setting his book on the chair. "Gonna check the vending machines."

Ivy waited until he was out of earshot before pushing the door open. The room was dark, the only sound the beeping of the machines hooked up to Jason Zimmerman. The man lay on the bed, his eyes closed. His midsection was bandaged, probably from the fractured ribs Ivy'd given him. She was lucky she hadn't punctured his lung or something else vital. An IV ran from a drip machine to his forearm, which was handcuffed to the bed. Likewise, his other arm was also restrained, along with his legs. He couldn't even turn over if he wanted.

"Come to beat on me some more?" the man asked without opening his eyes.

"Who are you?" Ivy asked.

Zimmerman chuckled, though it was obvious it caused him some pain to do so. "You already know that. You're the one who tracked me down."

"No," Ivy said. "Who are you, *really*?"

One light blue eye opened to stare at her.

"Why did you say those things to me?" Ivy asked. "Asking if I thought the place was familiar."

The man smiled. "Well. I guess you haven't figured it *all* out yet."

"Why even kidnap Jasmine Quinn? *Who is…was she to you?*"

"Is this an official interrogation, Detective?" he asked. Ivy didn't reply. The man licked his dry lips and glanced at the ceiling before responding. "I have a thing for little girls."

Ivy had to keep her stomach from turning. Zimmerman was looking for a reaction from her and she wasn't about to give him one. "You couldn't get to her that first night because your gas didn't work, right? She'd kept her window open. So you took the boy instead. But why? Why not just wait for another night? You could obviously get in the house whenever you wanted."

"Look at you, working out all the details," Zimmerman said. "Keep going."

"Cut the bullshit," Ivy said.

He smiled, then coughed once. "I'm not sure you know this, but that gas isn't cheap. I didn't have enough for another try. How's that for an explanation?"

"So you pawned off Albie Quinn on Margaret Weston?"

He shrugged. "I knew you'd be looking for me, so Weston seemed like as good a distraction as any. At least until I could get to the girl." He coughed once. "But you were too slow. I had to encourage you along."

"The anonymous call," Ivy said. "That was you."

Zimmerman nodded. "All part of the plan."

"The plan to kill her?" Ivy said. "You could have done that in her own home. You could have smothered her in her sleep. Or abducted her from school. Why the elaborate trap? Why take her down to that cabin?"

"Now, now, Detective, I'm not going to do *all* your work for you," he replied, grinning from ear to ear. Ivy wanted to reach down the man's throat and pull his heart out with her bare hand. He sat up, though it obviously caused him some strain to do so. "Just think, if you had killed me right then and there, she would still be alive. So really, which of us is at fault here?" He laid back down. "Ah, but then you wouldn't get the answers you need, would you?"

Ivy narrowed her gaze.

"See, I know you, Detective," he added. "And I know that fire that burns inside you. The one that has driven you all your life. The one that asks *why*. Why me? Why *my* family?"

Ivy's eyes went wide. She rushed the man, grabbing him by the collar and practically pulling him off the bed.

"Who are you?" Ivy yelled in his face, but he only laughed back in hers. A laugh that grew louder the more she jostled him.

"Detective!" Arms wrapped behind Ivy, pulling her away from Zimmerman. They were like being tased by an electric current and Ivy practically seized up before they let go. She turned to see Suarez, a scowl on his face. "Are you crazy? Do you want this whole case thrown out?"

Zimmerman only continued to laugh from the bed, though he was now askew with no way to right himself, given how he'd been clamped to the bed.

"No," Ivy admitted, breathing heavily. "I was just… I made a mistake."

"You better get out of here," Suarez said. "Before I'm forced to report this to Ayford."

"I'll be happy to report it!" Zimmerman said.

"Shut the fuck up," Suarez told the man. "Bishop, leave. Now."

Ivy took one more look at Zimmerman before turning her back and heading for the door.

"Don't worry, Detective," Zimmerman called after her. "I'm sure we'll be seeing a lot of each other in the coming weeks! Maybe they'll even let us share a cell!"

Ivy ignored him as she headed out into the hallway, fuming. Zimmerman knew more than he was saying. He knew something about her family. And Ivy wouldn't stop until she found out what.

"Hey, stranger."

Ivy glanced up to see Alice standing in the hallway, her hands stuck into the pockets of her overcoat as she leaned up against the opposite wall.

"Oh," Ivy said. "What are you doing here?"

"You know me, too nosy for my own good," she said. "I went to your room but they said they didn't know where you were. Apparently, there are some forms you need to sign before they'll discharge you? Anyway, I was hoping to get a statement about what happened."

Ivy turned and headed down the hallway. "I'm not supposed to talk about it."

Alice fell into step beside her. "Off the record, then."

Ivy glanced over for a second before turning back. "I'm already in deep shit. I don't want to dig myself any deeper."

"Hey," Alice said, stopping her in the hallway. "You *owe* me. You left me in that godforsaken place and there happened to be an underground bunker there the entire time? That would have been a pretty big fucking story."

"How do you know— you know what, never mind." Ivy knew Alice had sources and no doubt word about what happened was spreading fast. "You putting it on the news tonight?"

"If I can get enough for a feature, yeah," she replied. "It's my job. Remember?"

Ivy scoffed.

"Look, I wanted to come down here to give you the chance to set the record straight. Because from what I've already heard, things kind of got out of control down there."

"Out of control?" Ivy asked, bemused. "I'd call that an understatement."

"Okay," Alice said. "So give me your version. What happened?"

"I screwed up, that's what happened," Ivy said, turning and heading back for the elevators again. "And someone died."

"I'm sure that's not all of it," Alice said, softening a little.

"No, that's about how it went," Ivy replied. "An innocent kid lost her life. What's worse is I don't even know why." The two women stood side by side as they waited on the elevator. "I'm sorry I left you there alone. I… froze."

Alice shrugged. "It was a creepy place. Obviously."

"That wasn't it," Ivy said. "It's like I couldn't help it. I wasn't ready for how hard that place would hit me."

"Hit you?" Alice turned to her. "Had you been there before?"

She thought back to Zimmerman's words— his little quip about the cabin being familiar. Ivy had spent all her time waiting for the doctors scouring her memory. And she hadn't been able to come up with anything. But the problem was her memory was incomplete. It was missing two weeks from when she was twelve.

Two weeks and a night when anything could have happened.

"I… don't know."

Chapter Thirty-Four

IVY FOLLOWED her boss into his office, having been escorted up by Officer Ann Touley— the woman shooting her glances the entire trip. Not one person would meet her eye as she made her way through the precinct. She wasn't surprised. She had never made a lot of friends here so why would anyone go out of their way to comfort her now? She'd also noticed Jonathan's desk had been empty as Touley finally handed her off to Ayford, who didn't say a word, just turned around and made a beeline for his office with Ivy reluctantly in tow.

She took a seat across from the man, adjusting her collar. She'd actually put on a suit for once in anticipation of the inquiry later today, but it was chafing at her neck, feeling something like a noose.

Ayford sat down across from her, but also neglected to meet her eye. Instead he turned to his computer, typing something before clearing his throat.

"I spoke with the Quinn family yesterday," he said. "And offered our most sincere condolences." Finally he turned to Ivy. "As I'm sure you can imagine, they are going through an incredibly difficult time right now."

Ivy nodded.

"So difficult, in fact, that I didn't actually deliver our condolences to the family themselves," Ayford amended. "Instead it was to their lawyer."

"That didn't take long," Ivy said.

"No, it did not. We expect to receive notice in the next few days that the department is being sued for gross negligence."

Ivy hung her head. "It's not the department's fault."

"The department hired you, so therefore it's the department's fault," he said. "I won't sugarcoat this: it's not good, Bishop." He sat back, sighing. "Even if you had done everything right, gone in there with proper resources, called for backup the minute things got out of hand… we'd still be facing a lawsuit. But at least that would have been one we could defend. This… well…"

"I understand," Ivy said.

"I hope you do, because as the junior-most detective in the department, it doesn't look very good when you go off on your own without informing *anyone*. What exactly was your plan, anyway?"

"Does it really matter?" Ivy asked. "What's done is done."

"Humor me."

She sighed. "I was just going to check the cabin for any evidence Zimmerman had been there. I didn't actually think I'd find him. I was hoping the tank might give me a direction of where to look. I literally just… stumbled onto him."

"And the hidden room?" Ayford asked.

Ivy hesitated.

"Look, I'm not asking you anything they're not going to ask this afternoon in your inquiry. So you might as well get it all out now."

"What's the point?" Ivy asked. "They're going to terminate me no matter what."

Ayford worked his jaw for a moment. "Maybe. Probably. But if you don't have an explanation of how you found that room, then they might start to suspect you were in on it with Zimmerman all along."

"*In* on it?" Ivy shot back. "Are you fucking kidding me?"

"Watch your tone, Detective," Ayford said.

Ivy bit her lip. "I heard something… or I thought I did. Behind the wall."

"What?"

She shook her head. "I don't know." She wasn't about to tell him she wasn't sure she'd heard *anything* at all. Something had drawn her to that wall, she just hadn't known what. But if she couldn't even explain it to herself how was she supposed to explain it to the inquiry board? Did they really think she could have something to do with all this?

"Why didn't you call for backup the minute you found the tunnel?" Ayford asked.

The truth was because that place— whatever it was, had felt very personal to Ivy. She went there knowing there was a possibility it was dangerous and she'd elected to go alone anyway. No one was going to put themselves in harm's way for her, not again. She never should have agreed to examine that cabin with Alice. She should have just gone there by herself in the beginning and maybe none of this would have happened.

"I didn't have any service and I was investigating the area. I thought if I left, it would potentially give our culprit time to escape."

"So you decided to charge in there on your own, and no one even knew you were there."

She nodded, casting her gaze to the side again.

"Detective, I'm sorry but that demonstrates a *serious* lack of judgment."

"I know," Ivy said softly.

"I think I'm beginning to see what Lieutenant Buckley was talking about. You have great instincts as an investigator and you're one of the most determined and dogged detectives I've ever met, but your decision process is *highly* flawed. We follow procedure in this office, Detective Bishop, and not just when it's convenient." He let out a long breath. "I'm afraid I'm going to have to recommend to the review board that you be removed from duty."

Ivy scoffed. It wasn't as if she was surprised, it was just one more thing to add to the mountain of shit she'd buried herself under.

Ayford checked his watch. "You have three hours until the inquiry. You should take the time to prepare any statements you wish to make because this may be the last time you can make them. Do you understand?"

"I do," Ivy said, feeling like a scolded child who'd just gotten caught running away. She'd spent her entire life looking for something— a purpose that would explain that night. And she'd been sure becoming a police detective had been the path that could lead her to the answers she'd been searching for over the past fifteen years.

But that was all about to come to a crashing halt. They wouldn't demote her— they'd just suspend her indefinitely, until the details of the lawsuits became clear. Then they'd use her as a scapegoat for the department, an example to hold up and show the community that the police were *repentant* and willing to do anything to make this go away.

And the entire time Zimmerman would sit in his cell and await his day in court, probably not for another three years.

"Alright, that's it. You're dismissed," he said, standing. Ivy matched him. "Oh, I almost forgot. I need your access card. If you need to enter or leave the building, you'll need to check with the desk sergeant at the front."

Ivy pulled the card off her belt and laid it on the desk between them.

"I really wish it didn't have to be this way, Bishop. But we have to remain accountable. Otherwise---"

"No, I get it," she said. "Someone's got to pay. I broke protocol. It only makes sense that it's me."

"If I don't see you again," he said, "I wish you the best of luck in whatever you end up doing next." He held out his hand. Ivy winced, but took it, shaking it quickly before letting go, hoping he didn't interpret the discomfort on her face as anything to do with him. Hopefully he'd just assume she was upset about this situation, which she was.

As she left Ayford's office, she couldn't help but try to take in everything as she left. This might be the last time she ever saw the inside of this station and she wanted to remember it as best she could.

When she returned to her desk, she found all her personal items had already been removed and placed into a box for her. Jonathan's desk was still dark. She wasn't sure she wanted him at her inquiry later— it would only make things worse. Maybe she should just go home and come back before the inquiry. She wasn't sure she'd be able to stand just hanging around here all morning, fielding pitying looks from everyone else in the office. And the last thing she wanted to do was run into Armstrong— who apparently *would* be at the inquiry, just waiting to fire her at the first word from the committee.

She didn't want to be here. And it was pretty obvious no one wanted her here, either. So why stay?

She headed down the stairs and back outside, the door *clicking* closed behind her as if to say *You're never coming back.* Ivy slid behind the wheel of the Datsun and turned the engine over, the roar drowning out her thoughts for only a short moment.

Questions swirled around her brain as she drove. Who had built that torture room, and why? And had Zimmerman always known about it? Or was he the one who built it? What's worse, why did he go through the extraordinary effort to kidnap Jasmine Quinn? There were so many variables here that she wasn't even sure where to begin. But at the same time, that bastard had cost her everything she'd worked for her entire adult life. She couldn't just let that slide.

Twenty minutes later she pulled up to Oliver's house. She hopped out, through the gate and up to the door, barely stopping using her key to get inside.

Inside, she came face to face with Oliver, his robe hanging open as he attempted to hobble back down the hallway.

"Ivy! Jeez!" he yelled, pulling his robe tight and nearly losing his balance in the process. "What the hell?"

"You often walk around with everything just hanging out?" she asked.

"In my own home, yes. Don't you knock?"

She motioned to the door. "You told me to use my key last time. I thought that meant it was a standing invitation."

He shot her a look before taking in her appearance. "Whoa. What's the occasion? I don't think I've ever seen you in a suit before."

She sighed. "I have a disciplinary hearing this afternoon. They're going to fire me."

His eyes went wide. "Fire you? For what?"

Ivy looked around. "Do you still have those wine coolers? I need something to take the edge off."

"Of course I do, I can barely drink the things," he replied. "Hang on."

Ivy headed to the living room while he hobbled back to the kitchen. "I'm surprised Carol didn't call and give you all the sordid details, since you guys are BFFs now."

Oliver returned to the room a few moments later. He was getting quicker, but obviously still had some trouble with it. "We just talk about Hero," he said, handing her one of the wine coolers. "Why do you have a hearing? What happened with the case? All I got was a text from White yesterday saying he'd found you after all."

She nodded. Thankfully they'd avoided the late-night news last night thanks to Alice helping to suppress the story until the family could be informed. But she expected it to hit the airwaves any minute now and would probably be the leading story for the next week on the local news.

Ivy popped the top of the bottle and laid out the whole thing for him. Starting with what she found in the cabin all the way up to this morning.

"So… they're going to fire you?" he asked.

She nodded. "For improper procedure. I never should have been in that cabin without backup. Especially after finding out it was connected to Zimmerman."

"Fuck," he said, taking a sip of the wine cooler. "Isn't there anything you can do?"

"Like what?" she asked. "They're not wrong. It *was* my fault."

"But if you hadn't arrived, wouldn't he have just killed her anyway?" he asked.

Ivy stared at the bottle for a moment. She wasn't sure he would have. He had plenty of time before she arrived. It wasn't like she'd interrupted anything. So why had he waited? Was he waiting for *her*?

"Do you think you could find anything on this Zimmerman guy? Anything that might explain some of this?"

"It can't hurt to look," Oliver said. "You said he lived in that cabin fifteen years ago?"

"I don't know if he lived there or not, but I do know he shipped the tank of Vapoxil there. Whatever was happening, he was there fifteen years ago."

Oliver nodded. "The same cabin where you suspect Nat was keeping information about your family. At the same time."

"I know," she said. "It's no coincidence. *Something* was going on there. And yes, I'm very aware there were *three* chairs in that dungeon. But Oliver, I wouldn't have forgotten something like that. If my family had been down there… if… something happened… I would know."

"Are you sure about that?" he asked.

"Yes," she said, but she had to admit she was beginning to have her doubts. What if something terrible *had* happened to her family in that room, and she'd just blocked it out?

"I'll see what I can find," he said. "But it may take me a little while."

She shook her head. "I didn't expect it to happen in a few hours. My fate is sealed no matter what happens." Ivy stood up. "I just have to accept it."

"Maybe they'll go easy on you," he suggested.

Ivy headed for the door. "If I'd walked away with the Quinn girl unharmed, maybe. But someone has to accept responsibility for what happened. And that someone has to be me."

Chapter Thirty-Five

NAT BREATHED in the scent of the apartment. The smell of old clothes lingered in the air, like someone hadn't done laundry in a while. She closed the door behind her, making sure to lock the deadbolt as she walked into the space.

Ivy's apartment. She hadn't been here in a while, but little had changed. Ivy wasn't exactly an interior decorator. There were a few pictures scattered about, but mostly there was some garment or another draped across every piece of furniture. Using her gloved hand, Nat ran it across the countertop in the kitchen right off the front door. A thin layer of dust came along with it. She moved to the fridge, opening it to reveal an empty case of beer, a jar of pickles that had long since expired and a Tupperware with the remnants of some meal— most likely a gift from Carol. The freezer contained a few microwave meals and not much else.

Nat laughed to herself. Ivy hadn't changed a bit. Of course she'd been watching her carefully ever since she began as a patrol officer, but she hadn't seen Ivy's personal side. Not really. Ivy had hidden that part away, pulling back as Nat had decided to be more cautious around her. The older Ivy got, the more likely something bad would happen— it was only a matter of time. And now, it finally had.

She'd been too late.

Nat had hoped that she still had time, a few more months at least. But then somehow Ivy found out about the cabin, setting everything into motion ahead of schedule. And it wasn't like she could count on Mike to help her out— he'd long since been out of the game. No, she'd had to move up her timetable; she just hoped she could get Ivy to agree without much fuss.

Who was she kidding? The woman would put up a fight *because* it was Nat, if for no other reason. But she was the only one who could convince Ivy. And she was finally ready, even though it had come at the cost of… *everything*.

Nat took a stroll around the space, taking in Ivy's personal effects. Tools from the garage downstairs, as well as random parts she'd brought up for one reason or another. Along with a smattering of books stacked haphazardly along the single shelf above the couch. Nat took note to memorize the books. Ivy might need some of them.

She checked her watch. It was closing in on five. The hearing would have ended an hour ago— so where was she? Did she decide to head to Carol's for consoling? Not likely. Maybe instead she went to a bar to drown her sorrows. But Ivy wasn't the kind of person who got drunk when things went bad.

There was another possibility of course… she had been arrested for what happened. Nat didn't think they'd do it so soon— it had only been a day since the girl's death. But Burns was studious, maybe she'd found a way to put the pieces together, show that Ivy—

The sound of a key in the deadbolt stopped Nat in her tracks. She shuffled over to the far side of the apartment, out of sight as Ivy opened the door and came inside. Thankfully, she was alone.

The woman didn't slam the door, but she closed it with a good amount of force, throwing her suit jacket on the nearest chair. Her blouse was unbuttoned and wrinkled at the top, as if Ivy had been pulling on it during the hearing.

Ivy headed to the refrigerator— no doubt in search of that last beer, when Nat stepped out of the shadows.

Ivy froze.

"Hi, Ivy," Nat said.

"What are you doing here?" she asked, stopped dead between the kitchen and the island.

"How did the hearing go?"

"Answer the question," Ivy demanded.

"I'm here because we need to leave," Nat replied. "Right now."

Ivy both scoffed and forced a laugh at the same time. "You must be joking. You're supposed to be in San Francisco."

"My old *phone* is in San Francisco," Nat replied. "Let me guess, you recruited Oliver to track it for you. Speaking of which, hand over yours."

"No," Ivy replied.

Nat sighed. She didn't want it to go this way. But she didn't have a choice. Ivy was a danger to herself and everyone else around her. She pulled her firearm from under her coat, pointing it at the woman she had known for over half her life. "Don't make this difficult."

"Nat, what the fuck?"

"Your phone. Slide it across the counter."

Reluctantly she pulled it from her pocket and did as Nat asked. Without missing a beat, Nat grabbed it, powered it off and slipped it in her pocket. She exchanged it for a pair of zip tie cuffs, which she threw to Ivy. "Now put these on. And make sure they're tight."

"No," Ivy said, defiant. She had that look in her eye, the one that Nat recognized she'd already been pushed to her limit. She was calling Nat's bluff. "I guess you'll just have to shoot me."

"I'm not going to shoot you," Nat said. "At least, unless you give me no choice."

"What the hell is that supposed to mean? What are you doing here? Why are you pointing a gun at me? And what the hell happened in that cabin fifteen years ago? Did you know about the torture chamber?"

"So you found it," Nat said. "I figured that's probably what happened. And that's how the girl died. The blade."

"You *knew*. You knew this entire time and you didn't say a fucking thing!" Ivy took a step around the counter, but Nat trained the gun on her again.

"Nuh-uh. I will put one in you if I have to. Trust me, this can go one of two ways. You'll want the easier way."

"*What* can go one of two ways?"

"This," Nat said. "You're coming with me. It's the best thing for everyone. Trust me."

"Not in your lifetime," Ivy growled. "I'm not going anywhere with you."

"You are. It's for your own good. We need to get you away from here— to somewhere where you can't hurt anyone else."

Ivy furrowed her brow. "Hurt anyone else? What are you talking about? Wait, are you the one who has been sending Jonathan those texts to stay away from me? You think I'll hurt someone?"

"The girl… Jasmine Quinn. You killed her, didn't you?"

"No," Ivy replied. "Some psycho named Zimmerman killed her. I… I just couldn't stop him quickly enough."

Nat paused. Could she be telling the truth? Or had she realized what she was, and was lying to cover up the facts? She'd be able to find out in due course— she still had some friends in the precinct; she needed to get a hold of the case record. But regardless, even if Ivy hadn't killed the girl, the madness was coming. She knew too much to keep it all buried any longer. This situation was nothing more than a predictor of the true horror that would arrive if Nat didn't do something.

"Nat, do you really think I could have done that?" Ivy asked. The question seemed genuine enough, but Nat wouldn't be fooled. She was the last line of defense, and she couldn't fail.

"I do," she replied.

"Why?"

Nat took a deep breath and gripped the gun tighter. "Because you've done it before. When you killed your family."

To be continued…

Want to read more about Ivy?

ONE DARK NIGHT CHANGED EVERYTHING. NOW IVY BISHOP must face the truth she's spent a lifetime outrunning.

Haunted by the fallout of a case gone tragically wrong, Detective Ivy Bishop is forced to confront the one mystery she's never been able to solve—her own. When new evidence resurfaces about the night her family was destroyed, Ivy is pulled into a web of secrets that stretches deeper than she ever imagined. But the truth won't set her free. It might even break her.

As she investigates the shadows of her past, Ivy is also reckoning with a failure she can't forgive: the young victim she couldn't save. With the weight of two tragedies threatening to consume her, Ivy must decide if she's still the protector she set out to be—or just another ghost left behind by the darkness.

Some wounds never heal. Some answers only lead to more pain. But Ivy Bishop isn't done fighting.

Not yet.

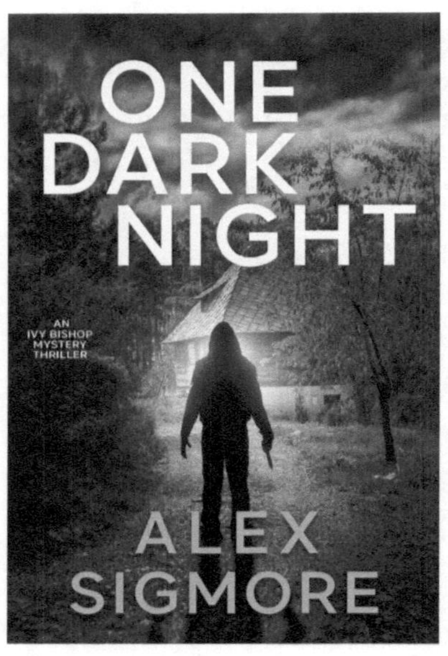

To get your copy of ONE DARK NIGHT, CLICK HERE or scan the code below with your phone.

FREE book offer!
Where did it all begin for Ivy?

I HOPE YOU ENJOYED *HER HIDDEN LIES*. IF YOU'D LIKE TO learn more about Ivy's backstory and how she became a detective, including how she originally met Jonathan, then you're in luck! *Bishop's Edge* introduces Ivy and tells the story of the case that both put her career on the line *and* catapulted her into the VC Unit.

Interested? CLICK HERE to get your free copy now!

Not Available Anywhere Else!

You'll also be the first to know when each new book in Ivy's series becomes available!

CLICK HERE or scan the code below to download for FREE!

A Note from Alex

Dear reader,

I know, you're probably not very happy knowing you'll have to wait to read more of Ivy's story. You'll have to chalk it up to my more sadistic side—the part where all my villains come from. They forced my hand :D

Personally, I can't believe we've already been through four books with Ivy and the gang. It seems like just a few days ago that I was working up the courage to craft her story and build out a brand-new set of characters. And I'm so happy with how these books are turning out. Ivy is a very different character from Emily so I've enjoyed writing in her world.

As always, I have you to thank for these books. If it weren't for your support, I couldn't continue to do this job I love so much.

If you enjoyed this book, please leave a review or recommend to your friends. Writing is my passion and I want to continue to bring you many more books in the future!

Thank you for being a loyal reader,
Alex

The Ivy Bishop Mystery Thriller Series

Free Prequel - Bishop's Edge (Ivy Bishop Bonus Story)

Her Dark Secret - (Ivy Bishop Series Book One)

The Girl Without a Clue - (Ivy Bishop Series Book Two)

The Buried Faces - (Ivy Bishop Series Book Three)

Her Hidden Lies - (Ivy Bishop Series Book Four)

One Dark Night - (Ivy Bishop Series Book Five)

The Emily Slate FBI Mystery Series

Free Prequel - Her Last Shot (Emily Slate Bonus Story)

His Perfect Crime - (Emily Slate Series Book One)

The Collection Girls - (Emily Slate Series Book Two)

Smoke and Ashes - (Emily Slate Series Book Three)

Her Final Words - (Emily Slate Series Book Four)

Can't Miss Her - (Emily Slate Series Book Five)

The Lost Daughter - (Emily Slate Series Book Six)

The Secret Seven - (Emily Slate Series Book Seven)

A Liar's Grave - (Emily Slate Series Book Eight)

Oh What Fun - (Emily Slate Series Holiday Special)

The Girl in the Wall - (Emily Slate Series Book Nine)

His Final Act - (Emily Slate Series Book Ten)

The Vanishing Eyes - (Emily Slate Series Book Eleven)

Edge of the Woods - (Emily Slate Series Book Twelve)

Ties That Bind - (Emily Slate Series Book Thirteen)

The Missing Bones - (Emily Slate Series Book Fourteen)

Blood in the Sand - (Emily Slate Series Book Fifteen)

The Passage - (Emily Slate Series Book Sixteen)

Fire in the Sky - (Emily Slate Series Book Seventeen)

The Killing Jar - (Emily Slate Series Book Eighteen)

The Oak Creek Mystery Series

The Darkest Game

Never Strike Twice

Standalone Psychological Thrillers

The Forgotten Wife

9 781957 536934